Transitory

by Ian Williams

Cover design by:
http://www.selfpubbookcovers.com/RLSat
her

This book has been professionally edited.

Table of Contents

Chapter 1 1

Chapter 2 8

Chapter 3 12

Chapter 4 27

Chapter 5 41

Chapter 6 58

Chapter 7 69

Chapter 8 77

Chapter 9 89

Chapter 10 109

Chapter 11 120

Chapter 12 129

Chapter 13 150

Chapter 14 162

Chapter 15 175

Chapter 16 189

Chapter 17 206

Chapter 18 219

Chapter 19 229

Chapter 20 234

A Thank you 239

About the author 240

Other books by Ian Williams 241

Connect with Ian Williams 242

Chapter 1

Nate Maddox sucked on an ice cube from his scotch. It floated around in his mouth, surrounded by a layer of liquid that hung to its quickly melting surface. Occasionally the taste of his favourite tipple numbed his tongue as he tried to pin the ice against the bridge of his mouth. Within seconds it was once again rattling around, hitting his teeth as it squirmed away from his tongue. One of many things that annoyed Nate about zero gravity, he could never keep things from flying out of his reach. Nothing a large dose of mass could not correct.

A glistening light interrupted Nate's battle with a lack of gravity. He lifted the blind and peered out of the small window he had neglected to use the entire journey. His hand lingered on the blind, along with his eyes over the view. It was not the empty space he had become accustomed to over the course of his journey, but something bright and emblazoned with colours.

"It's beautiful, isn't it?" Helen said, while leaning over to look through the same window.

Nate rolled the ice to the other side of his mouth. He was forced to slurp loudly as a drop of liquid threatened to fly out. "It certainly is," he replied, with a slur.

"So I trust you've changed your mind about this visit?"

"Let's not get ahead of ourselves," Nate said through his teeth. The ice kept his tongue too busy to talk properly. "I think a bath, and a scotch that I don't have to squeeze

1

into my face, is in order before I answer that. I mean, how are we supposed to enjoy a drink when it wants to fly away? What I'm drinking is nothing more than a chilled scotch bubble with one ice cube."

Helen laughed and leant back. "Quit moaning," she said with a wry smile across her face. She reached into a pocket attached to the seat in front, produced a dark brown folder and began to sort through the papers. After a few seconds she found the one she wanted and offered it to Nate, being careful not to allow the others to escape. When she noticed he had become transfixed by the view once again, she let out a derisive tut.

His attention had now completely drifted away from her. The sight had become so surprisingly detailed and pleasing to behold, that his focus had no room spare for anything else. He had spent so long looking at the brochure before the flight that his expectations had become diluted, like his scotch. In the pictures he had seen a soft, slightly out of focus ring around a creamy yellow coloured planet. What he saw in reality was a spectacle that his eyes struggled to take in and his mind refused to ignore.

An enormous gas giant encircled by a light scattering disc of visible, icy material had gradually come into view. Instead of marvelling as they had approached, he had pondered over the drinks selection and on-board entertainment.

He quickly brushed aside his obvious error and allowed his eyes to wander over the planet's interacting bands of yellows and oranges. He could now make out the distinct details that made the view so much more enjoyable than the pictures had suggested, even down to the individual rocks, boulders and moon sized pieces that made up the planet's icy rings.

Nate's sightseeing was interrupted by something digging in his arm. When he turned he saw that Helen had grown frustrated with his lack of attention and had taken to prodding him. She was not concerned with what hovered,

2

serenely, outside like a swirling ball of cream and caramel. There was work to be done and she intended to finish it.

"We'll be landing soon so you need to look over this leaflet. It's about the festival tomorrow evening," she said.

Nate gave it a quick look, paying all of his attention to titles and pictures. He was not feeling in the mood to read. Once he had absorbed the ten percent he needed to feign interest, he placed it on his lap. He quickly slapped it back against his legs as it began to venture away. He could not wait to feel gravity's comforting influence once more.

"Fine, I'll tell you then." Helen turned in her seat to face him with obvious excitement. "This place is incredible. The festival tomorrow evening takes place once every 2 years."

"I thought this vacation was supposed to be relaxing?" Nate said abruptly, surprising even himself with the sudden interruption. He sucked in, forcing a drop of cool liquid down his throat that made him cough as he spoke. "Does a festival really qualify?"

"Relaxing? What gave you that idea?" she replied.

Nate shook his head in amusement. "Never mind." He coughed again. "Carry on."

"So the festival happens every 2 years, when the moon we're staying on passes close to one of the rings, through…" Helen referred to her own copy of the brochure before continuing. "…something called Orbital Resonance."

"Great, now when you say moon, do you mean a small grey dusty rock with no atmosphere, and no pool?" Nate could see the beginnings of a frown form on Helen's face— a cue that he was pushing it now. "Sorry," he said, as he raised his hands in defeat.

"Maybe that bath and scotch should come first. Zero-G seems to make you grouchy. How about I tell you properly when we're settled in?" she conceded. "By the way, it's that moon there. And it's not small. It's roughly Earth sized, smart-arse."

Nate followed the line of Helen's finger out the window and into space. The view was even brighter now as they passed, what Nate thought to be, only metres above the planet's rings. He could see Helen was pointing to a region between two of the bands of the rings.

Hiding there was their destination. A moon comfortably bigger than anything the rings contained, but still a tiny dot against the backdrop of the gas giant behind it. In comparison, Nate found it looked closer to an annoying smudge on an otherwise perfect oil painting, than it did another world.

He returned to his drink and allowed the scene to develop in the corner of his eye. Once every last drop of scotch had been released from its Zero-G plastic sachet packaging, he tucked it away in the side of his seat. He estimated another hour or so until they would arrive, plenty of time for a little nap.

***

A few hours later, Nate found himself in more comfortable surroundings, with a bed big enough to stretch out all of the aches and pains his journey had stored up in his body. He lay straight, staring up at the ceiling. If he concentrated hard enough he could swear he was back at home; at least for now that was enough to keep him relaxed. Tomorrow he would begin his vacation officially, he decided.

The moment he felt he could happily slip into a calm and welcoming sleep, a knock at the door brought him right back. He lay still for a few seconds before deciding to see who it was. Sleep would have to wait just a little longer. As he cumbersomely lifted his tired body up and shuffled slowly into a seated position, he immediately remembered how much of a bitch gravity could be.

Once to his feet he shuffled to the door. But before his hand had even made an attempt at the handle, someone began to push it open from the other side.

"Nathan, you in?" Helen jumped back the moment she spotted Nate standing by the door like a well-trained puppy, waiting for his owner to arrive. "Oh, you startled me. You have a minute?"

"Sure, what's up?" He hoped a minute was all the impending conversation would require. The clean, soft duvet was calling to him with promises of a peaceful slumber. It had already moulded itself to his body, so it seemed only fair he should oblige and fill in the grooves.

"I thought we should go through some things before you sleep."

Always the eager type, Nate noted. It was one of the things he had always liked about her; she was never one to delay things. On any other day he would have appreciated her keenness, but his dire need for rest was putting an altogether different spin on things. He was not as likeable when his head yearned for the cold side of a pillow.

"This has to be done now?" he said, trying to hide his tired frustration.

"Best now while you're awake."

Nate could not really argue with her logic. The task was to be done there and then whether he agreed or not, and whether he was awake or not. He was sure if he had dozed off right in front of her that she would have placed a pen in his hand and signed away until her work was done. The more he thought about it, the more he liked that idea.

"Besides, Stuart made it clear I'm here to sort everything out," Helen continued. "He doesn't want you to have to lift a finger while you're here." She brushed past Nate, sat on the edge of his bed and ran a finger through her paperwork, licking her finger between pages.

"Ah, Stuart, yes, I remember him. Short, balding guy, sort of yay wide?" Nate held his arms wide apart, then pushed the door shut as he brought them together, all in one satisfyingly Zen like move.

"Very funny. I think it's generous of him to hold the fort while you rest up. Even the mighty Nathan Maddox needs a break once in a while."

"Hey, I'm kidding. I know Stuart's been concerned about me. He's been great since my father retired. I couldn't

5

have taken over the company without him. He's helped my family a lot over the years. Hell, he's pretty much an uncle. A creepy uncle." He paused. "Don't tell him I said that."

Helen pinched her lips shut with a finger and thumb, indicating the secret was safe with her. "My lips are sealed. Now, first thing is this. He's your assigned bodyguard." She handed him a piece of paper, then neatly tucked the rest back into her folder.

Nate rolled his eyes as he went over the man's record sheet. Without really reading any of it, he handed it back— reading even his usual ten percent felt too much of a chore in his sleepy state.

"Looks fine," he said.

"He's not. His record isn't worth sneezing on. He's got this one last babysitting job ..." She shot a look of apology to Nate. "If he screws this up, he's out, so keep an eye on him. He'll report to you tomorrow."

"Fine, now shoo," Nate said as he ushered Helen in the direction of the door.

"You know, you really need to work on those manners."

"Duly noted, now go away." He waved as he pushed the door shut. The inevitable exhalation that followed effectively pushed him to the drinks dispenser, sat on a desk in his room.

He fumbled for the light on the corner table, before looking over the puzzling device. For something only created to provide drinks, it had a dizzying array of buttons. Unfortunately for him it had no button marked Scotch. He was not remotely in the mood to work the device out, except his drink was trapped inside it. Finally he found the right button combination, and within seconds his drink materialised already in its glass.

He sipped at his beverage as he instinctively wandered to the balcony. The breeze was fresh, temporarily counteracting the alcohol's numbing sensation. But his senses could immediately detect the breeze's unnatural origin. Whoever had designed the hotel had done a commendable job, making it feel like some kind of oasis. If not for the enormous icy rings above that kept the moon's night side sky more of a continuous twilight than a starry black, he would have believed it was genuine.

Past the hotel, with its pool and bar in full view downstairs, Nate could make out figures scurrying about in the distance. He followed them as they ran either to or from a large single story stone structure that resembled an unfinished pyramid. They were all busy in preparation for the festival Helen had told him about, although he did not care much for large celebrations.

With his scotch finished the night was finally at an end. He said goodnight to the busy bees as they built whatever was centre stage for tomorrow's celebrations and then headed back into his room. As he turned, his eyes caught a sparkle from the rings of the planet above. He remembered Helen had told him that their little piece of paradise was due to touch a layer of the rings. It still surprised him how close they were.

Another item added to his list of things to be bothered about tomorrow.

Chapter 2

The next morning, Nate made a point of having his breakfast by the pool, in shorts he would never normally dream of wearing.

He was not one to waste a morning, so he had found his dining guests in short supply. For nearly an hour his only companions had been his new bodyguard, Cameron, and a serene looking character who sat next to a small fountain in silent meditation across the pool from him. The man's clothing was long and loose, with overly large sleeve openings, almost oriental in style. A curious sight, Nate thought, but in keeping with the mystical look he had noticed his setting displayed.

As he relaxed, the other guests slowly began to appear. He had not noticed that many people last night, or was it the morning? The permanent twilight was causing havoc with his sense of time. Now, as he watched them in all their different shapes and colours, he could gauge just how important this festival was.

He had rarely seen so many races from so many different worlds together in one place. Some of the races he could name, others he was not so sure he had ever encountered before. Something very special appeared to be attracting them. Something he was beginning to realise he had underestimated.

"So, how's the CEO of Maddox industries this morning?" Helen said, pulling out the seat next to him. "Sleep well, Nathan?"

He could not help but admire her casual appearance. Her usual neutral coloured clothes and tied back hair was now replaced with a loose fitting, flowery dress and free flowing blond hair. He had never seen her like this before. She was essentially the same, but with a new lick of paint, a vibrant and invigorating palette to compliment a natural beauty he had always seen.

"Fine thanks, but for the next few days I'm just Nate OK? No Mr. Maddox or Nathan Maddox from now on," he replied with a broad smile across his face.

"Whatever Sir requires." She sent him a quick wink. He shook his head in response. "So you ready for this evening?"

"Yeah, about that," Nate said. "What exactly is it again?"

"Sure, it's not like I gave you a brochure to read or anything."

Nate laughed and leant back in his seat. "You know me so well."

"Too well," she said. "Right, this evening you will be attending what the locals call the Passing. They say there's some kind of ethereal life that exists within the planet's rings. The festival is to celebrate the Beings' temporary visit as the moon skims the rings. Of course you would have known that if you'd read the brochure."

"Sounds great." Nate put his thumbs up to emphasise the friendly sarcasm in his voice.

"There's more to it than that. I'll let you know the rest later. By the way, how's our mutual friend?" She indicated to Cameron with a nod of the head, accompanied by the judgemental raising of an eyebrow.

"He seems OK, very quiet. He does tend to hang around in the most conspicuous places though. He's not very good at blending." Nate watched as his newly assigned bodyguard assessed the threat level of a row of potted plants, on the other side of the pool.

"That's apparently one thing he's very good at, blending ..." Helen's eyebrow raised again, almost automatically. "His drinks that is," she added.

"Really? Shall we meet by the water-cooler the same time tomorrow?"

"I'm just saying, keep an eye on him."

"Will do. Now what time does this festival kick off?"

"This evening, about six," Helen said as she stood and glanced at Cameron one more time.

Before Nate could question her further she had already begun shuffling away. Something else important needed doing. She was all work and no play with him these days. A shame, he thought, he could see himself asking her to dinner one day, only to be declined.

She had only moved over to work with his adopted uncle, Stuart, a few months ago. During the two years before that she had never been more than four rooms away from him. This had allowed them to quickly become friends. But since then she was more focused than ever. Perhaps for the best anyway, he had regularly told himself; better that she were a friend than an ex.

He decided to head to his room and change, ready for the evening festivities. Something thin and loose. Despite the twilight it was warm enough to wear little. Maybe not the shorts again, he decided. The vacation was starting to sound interesting. It was not simply a desperate attempt at finding relaxation anymore, his curiosity had gotten the better of him. The least he could do was dress appropriately.

As he packed his things he looked to see if the meditating man was still there. He was, and had not moved an inch. Absolutely no part of his wrinkled and pale skin appeared to have budged at all. Somehow his serene state had remained intact, even with the small crowd that seemed to have congregated around him. Nate found the man's state both puzzling and enviable at the same time.

He could not quite place the man's species though. He had seen many different beings during his career and the man was not from one he could instantly recollect. The others he had not recognised were just guests, like him. The meditating man on the other hand was of obvious importance, someone the visitors knew and highly respected.

After a second or two he gave up trying to name the meditating man's species and waved to Cameron, who dutifully joined him.

"Yes, sir?" Cameron said.

"I'm heading to my room now."

"Right behind you, sir."

Nate led the way, making a mental note of how nervous Cameron sounded. His demeanour did not resemble that of a bodyguard at all. He was not remotely imposing or, unfortunately Nate saw, competent at portraying a sense of authority. It seemed a shame to him that the guy was probably not going to be under his employment when they got home.

Nevertheless, he was assigned to Nate for the duration of his stay. He brushed it under his proverbial carpet for the time being. He had to get ready to celebrate the Beings from the Rings of Ice and Dust, or something. He admitted he really should pay more attention to Helen when she explained things to him.

Chapter 3

Nate hesitantly made his way toward a growing crowd, just outside the grounds of the hotel. He had picked his clothing almost randomly, going for what felt most comfortable rather than any particular style. The choice had at least managed to meet his criteria of looseness: a blue, short-sleeved shirt paired with beige trousers. And as it turned out, his choice to wear trousers had been spot on. His bare legs would only have attracted the tiny, glowing bugs that whizzed above his head.

The time had finally come for the festival to begin. The attendees further ahead all hurried to find a good spot, while he walked among a shuffling mass of people who were clearly unsure of what was ahead. He would have said they were in the same boat, but the amount of people that appeared to share his trepidation would require more of a cruise-liner to be accurate.

Helen walked beside him with an arm on his sleeve. Cameron, however, was just ahead and making everybody aware of his presence. As the crowds began to swamp them he still stood out in his black suit, white shirt and brown tie combination. Subtlety was obviously not his strong-suit, choosing of course to top off the ensemble with a pair of black sunglasses. Even so it gave Nate the required level of security to make the crowd relatively comfortable to traverse.

As the path narrowed in front of them, they slowed to a crawl. Everyone seemed overly calm and polite as they tried not to land an elbow into their neighbours while finding room. If they had not been so pleasant, Nate would have turned around and headed back to the hotel. He cared little for large gatherings.

So far the evening was not going as Nate had foreseen. He had expected blinding lights and loud noises, either from some God awful music or suspiciously excited crowds. This was something altogether more civilised and controlled, precisely his kind of festival.

Up ahead, the single story structure he had seen the night before was gradually coming into view. As the crowd parted he could see it had now come to life, with small fire torches bathing it and the surrounding area in a mystical flicker of dim light.

There was no doubt in his mind this was all to add to the belief that something amazing was soon to occur. He was not so sure it was going to. Nothing more than some well-planned marketing ploy, he thought. Nevertheless, he tried to ignore his wallet-stretching concerns and decided he would simply enjoy it. For Helen's sake at least.

People in front of him bunched up as they found friends, family or just a spot they liked the look of. While being as polite as possible he pushed his way past them to find his own space, he remembered his misspent youth battling to be at the front of so many live music concerts as he did so. The art was to apologise just before making a move. He felt no shame in it, just a case of every man for himself.

Eventually Helen guided Nate to the spot reserved exclusively for him. It was not anything fancy, just a clear space on the floor. But it was closer than he would have managed otherwise.

He sat on the cold ground and felt the stone slabs with his hands as he found a comfortable position. He could not help but notice the unnaturally symmetrical way in which they had been placed. The entire area had been carefully built around the central structure, which by now had been completely surrounded by hotel guests. The level of orchestration he saw around him was admirable; everything was where it needed to be.

The excitement in the air was palpable and felt by all around. Yet for Nate the unknown only made his mouth dry and his limbs shaky, and unsure. Also, a slightly metallic taste had taken up residence on his tongue and was refusing to go. However many times he swallowed, it stubbornly remained.

"So," Helen began. "There're some things to go over before it starts."

As she went through the checklist, Nate watched the last minute preparations being carried out by the local inhabitants. He nodded at the first few items she read out, but something in the middle caught him by surprise.

"Say that again," he said.

"What? The doorway bit? Well, it will open in front of you. That's why everyone's keeping space free."

Nate had not even noticed. He quickly scanned around and found that each group had indeed left room between them. An odd sight, again nothing like the festival he had envisioned. He was more caught up in the atmosphere than he had first thought—surely he would have noticed otherwise?

"What's the doorway *to*?" he asked, feeling a sense of confusion building in him.

Helen's lips parted and she was ready to speak, when someone else answered for her.

"To whatever past events the Gods have deemed important, and enjoyable, to you," someone said.

Nate turned and was shocked to find the meditating man from the pool taking a seat next to him. He lowered himself into place carefully, crossing his legs underneath. His loose sleeves flapped open to reveal thin and bony arms hidden inside. They were as wrinkled and pale as the rest of him, and contradicted his slightly chubby torso. Perhaps a trait of his species rather than an indication of his lifestyle.

14

He had Nate curious, nonetheless. This alien was more interesting than the others.

"I sense you are feeling some trepidation about the gift you are about to receive," the man continued.

"I suppose I am, yes. I'm Nathan Maddox." He extended an unexpectedly clammy hand to greet the man, which was appreciatively received. They shook hands enthusiastically as they spoke.

"Welcome Nathan Maddox, my name is L'Armin Hes. I am the spiritual leader here and I guide those who seek the Gods during the Passing."

After a few shakes the man seemed unwilling to let go. Nate normally expected a handshake to last, at most, three to four seconds—enough time to make your confidence known. He was already at six seconds and the man showed no signs of stopping. If anything the shaking was speeding up.

"Pleasure to meet you," Nate said.

"You have questions?"

For a moment, Nate found himself suspecting the man had read his mind through their vibrating limbs. He quickly brushed off the absurd notion, despite the deeply intense, and intensely deep, stare directed at him.

"Just a few," he said.

"I think I'll leave you with ... L'Armin?" Helen checked her pronunciation before continuing. The man nodded his approval. "I've got some things to attend to," she continued. "Cameron is fully aware of what to do when it starts, by the way."

"You're not staying?" Nate said.

"No. You'll be fine. Have fun." Helen carefully stepped around a mother and child—both of a species Nate did not recognise. She then delicately picked her way through the scattered groups, tip toeing like a child trying to leave a classroom without disturbing her classmates. Soon she had stealthily disappeared amid the shadows—an easy feat considering the permanent twilight.

15

"Only those who wish to witness the power of the Beings remain," L'Armin said. "If you choose not to see your own past, you must avert your gaze when contact is made with the rings. So, do you wish to see, Nathan Maddox?"

Nate took a few moments to decide. He could see the excitement growing among the crowd. Some of the more enthusiastic members had begun wandering around and handing out flowers, while conversing with complete strangers. Something was beginning to stir and he could not help but smile at what he was seeing.

He took a moment to absorb all he could from the scene, allowing it to mix with his senses. The refreshingly dynamic crowd he found himself in was like nothing he had ever experienced before. Their fragrances were both alien and familiar. Some tickled his sense of smell like the scent of a flower—only not a flower he had ever known—while others invaded without warning.

The noises they made were equally as strange. But the emotions they portrayed were interpretable, some even unmistakable. All in all there was nothing remotely threatening that he could see. Perhaps something great *was* about to happen after all.

"Let's give it a go then," he finally said.

"As you wish."

"What do I have to do?"

"In a short time the beacon will be activated, calling upon the Gods. You must allow them to join with you. Only then will you be given the gift of re-creation."

"They'll let me re-create what ... exactly?" Nate said, still more confused than he would have liked.

"Physical re-creations of memories or memorable experiences. Each will uniquely reflect the path the participant has walked in life. The gift of the Gods allows you to see again, Nathan Maddox. Are there not times you wish you could return to?"

Nate felt a lump form in his throat. If only he had listened to Helen earlier. He did not see such power as something to be treated so lightly. Some past events he knew he would rather leave alone. He certainly did not want to have them dragged back to life, kicking and screaming like an unhappy newborn. No, he would rather keep them to himself—some deeper than others.

His left foot began to twitch nervously, tapping against the stone slab beneath him. He suddenly realised how completely unprepared he was.

"Enjoy the peace The Passing will bring you," L'Armin said, his tone reassuring and soft.

Nate remained still—all except for his foot—as L'Armin stood and sauntered off in the direction of the central structure. He turned back with his hands placed together and bowed, before then continuing on. Nate was surprised to notice that the ruffles of skin ran right over L'Armin's head and to the nape of his neck. Was any part of him not entirely covered in wrinkles?

Soon though, only one thought rattled around Nate's head as he watched his guide finally disappear into the crowd: was it too late to back out? A rush of loneliness made him check that Cameron was still there. He was, but it settled Nate's nerves only temporarily.

He did not know the man that was now responsible for his safety, how could he confide in him? More than anything he wished for Helen to be there with him still. She could always calm his nerves with a cheerful smile or a sarcastic comment. Exactly what he felt he needed.

For the next few minutes he sat in silence, more nervous than during the monthly board meetings he held at Maddox Industries' headquarters. The last of which had been riddled with doubtful whispers about his leadership. A weak portfolio for their asteroid mining endeavours meant a weak leader. Plus their usual competitor had won a big contract and somehow it was entirely his fault.

His father had proven them wrong enough times in the past, and he knew he could do too. At least with this Passing thing he did not have to face the usual torrent of questions that followed the meetings. It was not much, but the thought was enough to take his mind comfortably away for a few seconds.

As he waited, the nearest group began to offer him some of their friendly advice. Either because of the look on his face or possibly the noise his foot continued to make as it repeatedly, and automatically, tapped the floor. For whatever reason, he was just grateful for the support. Except for one problem: none of them spoke any Human languages. They resorted instead to gestures and overly animated enactments, to get their tips across to him.

One of them drew in a couple of deep breaths and then pushed against Nate's chest. When he repeated the action, the man grabbed his left shoulder and shook it—he assumed this was equivalent to shaking hands. Another of the group then pointed at her eyes, held wide open. He could interpret this well enough but copied her anyway, to her delight.

The third suggestion, however, had him slightly concerned. As well as keeping his eyes open and controlling his breathing, he was to expect a slight kick at the back of his head—demonstrated by the entire group suddenly slapping the rear of their skulls.

Laughter rippled through the group as they acted out the events that were only moments away. Nate found their joyful interactions an effective remedy to his stressful ills. More and more his mind was able to form an expectation of what was to come. It almost sounded fun to him now.

When the group stopped and turned to face the stage, it was clear the festival was about to begin. There was no backing out for Nate now.

A cheer erupted as a man appeared on a raised podium in front of the crowd. He raised his arms, quieting them to near silence. No words were spoken, or even required, such was his command over the crowd.

Nate had to squint to make out the figure that had brought the group to a deathly quiet. The power he had over them impressed him. It took him a few seconds to realise it was L'Armin. The softly spoken man that had remained so still and quiet earlier, was well and truly in charge of proceedings now.

Everyone watched with wide and focused eyes. Nate was not sure where to look, their reaction intrigued him as much as the proceedings ahead. If he concentrated on them too much he was worried he would miss something L'Armin did. The spectacle was beginning to draw him in, which was a surprise, but not a disappointment.

L'Armin looked up to the rings above, speaking words of worship into the sky. The crowd began to chant along with him. The language was not one Nate recognised, but those around him certainly did. His words were repeated as a near silent chant that began to work its way toward Nate, as though carried on the breeze.

A signal was then sent to a man to L'Armin's side as the chanting intensified unexpectedly. The volume of the voices all around increased in anticipation.

All Nate could see was a man approaching the large central structure behind L'Armin. He climbed its single structure and then ceremoniously bowed. He was clearly of the same race as L'Armin, but without the baggy clothing that concealed his body shape. The topless figure's limbs were the same as L'Armin's too, skinny yet able to support a surprisingly bulky upper body.

After he had shown the correct amount of respect, he put as much theatrical exaggeration as he could muster into pulling a large lever in the middle of the structure. Nate was mesmerised. The man moved like a magician, revealing an intricate workings the eye did not see. He struggled at first to move the lever fully across from left to right, stopping occasionally before continuing. Eventually it clicked into position, locking in place with a satisfying *clunk*. Then silence again.

Nate went to clap in appreciation, before noticing in the corner of his eye that everyone remained still. They were held by something he did not understand. His hands hovered a few centimetres away from each other, he had just managed to stop them slapping together in time. Was that it? he thought.

A woman screamed excitedly somewhere near the back of the crowd. It startled him, but only briefly. What followed was much more dramatic—and loud—as something on the stage exploded. Whatever had sent the woman into a frenzy had suddenly come to life. The festival had definitely begun now.

"Christ!" Nate shouted, as a bright blue beam of light, nearly two metres in width, shot out from the centre of the structure and straight up into the sky. It continued on to the sparkling bands above at a tremendous speed. The beam reached so high and so quickly, that within less than a second the top of it had narrowed into a thin streak of laser-light as it raced away.

In reality it had travelled at an incredible velocity to far beyond the moon's atmosphere, where it had gently tickled the edge of the rings high above them. He could see the light as it eventually hit, diffusing as it made contact. The distance dazzled him; he guessed it must have travelled tens of thousands of miles at least.

Then ten, maybe eleven, seconds after reaching its destination something began to happen. It appeared to vaporise a small area of the rings, now connected to their tiny moon by the light beam. There, a small blue luminescent cloud, perched at the top of the beam, began to build.

Nate's neck retorted at the sudden jerk upwards, as he had tracked the light. He placed his arms on the ground behind to support himself. If he had not, he was sure he would have fallen back and cracked his head on the stone floor. He quickly realised he was witnessing something that would stay with him for a lifetime; he did not want to miss a thing. Even so his eyes began to sting as he fought to keep them open. They soon began to water uncontrollably as the urge to blink became too much.

He decided, against his better judgement, to stand and take a better look at the source of the light beam. It emanated from the bowels of the stage in front, a bright structure of light that appeared as solid as anything else around him.

A rumble of voices said something to him, but he was too immersed in his own thoughts to pay attention. As he did with any magic trick, he searched for the things you were not supposed to see. To him the light must be a spectacular distraction. Except nothing appeared out of place, no loose props or hidden doors. Even the man who had activated the device was standing in awe of the beam.

As he kept his thoughts busy with peeking behind the curtain, he failed to spot what those around had tried to warn him of. The luminescent cloud that had been building at the top of the beam was now hurtling back down it like a violent two metre wide glowing tornado. When it hit he realised those around had been trying to tell the *moron* standing up, to sit his ass back down, lest he fall flat on his face. An apt prediction, Nate soon found out.

The cloud hit the ground with a dull, almost inaudible thud and immediately began to spread out across the surface in one vaporous wave. Nate felt it hit with surprising force, sending him stumbling into the group behind. A small child yelped as he trampled over its tiny hand before he finally lost all control of his fall.

The floor welcomed him with a generous clout to the back of the head as he landed. The family he had crashed into kindly propped him up again. One of them then slapped the back of their own head to reiterate what they had told him.

Everyone in the group took a deep lungful of air in unison, holding it in for a few heartbeats before slowly exhaling. Those around Nate gestured to him to focus his breathing in the same way as before. He copied as best he could, but the fall had winded him slightly, making each breath wheezy and laboured. He followed their actions whether he thought it would help or not. He was just grateful to accept their guidance once more.

As the air cleared and the sky returned to its usual twilight hue, Nate could feel something odd. He hoped he had not cocked it up for himself as he watched the vapour cloud fade to nothing. His head buzzed with an unknown energy that permeated his entire skull. His thoughts were suddenly hard to form and fuzzy, like a TV showing nothing but static. Occasionally the seed of a thought sprung up, but was quickly lost in the interference.

Then came the forewarned kick, almost as forcefully as the cloud, right at the back of his skull. It quickly passed along with the static, before the crowd slowly came back into focus. He could see, but his balance was shot, causing him to unintentionally slump to the side.

But he did not hit the floor this time. Instead he fell against someone he had not even noticed had taken position next to him. Whoever it was he had held Nate in place, anchoring him to the spot.

"Are you all right, sir?" Cameron said with obvious worry in his voice.

After quickly gathering himself together, Nate tried to find Cameron, assuming at first it was he who had stopped the fall. Yet when he turned in his new spot, he was shocked to see L'Armin smiling back down at him instead. How long he had been there for, Nate could not tell.

A laugh escaped from the side of Nate's mouth. "That was a rush."

Cameron did not reply. The wide-eyed look on his face showed his composure had made a run for it as he had watched his career nearly disappear in front of him. He wiped a loose drop of sweat from his forehead and into his slick black hair. The collar of his shirt had turned a darker shade, a tell-tale sign of runaway perspiration.

Nate watched the others nearby. The ten percent of the brochure he had read had not covered any of this. So, unlike him they knew exactly what was coming next. They stood closely huddled together in a circle and held hands, then closed their eyes.

Another of L'Armin's race had joined the group next to him and was helping them along like an enthusiastic tour guide. Nate looked to the other circles that had spontaneously formed and noticed each of them now had their very own chaperon. He guessed L'Armin had been assigned as his.

A family much nearer the front were the first to reach the next part with their guide. Something was trying to form from nothing more than thin air, and Nate could see that those around were causing it somehow. In the middle of their circle, a small ball of glowing static electricity was popping excitedly, with a playful crackle. The more it sparked the more it effected those in the group, until every hair and loose piece of clothing had become stretched out horizontally, as though reaching for it.

Nate stood up again, determined to see what was about to happen. He balanced on his toes, akin to a ballerina, to see over the shoulders that hindered his view. Annoyingly they had started to sway from side to side, in some kind of celebratory dance. He tried to compensate but his balance was not good enough to keep up. For the time being he had to settle for an obstructed view.

With a final *pop* a fantastic glowing orb appeared with a flash, like a tiny pinprick supernova. At this point the swaying stopped, reinstating Nate's view of events. His mouth gaped open when he saw the object in its entirety and not just the aura of light that surrounded it.

The orb grew until eventually it was big enough to step through. Even though he could not see beyond its bright light, Nate could still tell something lingered beyond. Whatever it was it remained hidden behind a veil of luminescence. It did not appear to be solid, moving instead like a bubbling and frothy soup of pure light, without any permanent outline.

As Nate peered in, not sure if he could make out something inside, the father figure of the group stepped in and unexpectedly disappeared. He gasped as the guide followed closely behind. Then one by one the others casually walked through, until they were all gone.

So enthralled by the spectacle of it all, he had not noticed a number of other orbs had now opened for others to enter. His concentration was only broken when he heard a familiar voice next to him.

"Are you ready, Nathan Maddox?" L'Armin said, his tone once again distilling a sense of calm into the situation, despite what had just happened.

"I'm not sure. This is all new to me," Nate said, as he clasped his hands together—now drenched in sweat. "Sure?" It had come out more of a question than a statement.

"I will guide you as they once guided me. Do not worry. Close your eyes and clear your thoughts."

He followed L'Armin's instructions to the letter, for fear of some unknown fate. Perhaps the blue orb would disintegrate his entire body to nothing more than dust if he did it wrong, he was not sure. More importantly, he did not want to find out. L'Armin was his guide and he had his implicit trust. His curiosity was slowly beginning to overwhelm his usually cautious nature.

"As you let the Beings in, thoughts will spontaneously appear and disappear," L'Armin continued. "Try to concentrate on one in particular."

L'Armin's voice had become distant as Nate allowed his mind to race uncontrollably. Something weaved a path through his subconscious, appearing for one fleeting moment before burying itself deep once more.

Thoughts were somehow more real than they were before, like he could reach out and touch them. He imagined his hand out in front of himself, feeling around as if in complete darkness. It ventured, wearily, toward a thought as it floated around, only to come up empty every time he tried to grab one. The more he attempted to hold one the foggier the landscape became, as though each had turned to dust in his hand.

But sure enough it gradually cleared to reveal one coherent train of thought.

"You must choose where to go, Nathan Maddox," L'Armin said, his voice now almost impossible to locate.

Nate could see something forming in his mind. One thought had taken precedent over all others and it was drawing him in. He slowly moved forward, almost automatically. The sound of a child laughing took him by surprise, followed by the sensation of heat on his neck and then a rush of air on his face. Where had he felt this before?

His projected hand groped at the fog, as if to part it once and for all, revealing even more. There was something there, only his concentration had shifted to one particular sensation: the crunch of dry dirt under his feet. How his mind had arrived at this one thing, he could not say. He could not really say if *he* had done it at all.

"What the hell is that?" Cameron said.

The outburst immediately brought Nate back. His eyes rolled to the front as he opened them, like he had been abruptly awoken from a deep sleep. All he knew for certain was that reality had invaded and washed away the most vivid daydream he had ever encountered. It had quickly then become as foggy as any other memory.

With his mind now clear he could see the outcome of his short, but enjoyable, trip into his subconscious. In front of him now hovered a glowing blue orb of his very own. He could not believe it, it had the same structure and everything. The last, stubborn, bubble of doubt had finally popped.

"Are you ready to enter, Nathan Maddox?" L'Armin said, his hand perched gently on Nate's shoulder.

Nate did not speak, he was transfixed by the beauty of the orb. It beckoned him to enter, like a steaming hot bath. It promised to comfort him and protect him: *step inside and see*, it seemed to say.

He wanted to enter more than ever and if not for a lingering sense of worry, he would have dived straight in.

His eyes no longer saw a random light show, but one made just for him. This one was special, it was his.

He was finally ready to see exactly how much of the brochure he had not read.

Chapter 4

Ever so slowly, Nate took a step toward the glowing shape he had somehow conjured up from thin air. He hesitated before taking another step, gradually speeding up as his confidence grew. Just as he raised his right foot, in anticipation to enter, someone tugged at his arm. Had something gone wrong?

"I think it would be best if I went first, Mr. Maddox," Cameron said, as authoritatively as he could manage.

Nate did not argue. It was the obvious suggestion. He could almost hear Helen sighing in relief as he waved his bodyguard forward.

Cameron took the lead and headed in. The light enveloped him as he moved further into it, until only the back of his right leg remained. It hovered for a second like a ghostly severed limb. Nate could see the moment Cameron shifted his weight back to his left leg as he lifted his right in. This was the cue he was waiting for. He figured that as long as the next thing he saw was not Cameron screaming and writhing in pain, he was safe to follow.

The light was blinding. He had expected as much, but the urge to open his eyes as he had stepped through had been too much to resist. With each step the pain that itched at the back of his eyes subsided and gradually settled, until the light began to take on a yellow hue.

He soon noticed a warm feeling surrounding his body as he walked on, followed by a light, refreshing breeze.

Something was coming through and slowly but surely taking shape. When the floor began to crunch under his feet, he was positive. He had been there before.

A more natural and welcoming light soon took over. He rubbed his eyes on his sleeve to clear them of moisture. Eventually he was able to keep them open for long enough for them to adjust to the early evening sun, before blinking again.

He was shocked at the realism of the scene. His memory of the place was lacking so much that now existed in front of him. He could make out every blade of grass, every cloud in the sky, even the rust on the children's swings that stood in front of him.

"What is this place?" Cameron said.

Nate had not noticed him standing to the side, with the same look of wonder on his face. Was it all real? Nate could not decide. As he watched Earth's sun reflect in Cameron's pitch black glasses, he knew it was certainly impressive. His own recollections of this time in his life never seemed as beautiful.

"This is the park near where I grew up. Only I'd forgotten most of these details," he replied.

Cameron did not hesitate, he set about touching as much as possible to confirm it was really there. Nate watched him move around, envious of his confidence, almost as though he were scared he would break something if he tried to as well. He could not even imagine feeling any of it on his fingertips.

The sun was beating down overhead, and he could feel its warmth like a soft blanket. But he could not tell if it were a giant ball of plasma out in space, nearly 150 Million kilometres away, or a cleverly designed light trick hung metres above. Whichever it was he conceded it resided high enough to be out of reach, so of little consequence. The memory existed but this was not simply a recollection, it was something much more tangible.

"Bugger," Cameron called out from behind a tree Nate had not even noticed.

He headed over to meet Cameron. He had not paid any attention to the tree as he had entered. It had been such a huge thing to him as a young child, bigger than any other living thing he had seen at the time. It once again filled him with a sense of joy and wonder, even though he had aged considerably since then.

The gravel again crunched under his feet. It was a sound that jolted his memory into sync with his surroundings. He had never forgotten that sound. It conjured up countless memories of himself speeding through the park like his life were at risk. The imaginary creatures he had enjoyed evading at the time had since faded into obscurity. Nothing could bring them back, he realised. He was not sure his imagination could still create such vivid images anymore. Still it was something incredible to see all of this in front of him once again.

Cameron stood on the other side of the tree with a bloodied finger. Nate found him and at first glance was surprised to see he had removed his glasses to reveal two distinctly tired and heavy looking brown eyes. They appeared older than the rest of him, which Nate guessed was somewhere around the mid-forties—roughly the same as himself.

"What?" Nate said.

"I've cut my finger on the damn tree bark," Cameron replied excitedly.

Nate repeated Cameron's action of rubbing the tree's rough surface. Bits of it began flaking away and sticking to his palm as he moved his hand up and down. It did exactly what he expected it to. Even down to the inevitable splinter he could feel sticking into his skin. He had hated this as a child, but the sensation was too real to dislike now. He had found a link to his childhood and gradually he was beginning to enjoy it.

They shared a childish laugh as Nate wiped the debris onto his trousers. Cameron quickly moved on to the next thing that required exploring, showing an unrivalled amount of joy at the scene.

Nate watched for a second before deciding to continue wandering around the tree. He gently explored its surface by brushing his left hand across the bark. Soon he felt something curious, a defined shape, perhaps a letter carved into the wood. He then found others nearby. They were markings carved into the wood with a pocket knife, left by previous visitors. Some were crudely designed images, hard to interpret, while others were clearly marked messages of friendship or childhood loves.

A rush of heat travelled up his neck and to his forehead as he began to search for the one his own pocket knife had left. As he did he could remember the sweat on his hands as he had gripped the knife and spelled out his name so many years before. He had been barely nine when he had left the message, in a tree he guessed was now paved over in reality. But it was not there. He was sure he had left one.

Nate reminisced of the hours he had spent playing in this playground. He had so many fragments of good and bad memories, all among the swings and climbing frames. Like the time his friend broke an arm jumping from the top of the slide, or his own bruises from pretending to be a superhero, or even his first kiss, on the swings.

Each of them took place with a distant sparkle from the many skyscrapers behind, permanent glass-clad reminders of what his future would hold, not that he ever realised as a child. To him the buildings, with their swarms of flying vehicles whizzing by, were just cool.

It was the first time in years he had remembered such times; he was rarely relaxed enough to be able to. His vacation was finally beginning.

The sound of children giggling nearby took his mind away from the past. He peered around the tree and saw a group of kids swinging high and fast on the communal swings in the middle of the park. They were oblivious to the unnatural origin of the place in which they frivolously played.

It took Nate a few moments to realise they were part of the re-creation. They had to be, he had not seen any Human families during his flight or in the hotel. His mind hurt as he tried to comprehend how this was at all possible. Did they know he was there? Would he be able to interact with them, or was this simply a scene he could only witness?

The answer came to him like a wrecking ball through a weak wall. He was amazed to see Cameron pushing one of the children on the swings, a small boy. If any doubt remained it served as nothing more than structural support to the wall that had already fallen. Once they were gone the rest would come tumbling down around him.

"Strange, is it not?"

"L'Armin, this is fucking crazy," Nate said, his curse causing a nervous laugh to slip out. "Sorry. How is this possible?"

"Your question does not need an answer. It exists and is for you to enjoy. Do you recognise this place?"

"Yes, I used to live a few streets from here. Over there somewhere, I guess." Nate pointed in the direction of a row of houses to his left, past the swings.

But as his arm straightened out horizontally in the air—his finger extended—he noticed something odd about the child Cameron interacted with on the swings. It was a young boy around, he guessed, six or seven years of age.

The boy wore a bright blue t-shirt with scuffs and small tears on the elbows. Exactly the same as the scuffs his mother had complained about to him. *How do you keep ruining your clothes?* she had regularly said to him as a young boy. The answer was simple: in order to flank their imaginary enemy it was necessary for him and his friends to crawl through the bushes.

It quickly dawned on him that the child shared a lot more in common with him than he wanted to admit. The trainers he had loved as a child reached up to the sky as the young boy excitedly leant back into his swing to gain height. Cameron was completely unaware of who the child was.

"Shit, that's me," Nate shouted in amazement. "How the Hell." He turned to L'Armin, who watched his every movement with an air of amusement and curiosity.

"This is more than a memory, Nathan Maddox, it is a physical re-creation of the past. It is as real as you and I."

Suddenly, Nate realised something else. "That's why I couldn't find the carving on the tree, I hadn't made it yet." He hesitated before continuing. "Can I talk to myself, the kid me I mean?"

L'Armin nodded.

"I'm not sure my head would be able to handle that," Nate said.

The two of them stood watching Cameron as he explored the place in a way Nate wanted to, but could not. He was afraid if he altered anything it would damage the memory, corrupting it like computer data. Instead he let it wash over him.

The breeze had now lessened in strength and was breaking up less of the sun's heat than before, causing his skin to tingle. He licked a drop of sweat that threatened to drip from his upper lip. Was the sweat real? It certainly tasted real.

L'Armin was first to break the moment of quiet with a slap of his hands. "Would you like to move on?"

"To where?" Nate replied, his eyes never straying from the younger version of himself, smiling as he flew through the air, no doubt expecting to touch the clouds.

"Anywhere. The connection to the Beings should be strong enough now for them to guide you. Your mind is a land to be explored, let them explore it."

"All right, I guess we could. But how do we move on?" Before the sentence had completely escaped Nate's mouth, another glowing orb formed in front of them. "I guess that's how."

Without a moment's hesitation, Cameron stopped pushing the younger Nate and raced over to the doorway. His enthusiasm spurred Nate on to join him. This time Nate desperately wanted to go first. He had to jump ahead of

Cameron just to stop him charging through. Then a quick nod of the head between them confirmed readiness, with Nate first in the queue like an impatient and fidgety child.

Once again the sensation of a blinding light overpowered his senses. He fumbled the air for something solid but nothing obvious was there. Even the sound of his feet could not give anything away. He could have been entering a large hall or a tiny cupboard for all he knew, nothing was giving him any clues like before. There was not the warmth of before either. This at least suggested he could be entering somewhere indoors.

A low level hum of voices began to echo around him. A world beyond the blindness was coming nearer. The fog was once again clearing and voices were growing louder as he stumbled forward, becoming more defined with every step he took.

He continued to wave his arms ahead, eager to grasp something to anchor him to reality. When he finally felt something soft and padded he froze. Whatever it was, it had an owner and they were not happy with the unprovoked grope.

After an uncomfortable few seconds his sight adjusted to the light in the room, where he suddenly found himself face to face with a woman he did not recognise. He dared not look down in case the soft thing he had found to anchor himself to turned out to be a breast.

Eventually he removed his hand and was thankful to see it leave the left side shoulder pad of her formal suit jacket. She sent him a scornful look, regardless. There was no doubt the woman had seen, and felt him. A good reason to tread carefully, he decided. He would keep an eye on his wandering hands too from now on.

With an embarrassing incident averted, he took a look around. He was now in the middle of a crowded but intimate room full of elegantly dressed people. They conversed within small groups that occasionally mingled with others nearby.

"OK, this is cool," Cameron said from behind.

Nate turned to see him poking a man he had unintentionally bumped into. Unlike Nate, though, he annoyingly prodded the poor man like a plaything.

"Cameron, easy with the finger attacks," Nate said.

Cameron laughed as he stepped away from the confused man. "Sorry Mr. Maddox, this is just really weird. What is this place anyway?"

Nate scanned his eyes across the large, busy room. People stood talking among themselves, each one holding a glass of champagne. They were waiting for something to start, something he remembered straight away.

He found he could remember a lot more of this place than the playground; with its dim artificial lighting overhead—relaxing to the eyes—and the rubbing of shoulders as people politely competed for room. A thought of bubbles racing up his nose as he had swigged a drink came to mind. He could picture the tall glass in one hand, and something small in the other: a ring, hidden in the creases of his sweaty palm.

He grabbed two glasses from a tray as it was expertly manoeuvred past him and through the crowd. When he handed the second glass to Cameron he immediately remembered Helen's warning as the glass was taken.

A moment of worry that was put to rest by Cameron's attempt to stealthily place it down on a nearby table. Nate took note; no amount of paperwork would have picked up on that. Cameron was trying to beat his problem and he admired that.

The champagne slid around his mouth as he took a generous sip. The bubbles tickled the back of his throat as he swallowed, just like it had on the day. It did not last long either, only three swigs until it was gone. Slowly he found himself losing the cautiousness that had stifled his exploration of the park before.

He began to make his way through the crowd like he would any ordinary gathering of people, regardless of whether they were real or not. Even going as far as apologising for bumping into people and raising his glass when the risk of spillage arose, though only a drop remained.

Finally he made it to the front, where a large floor to ceiling glass window extended along the entire length of the room. He knew exactly what to look for, so as soon as the last few people parted he set about finding it. Everyone waited for what was due to take place outside, he just had to remember where.

Out in the expanse of space, one particular winking dot was about to provide their entertainment. He marvelled at the familiarity of the sight before him, but was frustrated by this one missing detail. Only one of the many stars he could see interested him, the others were just a distraction.

"We've got about five minutes until one of these stars goes supernova," he said, but Cameron had already disappeared into the swell of people.

He pushed his finger against the glass, where one of the closer stars—or bigger, he could not tell—resided. Any moment now he expected it to explode into billions of brightly coloured pieces, spraying its content across a huge area of space and hurtling massive amounts of energy into nearby nebulae, seeding future galaxies, an incredible aspect of nature that those aboard the ship had paid handsomely to witness.

"Kaboom," he said to himself. He had not realised someone was still listening to him. The field of stars had him transfixed. But someone had been there all the time, and they had enjoyed Nate's low-tech sound effect.

"Do you remember this place?" L'Armin said with a friendly smile. The tiny giggle he had let out quickly trailed off.

"You bet I do. When the star blows …" Nate pinched his fingers together as if to crush the star he had picked out of existence himself. "I get down on one knee and ask Gemma to marry me. Somewhere over there."

Nate's finger surveyed the crowd behind him and rested over a couple standing at the back. Immediately he recognised the blue shirt with narrow white stripes and black trousers he had worn to pop the question.

Equally, he remembered the black dress Gemma had effortlessly worn, with its well-placed slit down the side that framed her left leg perfectly. They stood close, his arm around her back and resting gently on her hip. Nothing—and no-one—mattered to them. The words exchanged were meant only for each other, spoken softly and directly into the other's ear.

"I was so nervous," he continued, never once letting his eyes move away from the intimate scene.

The other Nate rolled with laughter at something Gemma had said. For the life of him he could not remember what it was. It occurred to him that he had forgotten more about this day than he liked to admit. A smile still managed to invade his face at the once shared joke. The emotion was still as strong as it had been on the day, even if the details had become diluted.

It seemed contagious as L'Armin had picked up on the same thing, despite the joke having evaded Nate's best attempt to recall it. He and L'Armin were still able to appreciate the reaction it had elicited. It brought a smile that lingered on L'Armin's face for long enough for Nate to spot, and become slightly confused by.

"It's strange to see the past play out like this," Nate said, deciding to ignore the oddness of the moment.

"The memory must be strong for the Beings to lead us to it." There was a slightly questioning tone to L'Armin's words.

"It is. This was roughly 15 years ago. We're still great friends. Divorced. But good friends. At this point it couldn't get any better ... or it was all downhill from here. Both are true."

"Which is it at this moment?"

"Good question. To be honest it depends on my mood." Nate left it there. He quickly shifted his position to get a clear view of the stars, and to stop L'Armin posing any more questions about his failed relationship.

36

The star everyone had gathered to see was now due to amaze them with its violent death throes. The life of a sun was about to end in one of nature's most impressive processes, and trays of snacks were drawing all of the attention over on a small buffet table. Nate and Gemma were no exception, but they were interested in each other rather than finger snacks.

Nate was first to spot the increasing luminosity of the star of the show. It was roughly two inches or so further along the glass than the one he had incorrectly picked earlier. Soon enough it began to make itself known. The dark and featureless view was quickly becoming its stage to shine on. All others appeared to dim as its performance overwhelmed their amateur talents.

It soon became too much for his eyes to stand, stinging the back of them. He closed them but the light was stronger still. It shone through the skin of his eyelids, making them almost translucent. Only a hand over his already closed eyes could alleviate the pain.

Everyone was now paying attention. Some covered their eyes like Nate, while others adorned tinted glasses to block out the harmful brightness. After a few seconds it began to dim, along with the crowds audible reactions.

He was surprised to see it was over so quickly, but cautious enough to open his eyes away from the glass. When he did he was greeted by an ensemble of emotive faces, some of which showed their amazement, with mouths agape and half eaten snacks on full display.

"We've tinted the window to filter out some of the light, so go ahead and remove your glasses folks. Enjoy the view," a voice said through the speaker system overhead.

Nate turned back to see for himself. It was still the brightest thing in view, but with less strength than before. The star had completely torn itself asunder and would continue to do so for months now, and they were able to watch without a worry. He was sure, as he peered through the dimmed glass, that he could make out a bubble like shape surrounding the distant explosion. Either debris or the distorting effect of watching such a thing through a window, he surmised.

But it was not the immense scale or overwhelming beauty that caught him unexpectedly. It was something else. Something he could not possibly have appreciated at the time. As he watched the demise of the star for a second time, he realised what it was. It had become the perfect metaphor for his relationship with Gemma and the way in which it had ultimately ended. One minute it had been perfectly stable and full of wonder, and the next it drifted in a million pieces through the black of space.

The thought seemed to stick in his side. He was not bitter, but maybe a little regretful. Perhaps he was ready to try again? The star had released energy that would go on to seed other stars, why could not he do the same in his love life? His mind began to picture the same scene, except with Helen in Gemma's place, wearing the same dress and gracefully sipping on a glass of champagne.

"I think she is pleased, Nathan Maddox," L'Armin said.

"Huh?" Nate spun back around to face the crowd.

The question had been asked and he had completely missed it—too distracted by the view. The answer was obvious though. He remembered the relief as Gemma had accepted and thrown her arms around him. She had squeezed so tight that his neck had ached for at least an hour afterwards. He remembered it well and was strangely comforted by watching it play out again, despite his knowledge of the future.

But somehow things were not quite going right all of a sudden. He did not remember such a commotion in the background as he and Gemma had celebrated. Nothing obvious came to mind though, nothing he had forgotten. Still something was definitely very badly wrong.

He could see people pushing and shoving each other in the middle of the room, like a fight had broken out. The scuffle was beginning to spread, causing others to suddenly react to something Nate just could not locate.

38

"Get down," Cameron shouted suddenly.

Nate was shocked to see Cameron racing toward him and L'Armin, with a look of utter panic across his face. He pushed people in his way to the floor without any consideration. His sight was locked on and unmoving as he charged at them from the other direction of the disturbance. Everything was quickly going wrong.

Confusion took over as Nate could not decide whether to look at Cameron or to the crowd. Nothing appeared to be out of place to him. After Gemma had said yes, they had stayed to take in the view before going on to a well-planned night of celebration. He knew he had forgotten some elements, but this was totally different.

Cameron was more animated than ever before, suggesting something dangerous was happening. He had seen it and was reacting without hesitation. As Nate tried desperately to figure out what was wrong, Cameron had already parted the crowd like bowling pins. There was no more time to think as Cameron launched his entire body into a well-executed dive, knocking Nate and L'Armin to the ground with his full force. His weight landed in one heap on top of both of them.

Helplessly pinned to the carpet, Nate still searched for a possible cause. L'Armin, however, was more unfortunate and was knocked completely out of the way. He was sent rolling away, straight into a nearby table. Its contents catapulting across the room with such force that a few of the plates smashed against the window behind them.

Cameron fumbled with his holster and eventually unbuttoned it, freeing his side-arm. He pulled out a small pistol and waved it to the crowd, indicating that he wanted them to *back-off*. Each jumped away like any threatened person would, unwilling to see what Cameron's shiny black weapon was capable of. With a blinking red light showing the safety was off, he was ready for business.

"What the fu—" Nate struggled to speak under Cameron's bulky weight.

"Stay the hell down," Cameron barked back at him. "He's got a gun."

Chapter 5

What was once a treasured memory had somehow descended into chaos. The crowd had become a mass of panic. They had completely vacated the centre of the room, hugging the walls as best they could.

Nate could not understand what was happening. With Cameron in full protective mode and not letting him budge an inch, he found it impossible to see anything. Despite the fact that the extra weight was threatening to suffocate him, he fought for the strength to push Cameron off, but the man was strong. Too strong for him to move even slightly.

Just as his anger was about to boil over, something loud rang out that instantly released the pressure his anger had built up inside of him. For a few seconds he could not hear a thing and could only feel the ground reverberating as people trampled each other to get away. Though their voices were vacant. For some reason his ears hurt too, like someone had jabbed the inside of them with a hot needle.

After a moment his hearing began to return, revealing that some in the crowd were screaming hysterically. Everything was muffled, yet the sound was piercingly high pitched.

"What's happening?" he shouted to Cameron, whose reply became lost in the noise. Nate's own heavy breathing was rushing around his head like electrical feedback, drowning everything out, including Cameron.

Through the tiny gaps between people's legs he could see something intermittently, as they moved about. He was surprised to see a flash of Gemma on her knees, with her face in her hands. Frustratingly, someone's leg blocked his view once again. He struggled to move to see what she was doing. Each time his sighting was quickly cut short.

A feeling of claustrophobia began to take over as his limbs became trapped. Cameron continued to pin him down as any dutiful bodyguard should. At any other time he would have been grateful, but his view of Gemma was blocked. All he wanted was to move a few inches more to the side.

Finally Cameron leapt up, releasing Nate from his imprisonment. He moved ahead with his pistol drawn to clear the way as Nate followed suit and made it to his feet— albeit much slower than Cameron. Thankfully, the numbness that had come from a lack of blood to his extremities had subsided within a minute.

His legs were unsteady at first, sending him stumbling forward, and only just in a straight line. Then after a couple of steps they were swiftly propelling him toward the epicentre of the chaos, with the confidence his eagerness demanded. The closer he got, though, the more his mind was unsure of what he saw. Suddenly his legs were the most solid part of him.

Gemma had moved and was now cowering over a bloodied body sprawled out on the ground. She wept into the man's chest, leaving a slowly expanding wet patch on his blue shirt. Its familiar pattern of narrow white stripes was still visible through the red stain. Something awful had just happened, which Nate struggled to comprehend.

When he finally realised what had happened his jaw dropped to the floor in disbelief. His own double lay in a position he could not believe was even possible, with the left arm reaching around his back as if disconnected. Something violent had rocked through him, causing severe damage across the entire body. Not until Nate saw the top

42

of the body, though, did he realise the full extent of the injuries.

A weapon had been fired at point-blank range, right square in the victim's face. Except it had not just created a path through the skull of his double, it had created an entire bypass. The shot had also burnt the shirt collar as it had completely removed the head. He dared not look for long, the sight of his own demise made him sick to the stomach.

"Jesus Christ," Nate said, unintentionally aloud.

The shock made it hard for him not to feel like a ghost, newly released from the body and yet to find peace. Was he now haunting this place and did not realise? His thoughts raced as he made a vain attempt at understanding the situation. All he could see clearly in his mind was the image of his double laughing only moments ago.

He had not noticed that Cameron had vanished until he suddenly found himself alone. In desperation he searched for support, but could find none at all. If Cameron had spotted the dead man on the floor, Nate was sure he would have stayed. So where was he? As he struggled to calm his stomach he realised even L'Armin was now nowhere to be seen.

Gemma still leant across the body and sobbed uncontrollably. The incident had caused a torrent of tears that carried her mascara down her cheeks, in wet and dirty streaks. Nate instinctively reached out to pull her away and into his arms. She initially pushed him back, before then gratefully accepting help amid another barrage of tears. If there were doubts about the realism of this place before, they were washed away as her crying dampened his own shirt.

"It's OK, I'm here," he said, with no idea if she recognised him or not. It did not matter, at that moment he had to hold her tight. "I've got you."

She said nothing and only breathed heavily against him, stuttering every now and again as her weeping intensified. But she did not speak at all. Surely she would see he was unharmed and they could continue on to dinner? Lobster

43

and champagne, if he remembered correctly. He would enjoy that, he told himself.

Though she had become too distant to surely care about any of that now, to Nate's surprise, her reaction to the devastating scene slowly began to vanish from her face entirely. Something beyond terrible had just happened and she appeared to be OK with it somehow, and all of a sudden. This was not a human reaction at all, but an autonomous machine-like detachment.

Cameron reappeared suddenly, with his face red and his flushed cheeks almost purple. He inhaled in quick successions to regain his composure. His demeanour was that of a determined man rather than the nervous wreck that clung on desperately to the past, as Nate had soon become.

"Are you all right, Mr Maddox?" Cameron said between breaths.

Nate let go of Gemma and was disturbed to see an empty expression on her face. She did not recognise him, even face to face. Her eyes looked to him but they passed right through. He was a stranger and nothing more; a feeling far worse for him than anything he had experienced during the divorce. She was not there at all, nothing of the Gemma he knew was present anymore.

His shoulders felt suddenly heavy as she wandered off, giving him the kind of thank-you any helpful stranger would be happy with, a proverbial cold shoulder to match his own, which now felt the cold air rushing across drying tears. He began to doubt that she had seen anything there at all. Perhaps he was a ghost.

Her future husband now lay on the floor and was missing a pretty important part of his anatomy. Yet she no longer cared. She walked past people and waved, even smiled, as if the violent death a few moments earlier had never happened.

He watched as she eventually left the room through a door he knew he had used before, but could not use now—however much he desperately wanted to. If he could he knew he would try to re-create the night in the way it should have happened. As if this rewrite was permanent and lasting. The blood stains all over her dress would probably have made that plan a little difficult to pull off, though. They were hard to ignore.

Suddenly he began to regret his casual exploration, as though it had caused everything he now witnessed. How could things have changed so much? Did he alter things without thinking? He needed answers. If only to shake off the image of Gemma's dress soaked in red.

"What the fuck happened here?" he said through gritted teeth.

"Some guy in a hood ran in with a gun and blew that guy's head off," Cameron said insensitively, while pointing to the headless body now leaking blood all over the floor.

Nate's head whipped around so fast he thought it might twist off completely. He stared at Cameron, who did not initially notice. When he did his eyebrows began tunnelling down to his eyes.

"That guy was me. I'm dead right there. How is that possible?"

"What? I ... I ..." Cameron's sentence struggled for closure.

The crowd began to mingle again, ignoring the anxious conversation that continued by the body. They reacted to each other as though the incident had not occurred at all. Either they were unable to process it, or they were no longer aware of it, like a reset switch had been flicked that had erased it for them. Some even stood by the body, oblivious to the graphic nature of the scene. Nate was surprised, but too angry to think it over for long.

It was clear that something prevented them from reacting. This was true also for the re-creation of Gemma. None of them were real. They should only have acted out what really happened on the day. So what was the reason behind the changes?

L'Armin appeared through the dwindling crowd. He looked around, dazed but still intact overall. A collection of smears ran down his right side where he had been forced into a table full of half-eaten lunches. He wiped himself down to remove any of the remaining dirt. Though with each swipe of a hand across his garment, he managed instead to rub in the stains further.

"Thank God. L'Armin, what's going on?" Nate asked.

"This is odd indeed. The Ring Beings have chosen the new over the old," he replied cryptically. As he spoke he continued to make a mess of his clothes by pressing the dirt in even more.

"The guy was gone before I could see where," Cameron said. "I mean, I ran as fast as I could to catch up, but he was too damn quick. Once he stepped through the glowing entrance thing, I lost him."

Nate grappled with what Cameron had said for a few moments until it hit him. "Hang on. Are you saying this wasn't part of the illusion? L'Armin, is that possible?"

L'Armin did not reply. His eyes surveyed the room as if the answers were walking among the remaining crowd. It might have been too much for him to take, Nate thought. He stood motionless but for the occasional twitch of his lips. Clearly he wanted to speak.

"I'm saying this guy walked in, the same way we did, pulled out a fucking hand cannon and shot that guy … or you … whatever. He then legged it back out," Cameron said.

"This can't be real."

"If it wasn't real then why didn't he use one of the fake doors in here? It was real, sir, and the blood on your hands with it." Cameron only just managed to finish his sentence before he had to take another large breath, sating his lungs desperate want for air.

Nate looked down at his palms and was disturbed to find a sticky smear of blood stretching across them. Gemma's dress had been covered in it. He wiped them frantically against his arm sleeves, accidentally discolouring the cloth. To make matters worse his palms were becoming more and more red tinted, while parts of his shirt had been turned slightly purple. However much he tried, it would not go.

"Why kill him and not me?" he said, spitting in his hands and rubbing.

L'Armin stood over the body, a look of concern on his face. He knelt down beside it and closed his eyes with his hands clasped firmly together. The loss of a life had compelled him to pray, it seemed.

"I'm guessing, as far as he's concerned, he *has* killed you. Otherwise why bother?" Cameron said.

"So he was supposed to kill me." The shock had exhausted Nate, he had to sit down. He pulled out a chair from a nearby table and let himself fall into it. The red stains in his hands no longer bothered him anymore. The one still drying into his shirt would be much harder to ignore.

Cameron nodded in agreement.

They both watched as L'Armin carried out what they took to be an end of life ritual. He recited words under his breath, in a language neither of them recognised.

"But got the other me instead?" Nate continued.

Again Cameron nodded in agreement, accompanied by an automatic tap of a hand against his side-arm.

As they spoke they continued to watch L'Armin. He had begun to perform some kind of purifying procedure, waving his arms up and down the length of the body. He willed something to leave it. His motion showed a clear path for whatever it was to exit: a convenient hole someone else had created at the top.

Nate felt ever so slightly calmer as he watched L'Armin. He was comforted by the respect being shown. However unusual he found it, considering the dead man was not real. "I've got to get back to my room," Nate said.

With one last enthused thrust of his arms, L'Armin had removed whatever evil had remained within the body, and was done.

"I believe you have been given a gift, Nathan Maddox." He returned to his feet with the use of a nearby chair.

47

"A *gift*? How is this a gift?" Nate replied to L'Armin's absurd comment.

"By mistaking the past for the present, the killer has failed in his attempt to kill you. Yet he is ignorant of his failure. In here you are safe until he realises."

Cameron shook his head. "How can he stay in here? No, I need to get him off this bloody rock and back to safety," Cameron said.

He had completely changed within such a brief moment of time that Nate almost did not recognise him. No longer did he appear as the poor soul, clinging on to one last hope of keeping his job. In Nate's eyes he had reserved a permanent place by his side. He had proven vigilant and his actions had secured their safety. Cameron could have opened a bottle of champagne and downed the entire contents there and then, he would not have cared. Nothing of the man before was important to Nate now.

"You still do not appreciate where you are, Nathan," L'Armin said. He walked through the almost empty room with his arms outstretched. "To be in here is to be in you. You are the apparatus from which this projection emanates."

"Bullshit. We're leaving," Cameron said.

L'Armin's arms returned to his side with a slap. He sent an angry look to Cameron as he moved over to a table that had somehow been undisturbed by the chaos. Without a care he swiped his arm, knocking a glass off of the table beside him. It tumbled to the floor and landed in one satisfying crash, shattering instantly into hundreds of pieces. Shards were sent rattling across the floor as they bounced off of each other.

"The glass is broken," he said. "But the pieces are still there, yes? We can choose to leave them apart, *or* we can bring them together once more."

Nate was mesmerised by the demonstration. He looked at the pieces of glass littering the floor. He knew there was a point but he struggled to grasp it. More importantly, he was in no mood to try.

He placed his face in his hands and felt a warmth from them that was unwelcome and unexpected. He wiped his face instead. The stickiness from the drying blood had been made worse by a build-up of sweat. At no point did he consider the risk of accidentally smearing it across his cheeks.

When he removed his hands he was surprised to find L'Armin and Cameron waiting patiently for his response. Cameron's eyes had become wide and glazed, he was quickly appearing lost in thought. Nate found solace in their shared confusion.

"Listen, L'Armin, I'm grateful for your help, but I don't understand what you're getting at. I need to get away from this place and find Helen."

After a laboured nod in the direction of the exit, he stood and began to make his way toward it, with Cameron following closely behind. L'Armin stormed off in the other direction. He mumbled something in his native tongue, getting more animated the further out of Nate's earshot he got.

"I'll get us seats on the next flight off this rock," Cameron said while frantically tapping his fingers against a small holographic display, which projected from a tiny aperture on his wrist watch. He scrolled through a booking screen to find the earliest flight. Nate could see how urgently Cameron wanted him out of harm's way by the list he perused. From what he could see not one of the listed flights brought them anywhere close to Earth.

Their attention was torn away by a thudding sound from behind. Something was reverberating from a forceful hit. Then a second and a third. Whatever caused the noises had become determined to achieve something destructive.

"What the hell is he doing?" Cameron said. He immediately minimized his tiny holographic display and assessed the unexpected disturbance. His other hand gracefully moved over to his pistol, hovering there while he decided whether to use it or not.

Nate turned reluctantly to see what Cameron was complaining about. What he saw was hard to comprehend. L'Armin was smashing the end of a large metal pole into the wall of glass that kept space out. He could see the wire still hanging from the lamp shade L'Armin had pulled out of the wall socket and was now using like a battering ram. With each hit the glass wobbled more violently until a noticeable area of scratches began to form.

Nate shrugged his tired shoulders; the never-ending stress of the evening had begun to make him ache. Obviously the glass metaphor had not had the desired effect on him. But this new approach was even more perplexing.

"What are you d ..." Cameron's sentence was cut short by a sudden shift in tone of the glass wall, after yet another impact. It had quickly gone from a deep thump to a high pitched creek. The sound was no longer able to travel through the entire structure. Somewhere a crack had formed.

L'Armin stopped halfway through another hit and began to cautiously back away. A small but visible crack began to expand slowly from the impact point of the pole. More and more cracks began sprouting from the centre, like a spider unfolding its long knuckled legs, until there were too many to count.

"Shit, he's gonna kill us," Cameron said in a blind panic.

Nate felt Cameron grab his arm and force him in the direction of the exit. He really must arrange a pay-rise, he told himself as he was moved along. At the same time the buzzing sound of a device being activated came from Cameron's hand. He had drawn his side-arm again, without a moment's deliberation, and was one trigger-pull away from removing L'Armin from the equation. The lights on the side of his pistol again blinked a fierce and angry red.

"No," Nate said, placing his hand across the barrel as soon as he realised Cameron's intention.

"Seriously? He's trying to kill us."

50

In the background, Nate could hear L'Armin calling to him. "Wait, Nathan Maddox," he shouted, with both arms raised above his head.

The glass let out an ominous groan as it made one last attempt at withstanding the pressure deficit of space. But too many cracks had appeared for it to take much more. Its structural strength was suddenly laid to waste by the undermining weaknesses, shattering its entire surface in the blink of an eye. A massive explosion of glass and debris was propelled out into space, sparkling as they spun away, almost beautifully.

Nate instinctively clamped his hands over his eyes as quick as he could manage and drew in one huge lungful of air. He knew what was supposed to happen. His lungs should have been sucked empty in a nanosecond, squeezing every bit of air out. Followed by his blood boiling and escaping from any paths it could find, fizzling away into the black, cold death of nothingness. Not to mention being inevitably shredded by a billion tiny knives as he would then go on to join the expanding cloud of glass debris.

But none of it came. He dared not open his eyes in case he had somehow pre-empted his expectations. When his arms were eventually moved away by someone else, he knew for certain he was still alive.

"You cannot die by your own creation," L'Armin said calmly.

When Nate opened his eyes he found himself staring straight at L'Armin. Despite his best efforts he could not release his arms, they were locked in place. L'Armin had made his point and was not about to let him miss it. Even though he knew they should be dead, something told him to listen.

After enough time had passed that he could trust Nate would not just clamp his hands over his eyes again, L'Armin let go. He then stepped back and waited.

The freedom to move allowed Nate to take a tight grip of Cameron next to him. Just in case some kind of elaborate trick had been played on him and they were still about to be sucked into oblivion. But again nothing happened.

He could now see the large hole where once a protective layer of reinforced glass had separated life from death. In its place was a chaotic scattering of glass fragments spinning away in every direction, like tiny diamonds. Except now they were joined by any piece of furniture that had not been bolted to the floor: In less than a second the tables, chairs, cutlery and even parts of the wall had been sucked out. The room was now completely empty, but they remained.

"I can die if someone puts a gun to my head," Nate said, with a nervous wobble in his voice.

"Indeed."

"Spit it out, for Christ's sake." Cameron's voice carried across the room and back again. "What exactly are you saying, that needed saying like this?" He managed to say only slightly quieter.

"In here, we can find the killer. The Beings of the Rings have the ability to show us," L'Armin said.

Cameron waved his left arm in a dismissive manner. "Not this again." He let go of Nate and began to pace up and down a metre long piece of carpet. The gun continued to flash red in his hand. He had not yet decided whether he needed to use it or not.

Tension in Nate's neck was now causing him some considerable discomfort. He arched his head back to release the pain temporarily. After a few seconds staring at the ceiling he shook his head slowly, he could not quite put his frustration into words. He thought of joining Cameron in wearing out the carpet. But instead he let out an overly long moan.

"Your memories are the glass pieces," L'Armin continued. "We can put the pieces back together and witness its full form again. You must let the Beings of the Rings guide you in piecing your memories back together."

It was clear to see that things had begun to take their toll on Cameron. He leant on the back of a chair and allowed his weight to slowly shift from his right leg. The chair wobbled slightly as it reluctantly took the load. His pacing had only made things worse, he was almost out of breath.

Cameron had proven himself worthy of the job but his fidgeting was making it hard for Nate to decide what to do. Which made him think. It seemed strange how people had been so ready to write Cameron off, like a bad investment. What he lacked in intelligence he more than made up for in vigilance. What more was needed of him?

"OK," Nate said, finally having made his mind up. "So how would we do ... that?"

"We will allow the Beings to show us. You must understand that the answers will not be obvious at first. Let the Beings find them so we may interpret their meaning."

After taking the weight back off the chair, Cameron approached Nate. "Sir?" He whispered into Nate's ear. He cupped his hand around his mouth to conceal his words from L'Armin. "This isn't a good idea. You're not safe here with these bloody aliens."

"Mr Maddox?" L'Armin said.

The decision to follow Cameron had felt the most appealing to Nate, at first. But something lingered at the back of his thoughts, like the blood stains that refused to come off his clothes. Why him? He could not run away and put the entire situation behind him, he had to stay and find out why he had been the target. Except he could not tell what was behind the desire to remain: curiosity or revenge. Either way it was what the most emotive part of him wanted. He had to stay and find out why.

"I'm going with L'Armin," he said.

"But—"

"I've decided," Nate said, cutting Cameron off. "And I want you to guard the entrance back in the playground."

Cameron lowered his head in acknowledgement. "Fine. But take this with you." He bent down and unbuttoned a small holster—fastened just above his ankle. What he produced was more like a pen than a weapon, with no visible trigger. At the end, its two tiny barrels were more likely to confuse rather than threaten its victim. "It fires a low density beam. One shot is enough to put someone close face down on the carpet."

Nate took the weapon. "I'll keep it close." He placed it loosely in his pocket before offering his hand to Cameron.

"Make sure you do. Sir." Cameron solidly shook Nate's hand. "Just promise me you'll come get me if anything happens."

"I will, don't worry. One more thing, Cameron. Keep everyone out. I don't want people trampling around my memories."

Cameron nodded his head as he made the necessary mental note. "Got it," he said as he turned and headed for the exit. With a slight hesitation and one last look back for good measure, he stepped through and vanished into the unnatural glow.

It was not much, yet just enough to relax Nate and ease his racing heart. He felt safer knowing nothing else unwelcome could come bursting in. But an obvious vacuum had formed between him and L'Armin. He hardly knew the man that was about to lead him further into the realms of the weird and wonderful. At least with Cameron he had the familiarity that came with being of the same species.

"So how do we start?" he said.

With one raised finger, L'Armin silenced Nate's curiosity and took a couple of large strides to the right side wall, as though he were measuring the distance. Once there he moved slowly along the wall, his hands barely touching as he explored its surface.

His eyes closed periodically as something appeared to distract his senses. Nate could not see what, to him the wall was barely textured and only a painted surface. Yet somehow there was more that L'Armin was sensing. Eventually he found a spot that was apparently suitable for whatever he had in store. His arm remained outstretched with his hand hovering inches from the area.

"Here," he said.

Nate had watched with a great interest. It was matched only by an equal amount of confusion. Now he was expected to join in and with no clue as to what was about to happen. He hesitantly walked over to L'Armin. Again curiosity had gotten the better of him, but he was still cautious. A generous serving of nerves caused his steps to become smaller the closer he got.

"What are we looking for?" he said, still unaware of why the chosen spot was better than any other.

"This is a weak point." L'Armin almost rolled his eyes when Nate inevitably adorned the face of ignorance: eyebrows reaching for the sky, half of his lip upturned and an exhalation of breath in frustration. "Everything you see was created from your memories and experiences, yes?"

Nate only nodded in reply.

"Then, as with any memory, there are parts you will remember more strongly than others," L'Armin continued. "This area was less important, and as such a weaker recollection, or re-creation. Here."

Nate was ushered to the wall where L'Armin offered the position to him with an open palm. It felt odd at first, but somehow also right, as his hand made contact with the cold surface. There were no sparks or reactions from the inanimate surface, only an almost imperceptible softness to it, like he could push through if he tried hard enough. Perhaps the assumption that it was ordinarily impossible to do such things was all that prevented him.

"OK, that feels weird. What do I do now?" he said, his hand trembling slightly.

"Feel the underlying structure. Before we entered this place, do you remember what I told you?"

"About choosing a thought to focus on?"

"Yes. For us to proceed this time you must not. To find the answers you seek, you must allow the Beings of the Rings to search your mind. Close your eyes and allow them in."

He did as L'Armin asked and shut his eyes. He focused his sense of touch solely on the patch of wall his hand caressed. He tried to think of nothing else, except an image was beginning to form unintentionally in his mind. The cold slowly fell away as his body heat transferred to the metal. It temporarily broke the image apart, but something wanted it to appear. Something external, Nate suspected.

"Picture your body on the floor. Do you see it?" L'Armin said.

A hand was placed on Nate's back, pressing against him supportively. He leant into it without meaning to. Just having it there was enough to make him at ease with the experience, however strange it had become.

Even though he knew he was standing with his hand making damp patches on the wall, he could see another room just as real, though the room he was imagining was somehow to normal scale and physically within the infinitesimally small space between his eyes and the lids. Trying to picture what L'Armin had instructed became disturbingly easy. He had never known his imagination to be so real.

The body was still and lifeless, just as it would look if he had opened his eyes. But the blood had become more real now, like it was still flowing. He concentrated on the path the red liquid was taking and found that it led away from the contorted form on the floor. It had a life of its own, branching away like a blood rich delta across the ground. Some of the tendrils raced away and around the room as they searched for something. Every crack was a path to be exploited, until most of the room was glowing a vivid shade of red.

Their movements were purposeful and Nate was sure they were not driven by him, but by someone else. Unlike before he felt like a spectator in his own imagination, along for a ride the Beings of the Rings were in control of. They were busy too, seeking out every corner of his mind. He could feel them rummaging around and bringing forth feelings from the past.

"See the killer run through the rift. Now go through it. Follow him," L'Armin continued.

Nate could not help but notice how L'Armin's voice sounded. The words were so clear, like they were coming from inside his own head.

"I see him," he said, excited by the sudden chance to participate.

The figure was dark and hard to focus on. There were no details that he could make out, just a featureless form running for the exit his mind had conjured up. He followed as fast as he could until it vanished along with the room. As he tried to picture the scene again, he found he could not. His eyelids were once again the only thing in front of his eyes.

He felt disappointed to see the image disappear so suddenly. For a short while he thought he had done something wrong. But a warmth then began to build in his palm. He could feel it increase until unexpectedly the wall gave way. His fingers tingled as the sensation intensified. Something was there, but it was not solid like the surface he had felt before. It pushed back like a gust of air against his hand.

"There," L'Armin said.

Upon opening his eyes, Nate was at first blinded by the glowing light of another rift. He faced away, meeting L'Armin's stare unexpectedly. The wideness of his eyes suggested he had been impressed by the achievement—or just surprised.

"I have never helped a human do this before. We must be cautious."

Nate chuckled nervously as he pushed into the light. The further in he moved, the more the tingling sensation subsided.

"You first then," he said, not waiting for a reply. He was unable to see a single thing in front of him now. Even so, he wandered ahead. The rift was taking them even deeper into the unknown.

Chapter 6

Nate's feet landed quietly as he stepped through the newly formed rift. Again his sight was overwhelmed by an unnatural brightness that separated one world from another. With nothing to lead him through he took tentative steps, checking each time his feet touched the ground for something solid, before moving on. A look down confirmed his feet were there, but nothing appeared underneath them. He decided to keep his arms by his side; no accidental groping this time.

As his sight returned he found himself entering a dark and badly lit area. A faulty light flickered above him that he could not quite focus on, only seeing a blurred outline at first. Within seconds his eyes were able to see much more, allowing his surroundings to come into view, in all its dim splendour.

A long corridor, a few metres wide, stretched out in front of him. It curved to the left and out of sight. What lay beyond the bend was hidden from him, with the curve of the wall acting as a vertical horizon. For as far as he could see along the right side, there were rows of windows looking out into space. And on the left, a few metres or so apart from each other, were a number of airtight doors. All were sealed tight in case of a hull breach.

The lights that lined the ceiling were low, like they had been dimmed deliberately. Apart from the one above him of course, which was clearly due to be fixed. The advantage was that the low lighting let in a mesmerising image of space outside, an image he had marvelled at on many occasions.

A force was present to keep his feet on the ground, but he had experienced this unnatural version of gravity many times before. Unlike in the previous memory, this artificial gravity was originating from a much cheaper source. Not fancy, almost indistinguishable from real gravity generators, but the more affordable types his father insisted on having installed on his mining ships to cut costs.

It allowed for everyday walking, as long as the pace was consistent. It was much less effective at speed and often launched the more exuberant crew members into an unbalanced wobble. It was not that it did not work, it just had a reaction time that left a lot to be desired.

A loud pounding noise rang through the entire structure, bringing with it a sudden recollection of younger years for Nate. It was an unmistakable sound to him. The vibrations rattled his bones and sent a shiver up them in equal measures. His youth began flooding back to him, bringing a grin to his pale face.

L'Armin greeted Nate with a smile of his own, and as he entered he immediately began to look around. "Fascinating," he said, staring out the nearby window and into space. The pounding noise rang out again, causing him to flinch—which amused Nate. "What is making that awful sound?"

"I know exactly what that is." Nate began to walk at an excitedly brisk pace. He had to slow down soon after as his feet began to miss the ground. They wanted to skip or run, he was not sure. Instead they sped up, doing neither or both at the same time, again he was not sure. All he knew for certain was the artificial gravity generator was once again missing a beat. If he had not slowed down he would have lost his balance entirely.

After a few stumbles he made his way to the windows. There something large came into view outside. Tens of metres below their corridor system lay the rest of the ship, stretching out hundreds of metres ahead. It gleamed, with huge lights illuminating its surface and Lego-block like structures jutting out in a seemingly random way. The ship had undoubtedly been built for purpose, not aesthetics.

L'Armin joined him at the window and looked out at the ship. The expression of amazement on his face suggested he had never seen or heard anything quite like it before. His mouth remained open with his bottom lip hanging. When the pounding sound again reverberated through the hull it startled him, prompting his lips to slam shut.

"Incredible isn't it?" Nate said. "The noise of that thing nearly drove me mad as a teenager."

"Incredible indeed. What is it?"

"Welcome to Maddox Industries' flagship asteroid capture and mining vessel. Or the Miner's Folly, as we called it," Nate said with obvious pride. "This baby was my home from ages seven to eighteen. God I miss this place."

For a moment he was certain he was about to tear up. His recent brush with death had made him a mess of emotions. He really did miss the Miner's Folly, but thinking about it had never caused such a strong reaction in him before.

"An impressive sight. How does such a ship work?" L'Armin said, bringing Nate back from the brink.

"We grab the rock and break it apart." As Nate spoke a large glow began to emanate from the front of the ship. "The beauty of this system is its simplicity. We get what we can carry from each rock and make the fuel we need to get it home from the rest."

The pounding noise echoed through the ship once more. However, this time they could see where the sound was coming from. The glowing area at the front of the ship had suddenly burst into a highly energetic beam of luminescent yellow light, with sparks flying in all directions.

It shot ahead of the ship and silently struck the side of a large asteroid that had been hovering in the dark. Light from the beam scattered across its surface, revealing how much it dwarfed their ship. At more than three times the size of the Miner's Folly, it almost entirely blocked out the view of space behind it.

L'Armin leapt away from the window. The beam had taken him by complete surprise.

"Woah," Nate said. "Take it easy, L'Armin. They're just breaking pieces off for processing. Nothing to worry about."

"This is a dangerous endeavour, Nathan Maddox. One should not disturb the celestial realms." L'Armin continued to back away from the window.

"This is what I do, my friend. These rocks are lifeless, I assure you. And full of money making precious metals," Nate added with a smirk.

L'Armin's mouth drooped at the sides; the scene was proving too much for him to stomach. He turned away and sighed, choosing instead to ignore it completely. Nate's reassurance had done little to sway his obvious concerns. "A dangerous endeavour," he repeated, quieter this time.

Nate's excitement suddenly faded as he watched L'Armin's interest dissolve into something more akin to disdain. As he took in the sight it slowly dawned on him how ugly the concept must be for someone such as L'Armin. On display before them was a way of life that had absolutely no concerns other than how much profit was being made. It could not have been more opposed to L'Armin's—and his race's—reverence for the heavens. Or celestial realms, as L'Armin had called it.

He searched for something more pleasing to show his companion, but all he saw was heavy industry. His heavy industry. He wondered what his company would make of the beings L'Armin worshipped. Would they look past them and harvest the ring's ice for profit? He did not know for sure.

The sightseeing session had ended too abruptly for Nate, leaving an uncomfortable silence between him and his companion. He was finished showing off his ship and was now more interested in moving on. But everything appeared as he remembered, no nasty surprises were lurking in the shadows.

The pounding noise was continuing at the same regular interval he had lived by for so many years: four minutes and twenty eight seconds between bursts, he recalled. So why was he seeing this? It made no sense. The killer was not there, he was sure of that.

"I don't understand why they've brought us here," Nate said, breaking the silence. "This has nothing to do with what happened."

L'Armin walked ahead, mumbling something to himself. He held his hands together with his fingers interlocked as he calmly strolled away, leaving Nate behind and still waiting for an answer.

Whether he had been heard or not—or if he had been ignored—Nate could not tell. All he knew for certain was that something had drawn L'Armin forward along the corridor. Something his human hearing had not picked up.

"There is only so much the Beings can do," L'Armin eventually said. "Answers are here. We must find them buried inside."

Before Nate could answer, a raised voice echoed down the corridor. It soon returned to an almost inaudible level—for his ears at least. It had come from someone up ahead, who had appeared from one of the doors with another man.

Without meaning to, Nate quickly found himself overtaking his companion's more laboured pace. His feet now had a mind of their own and were missing the floor far too frequently, but he did not care. What was ahead had him excited. By the time he reached the pair he found L'Armin was a few metres behind and clearly taking his time with the inadequate artificial gravity.

As soon as he heard the voice he recognised his younger self, and the very obvious anger. They were still distant, but he knew exactly what the conversation was about and who it was with. He was able to work out roughly when this was as well.

When he finally arrived he was struck by how much younger and flustered his doppelganger looked. There, a much younger version of him stood red faced and frowning, with his arms crossed as a show of defiance. Next to him was his father, also younger and with much smoother skin than Nate knew him to have now.

"I've told you no and that's final. Why don't you bloody listen, boy," his father said. He wagged a loose finger as he berated his teenage son.

Suddenly Nate was back there and watching the same finger waving inches from his own face. The gesture threatened to re-ignite a teenage anger he thought he had long ago forgotten. He loved and respected his father, but at the time he had wanted nothing less than a resounding victory. What made his anger worse was knowing he would certainly not get one—stubbornness ran in the family.

"I'm nearly 18, it's my decision, not yours," the young Nate snapped back as he turned to walk away.

Nate watched, but the whole scene felt more like a dream from the third person perspective. He was completely lost in the moment and unable to make head nor tails of its relevance.

"If you leave when we get home, don't expect to come back after it all blows up in your face," his father said.

"Unbelievable." The teenage Nate turned back sharply to face his father as he spoke. "You think I haven't planned this out, don't you. You always do this."

"Of course you haven't planned it out. This is just another one of your pipe dreams. This is where you belong." His father slapped the metal bulkhead with his palm. "Here with me, on the Folly."

Nate could not help but smile at the way his father had made the point. It had never been enough to use merely words, a gesture was always worth ten times more. By slapping the wall, Nate had since realised, his father was making it about more than just the two of them. And he had been right. The young Nate was not just leaving his friends

63

and his father behind. The Miner's Folly had been his home, and he was planning on leaving *it* behind as well.

He watched the two arguing as they continued along the corridor. Both figures were so much thinner than he remembered. Still it did not deter the two of them from barking back and forth at each other like much bigger dogs than they really were.

When he passed the bulkhead his father had slapped, he placed his own palm on the same spot. It was pleasingly warmer than the surrounding metal and continued to heat up as he pressed it. He turned to L'Armin, who returned a perplexed expression.

"It's like he's here with me. I haven't had time to visit him much, since I took over the business." He slapped the bulkhead a few times to cement his own point before moving on.

"I see. May I ask you something?" L'Armin said.

"Sure."

They continued along the corridor with the much younger Nate and his father still arguing ahead. Their words were hard to make out as the echoes compounded against each other. Followed by the regular pounding sound that still interrupted the scene.

"Are there others who seek materials in this manner?"

"You mean asteroid miners?" Nate turned to face L'Armin, who bowed his head in acknowledgement. "Absolutely. It's pretty hairy sometimes actually. I remember once when a competitor approached a rock we were already surveying. When they saw us, boy, were they not happy."

"What did you do?"

"Well, let's just say that size matters a shit-load out here. And this baby's one of the biggest … look." Nate led L'Armin to a computer panel on the left wall.

It lit up immediately upon detecting his touch, throwing some welcome light across the still dim corridor. He tapped at the screen until a view of the ship's stern appeared. This time the scene was more serene and—to

Nate at least—beautiful. Even with tiny flickers of fuzz intermittently pervading the picture. He felt certain it would at least take the edge off L'Armin's inherently disapproving opinion of his company's operations.

The back of the ship appeared to stretch out almost equidistant to the front section. It put their corridor system somewhere in the middle, raised up by a few tens of metres. At the far end, positioned slightly above the hull, were enormous and bulging ovals. These were where the engines were housed and visibly alight. Their faint purple glow brought a much needed change to the black all around them.

"So there are many of these competitors who could desire your demise?" L'Armin said.

Nate had to take a minute before answering. He had been temporarily taken aback by the sudden interest, assuming the questions had been brought about by genuine curious. Instead, L'Armin was one step ahead and looking for the elusive clues. Even the impressive view to the rear of the ship could not tempt him to understand what Nate did for a living. He was all business for now.

At first the suggestion of a competitor wanting him dead shocked Nate. Partly because it had come out of the blue, and partly because the list he had quickly compiled had become quite long. Too long for him to keep track of in his head. It was undeniable that a few would hate him enough to want him dead. But which could have actually gone through with it?

"OK, I guess there's a few. So why are we here? Why aren't we checking one of them out instead?" he said.

No answer came. They began to walk toward the still loud voices. The argument appeared to be reaching its end, with the tone suggesting it was now more of a heated discussion than a shouting match, as it had been before. Although the conversation still carried enough baggage to count as an argument, it was a small one in comparison.

They were too far away to make out the actual words. They would have to get a lot closer to understand them.

65

Unfortunately, L'Armin had begun to drag his feet as he reluctantly followed. Something, Nate could see, had upset him. He appeared to be speaking under his breath like he had before, just prior to an outburst that shattered a perfectly good window.

Nate decided to leave L'Armin to himself and continue ahead on his own. The pair soon came into view as he walked along. The young Nate was stood in the entrance of a metal doorway with the words "Crew Quarters" written above in bold orange letters.

"I'll think about it, Dad, I promise," the young Nate said.

The relieved expression on his father's face was one he remembered well. Only it had been followed by one of bitter disappointment the next morning, he remembered, when he had finally decided to leave the Miner's Folly, a crushing blow his father had taken very badly. After that they had not spoken for nearly 6 years as Nate's plan proceeded to fulfil his father's prophecy, and duly blew up in his face.

But something finally felt wrong, or at least out of place, as he watched his young self and his father hug before parting ways. It took him a few seconds to realise what it was, by which time his father had slipped away through another door further ahead. The corridor was now empty, or so Nate thought.

His unique viewpoint allowed something he did not remember noticing on the day to be seen now. A few doors away someone else was watching from the safety of darkness. The person was obviously interested in the ongoing disagreement between the two generations of the Maddox family. He was also intent on remaining unseen, peering from behind a door only an inch or two open.

"Do you see that?" Nate said.

Even though he knew the other man could not see him, his footsteps were light and cautious as he approached. He snuck about in plain sight until a door behind him opened loudly and was then closed again. The unmistakable sound of metal hitting metal distracted him suddenly. The person that had exited the door simply wandered the other way down the corridor. He was of no importance and yet Nate had watched him just like the unknown man had.

Once silence returned, the man dashed out of the shadows and on to another door further up the corridor. His feet shuffled along, hardly making a sound at all. Annoyingly, Nate could not see who it was. It was difficult for him to judge whether the man was important or not at such a distance.

After quickly checking that L'Armin was in tow—and noticing how equally intrigued by the mystery figure he was—Nate continued on. When he turned back he was surprised to see the man had already reached the door and had begun tapping at the keypad next to it. A *beep* verified the acceptance of the entered pin, followed by a *thud* as the large bolt-locks slid into the open position.

It was an airlock that sealed their area off from the deeper levels of the ship, one Nate had used on countless occasions, but he had no idea what the pin was. It had been years since he had last needed to use it.

Knowing that he needed to get through the door if he had any hope of understanding the man's relevance, he launched himself forward. The answers were close and only a metal security door with an unknown pin number stood in the way. But his feet once again became light and unsure as the artificial gravity struggled to keep up. He was quickly losing his balance, and his temper, as he stumbled forward.

The only option he had left was to throw himself forward. To his delight the door and his outstretched left arm made contact just before it closed. He had slid a good few feet on his stomach to reach it, but he had managed to keep it open. Albeit by jamming his arm between the opening.

His hand reached through the gap while his face was forced into an uncomfortable sideways position against the door's edge. It squeezed his arm as he held it ajar like a squishy door-stop. Soon the pressure began to pinch. It threatened to cut off the circulation if he did not move. He pushed his arm and shoulder against the door and slowly it moved open further, until he could feel the blood rushing back.

When the gap was big enough for his head to turn in, he finally caught a glimpse of the mysterious man. He was confused to see someone he knew very well wandering away.

"Stuart?" he said.

Chapter 7

The face was unmistakable to Nate: a wide chin, small inset eyes and thin strands of hair that made little attempt to cover the top of the head. It was Stuart, but a much younger version. He had to know why this was important. The Ring Beings knew something he did not.

He pushed the door one final time, intent on stepping through, and readied himself to confront the much younger version of a man he thought he knew well. But it was not to be. As he slid through, what resided beyond the door withered away to nothing. Stuart was gone, along with something more important, the truth.

"Not yet, dammit," Nate said, infuriated at being taken away at such a crucial moment.

Instead of entering the room beyond, he was met with the same burning bright light he had encountered before. Except this time he had not expected it. His momentum carried him forward with little time to consider closing or covering his eyes. Rather than pushing through cautiously and allowing his vision to adjust, he had sped forward blindly.

As before, his sight gradually returned, but this time they were streaming with tears. Dark blotches hung in front of his eyes, like he had stared straight at the sun by mistake. Everywhere he looked they followed, hiding whatever was coming into view.

He began to feel bodies bumping into him as he walked on. To Nate the blotches were alive and grabbing at him, yet swiping at them did nothing. When he managed to hit something solid he realised the blotches were not real, relatively speaking.

The room he entered was vastly different to the one he wanted to be in. He began to make out its features piece by piece, as the dark patches slowly dispersed, like exorcised spirits.

The cold and dulled metals of before were replaced with soft, expensive looking wood and executive looking colours. The walls behind him and to his right had been painted a neutral cream, while the other two were floor to ceiling windows that overlooked a bustling city vista. The middle of the room was taken up by a large circular table—also made from expensive wood.

Rows of people lined the back of the room—a crowd of spectators—while the more important sat around the table in black leather chairs, ready for the meeting to commence. Everyone waited for a man at the front to begin proceedings.

Nate pushed his way through as he surveyed the room. His path was closely followed by L'Armin, who looked as alien as ever among the suits and ties. But this new place was not what he wanted. He fought the urge to return to the last area and ignore this one.

It was not until he had found a way through the sea of bodies that he realised where he was, and became instantly curious. When the final heads parted before him he could see the other side of the central table. There sat across from him was his father, Stuart and another Nate, all of a much older age than in the last memory.

The window behind let in a comforting orange glow as the sun began to set beneath an artificial horizon made up of smaller, surrounding buildings. The city was vast, but as a testament to his family's success, it all resided many levels below.

Nate turned to find L'Armin stood on his tip-toes in order to see past a young woman in front of him. The sandals he wore fell loosely to the floor under his feet, they only appeared to hinder him.

"This was only recently. Maybe two-and-a-half years ago," Nate said.

"Do you understand why the Beings have brought us here? It must be a relevant memory."

"Not yet, though the guy spying on my father and me earlier is now sat over there." Nate pointed at the three sat talking casually at the table together. "I don't know why, but these Beings of yours seem to think Stuart's important."

"Who is this man?" L'Armin said.

"He's been in the company since the beginning." Nate had to nudge a few people out of the way to make room for his friend beside him, as those nearby continued to fight for space. "He and my father have known each other longer than I've been alive. He's practically my uncle."

The room quickly hushed as Nate's father stood to address the still gathering crowd. This was the man he knew now, the youthful version had felt a little odd to him. More like an old recording of a man than a real, flesh and blood, living being. The same features were there, except they were now accompanied by the lines and creases that he was used to. Years of hard work had also pulled his stature downward into a frame more suited to boardrooms than hard labour.

"Ladies and gentleman," he began. "Thank you for joining us on this most special of occasions."

Finally Nate had pinpointed the exact day this was. "This was when I took over the business. Why was this more important?"

"Allow time, Nathan," L'Armin replied.

"As you all know," Nate's father continued, "I have been running Maddox Industries for a good few years. Too many some would say." A low level chuckle made its way around the room, louder at the table than elsewhere. "In fact this would be my 43rd year. And that is where the

71

meaning of this meeting lies. I have decided, with great deliberation, that this will be my last year at the helm."

Nate spotted a hugely obvious look of pride across the face of his double. He remembered exactly what that felt like. How bloody naive, he thought. If only he could tell his younger self of the sleepless nights and endless meetings the title carried with it.

The thought only lasted a second before it was stolen from him by the sudden sight of Stuart's expression. As his father continued his, as usual, well-rehearsed speech, Stuart sat with a look of utter worry. His fingers rolled over each other nervously. A bead of sweat formed under his highly groomed hair implants and rolled down to his brow. Nate kept his eyes locked onto him as the announcement was made.

"So I think it is the right time for me to step down. Now I know you'll all want to know who will replace me and I'm glad to say … I can." Another dull chuckle explored the room as Nate's father deliberated. "Nate, stand up for the ladies and gentleman and introduce yourself."

The other Nate stood and shook his father's hand. They exchanged a wide, enthusiastic smile.

"Thanks, Dad, but I'm sure everyone already knows me, and unlike you I'll keep this brief. It's a great honour, and to be honest, it's about time." Nate held up a glass to his father.

Those around the table with a glass of bubbly did the same as a toast to the outgoing leader. All except for Stuart, who took a deep swig of the glass before him. Nate had watched Stuart's face go through varying degrees of redness as the two Maddoxs spoke. The decision had taken him by complete surprise. Nate had never realised.

"It appears your friend does not find your succession pleasing," L'Armin said.

"I guess. I was so caught up in the celebrations, I never noticed he wasn't happy."

"Was he unhappy enough to tell you?"

"No. He obviously kept it bottled up. We're fine now though. I mean, I've been in charge for just over two years now." The words came out but Nate was not sure he meant what he was saying. Although their relationship appeared healthy on the outside, he had never understood Stuart like his father always had. He had been left to do his own thing and advising Nate took up less of his time these days.

The orderly quiet of the room gradually became a more social hum of chatting and cheerful exchanges. All around, Nate could see faces he knew well and even recognised some of the expressions he remembered from the day. His own double stood surrounded by a group of people all vying for the approval of their new captain. His father was already stepping back, obviously happy to give up some of the limelight.

Nate took a seat next to the still fuming Stuart. "He is really pissed."

"Does this appear to be the face of a killer?" L'Armin came right out with it.

"What? No, of course not."

L'Armin stood between Nate and Stuart, his eyes locked on his query. "His anger seems strong, Nathan." He switched back and forth between Stuart's eyes as though each told only one part of the story.

"OK, I'll give you that. But he's not involved in this." Nate rested his hands on his knees and lent in. "Besides, the guy Cameron saw was obviously younger than Stuart. This man couldn't outrun lunch let alone someone half his age."

Stuart's intense stare at the other Nate suddenly stopped and—like a switch had been flicked inside—he stood, put on a broad smile and brushed himself down as he headed for his new boss. He waded through the crowd and found a neat slot among the group. Nate followed and stood behind, able to see above Stuart's relatively low stature.

"Congratulations, Nathan," Stuart said. He extended his hand out and grabbed the other Nate's, rudely stealing it from another member of staff. "I think it's great your father thinks so highly of you."

Nate remembered how this had seemed a perfectly normal thing to say in such circumstances. But something pinched at the back of his mind this second time of hearing it. There was something else in Stuart's words that he had not picked up on as he had casually sipped his drink.

"I don't remember that sounding quite so snide at the time," he said.

"His words do not reflect his feelings…" L'Armin said, with a quaint nod of his head. He brought Nate's attention down to Stuart's stern grip on the other Nate's hand. "… Nor do his actions, Nathan."

Both of Stuart's hands were around his boss' left hand and squeezing roughly. His grip varied in intensity, almost exactly mimicking the clenching of his teeth as he feigned enthusiasm. Again, Nate did not remember paying much attention. After countless *Congrats* and *You'll do your father proud*, he had not had the room mentally to take anything else in, however unusual it may have been.

"If you'll excuse me, Nathan, I have some calls to make," Stuart said, his teeth barely separating.

The other Nate did not reply—an obviously unintentional snub. Instead his hand was snatched away by yet another smiling employee with a message of good will.

Nate stood aside and allowed Stuart to depart the festivities. "Where are you running away to?" he thought out loud.

He was about to follow Stuart through the crowd when he spotted a comforting face. The young woman he saw was trying her best to get the other Nate's attention: bobbing her head about into any and every empty space that appeared between those in front. It took immense patience, Nate saw, for Helen to find the right moment to make herself known. And when she did she took no prisoners, nearly elbowing another person in the face as she forcefully made room.

"We should continue our journey, Nathan," L'Armin said from behind. "We may be close to answers."

Nate was surprised at how pleased he was to see Helen stood before him. After the recent events she imprinted a sense of peace on an otherwise chaotic situation. Her great smile and large blue eyes drew him in every time. Now more than ever, he wanted to stay and lose himself in them like a sailor on a calming ocean.

Eventually his double spotted her and immediately became more interested in leaving his current conversation. He introduced himself, and from that grew a healthy chat about how much he hated all the attention. They laughed together. Nate remembered how, for the next month, they had been inseparable. He was sure that if she had not become Stuart's assistant they would have hooked up. At least he hoped they may have.

"Nathan." L'Armin put his hand of Nate's shoulder and began to gently turn him away. "We must continue."

"Right, sure, sorry. Where is he?"

L'Armin pointed at the large doors they had entered through. Nate eventually spotted one side of the double doors swing open and nearly knock a tall, thin man flat on his ass. Whoever had just used the door, he did not care much for others.

"That'll be Stuart," Nate said.

They both hurried through the bustling crowd. When they reached the doors, Nate stopped and peaked through its clear circular window. By now he was becoming acutely aware that every time he ventured through a door it could take him somewhere else. This time he wanted to make sure he did not miss anything before entering.

He caught a glimpse of Stuart speeding off in a huff. Quickly he disappeared around the corner of the corridor, heading for the lifts. Nate ran through the layout of the building in his head.

"Let's go," he said. "He's heading to his office on the 160th floor, I think."

And sure enough, as he pushed open the door, everything faded to an intense white. He could not decide whether he had caused it to happen because he had expected it to, or if it had simply been a coincidence. Nevertheless he continued.

He was starting to understand why the Ring Beings were so revered. The power they had was incredible. Past times, that he thought he had lost to forgetfulness, were once again restored. The synapses had reconnected and he was experiencing the memories anew. If only the rest of his memories could remain this vivid.

They had a great knack at moving people on to the next important memory too. He just hoped they would make their point sooner rather than later. His patience was slowing wearing thin with their insistence on focusing on Stuart. Why did they have such an interest in him anyway?

The voices of the boardroom behind became more and more echoed and distant, until another sound overtook them: a familiar deep hum, followed by his shoes making a *thumping* noise as they landed on metal.

This time he decided he would be more careful with L'Armin. The last thing he wanted was to show another part of his life that might upset him. Thankfully, he recognised the noises around him straight away. The Miner's Folly was once again ahead of them.

Chapter 8

The light abated, to reveal that they were again aboard the flagship of Maddox industries' fleet. This time things appeared more lived-in than before. The metal walls were clean, but contained gouges and scrapes along their surfaces after countless run-ins with heavily clad crew members.

This part of the ship was less impressive and a whole lot more practical than the previous area they had visited. It also desperately needed a new coat of paint to replace the now peeling layer of ocean blue that adorned its walls.

"We are again on your ship, Nathan," L'Armin said. "Which path should we take?"

Nate found the way L'Armin had asked mildly comical, and he was not sure if he wanted a literal or a philosophical answer. His unintentional smirk elicited a confused look from his companion.

Before them lay a seemingly endless corridor, devoid of any windows or signs. Where previously there had been thick glass windows, linking them to the outside world, now nothing but walls and doors lined their route. There were no markings around them to give away their position on the ship and no obvious direction for them to travel.

But this corridor was busy and provided an obviously important path for the crew. Nate placed it somewhere within the bowels of the ship, where the real work was done. This was a purposeful corridor.

Standing directly in the middle of the corridor proved an unwise choice for Nate and L'Armin. Within a minute of entering they were swamped by a group of crew members heading for the mess hall, all dressed in baggy blue overalls. The men were an enthusiastic bunch that took no time at all to shove Nate to the side. Once out of the way he could see just how busy the ship had become since their earlier visit.

Along the walls stood others who had been moved aside by the stampeding men. Some wore overalls, while others wore roughed up trousers and heavy boots with—more often than not—greasy tops to boot. Those with cleaner clothes were clearly just about to start a shift. They mingled casually along the corridor, some catching up on gossip and idle chat as they walked.

No-one along these corridors ever wore a suit and tie; the Minor's Folly was not a place for soft clothing. If it could not take weeks of sweat and grease then it did not belong on the ship. The same went for her crew. Nate tried hard to remember the last time he had worn anything that did not have a designer brand-name on it somewhere.

"I suppose we need to figure out where Stuart should be," he said, unwilling to address how much he had changed.

He took a few steps forward, past another static group of workers, and activated a small screen on the wall. "Now this system was never that advanced, so it can't tell us where he is. But …" He tapped the screen which in turn lit up, and then began scrolling through its options. "Got it."

L'Armin joined Nate at the wall screen with a curious look on his face. "What has the wall given you, Nathan?"

"Not literally," Nate said with a laugh, in a much more disparaging way than he would have liked. "It says here the date is August 5th, 2131, and here's the work schedule for the day …" He slid his finger down the screen as he surveyed the list. "A repair team is working on the fore antenna array which was damaged by debris during the last job." He swiped his finger across the screen, removing the list, and opened the map of the ship.

After re-familiarising himself with the ship's layout, he pointed the way ahead. "This way, come on," he said. "The forward access airlock is this way."

"Is this the place Stuart will be?" L'Armin asked as they set off along the corridor.

"If I remember right, yes. This was only months after I returned to work for my father. I was twenty four. He wanted to punish me for leaving years earlier, I think. So I got a lot of physically demanding jobs. One of which was to do outside repairs, like fixing the antenna arrays. And Stuart was supervising the job."

Nate could feel a sickness rising from his stomach as he remembered the countless space-walks he had had to endure, the sensation of all of his internal organs moving about, bumping into each other. He had found a way to counter the effects eventually with two fingers of something strong, usually scotch. It made him really appreciate the artificially produced gravity pushing him into the floor; everything back neatly in their place.

As they wandered through the ship, Nate spotted a few of the crew members he had once known. He had served on the ship long enough that he knew most of them by name, after working alongside them. He resisted the urge to try and talk to them. They were not real after all, and he desperately wanted to get to the reason behind Stuart's importance.

It still felt a shame to see the faces he thought he had forgotten, flying past without so much as a *How have you been*? It did not matter that they could not see him, it somehow felt like he was being rude.

When they reached the airlock control room they were swamped by busybodies on their way out. Inside, only a handful of crew members remained with the rest having exited and sped off down the corridor. Whatever purpose they had been brought in for had been fulfilled and they were not hanging around any longer than was needed. A clear sign that Stuart was in charge here, Nate knew.

The large, sealed airlock doors stood broadly next to the control room. A spinning orange light above warned of it being in use. This was where the inside and out were at their closest, with nothing more than a layer or two of steel and hull plating to keep the two apart. Like arguing siblings, the two just did not play well together. Because of the dangerous nature of their work, only the most professional people were ever allowed inside this control room.

A sudden crackle of static echoed out of the door as it swished open. Another crew member exited and purposefully dashed off down the corridor, brushing past Nate and L'Armin.

"Ryan, come in, over," a woman said over the speaker system, just about managing to break through the static.

Nate stood in the doorway and watched as the crew interacted. It felt so natural to him. If it were not for his companion beside him, he could have sworn he was back there and could have happily ignored his current predicament. He certainly would not be second-guessing everything he knew about Stuart.

A man wandered casually over to the control panel and held down a yellow flashing button. "What's up now? Over," he said jokingly as his finger lifted back off the button.

"Er, we've got a situation here," the woman said. "There may be some cleaning required when we get back in. Over."

The man turned to one of his companions and rolled his eyes. "Five bucks it's him again." The other man laughed and nodded. "Roger that," he continued, speaking through the microphone again. "Please clarify, what exactly needs cleaning? Over."

"Yeah, Nate's puked in his suit again. He's managed to clear some of it but visibility is somewhat compromised. Over," the woman said.

Nate recognised the voice immediately; it was Gemma.

"Noted. Are you on your way back yet? Over," the man—Nate knew was called Ryan—said.

"Yes, but I'm having to guide Nate." Gemma's voice was followed by a crackle of static as the radio connection intermittently cut out.

The man sat down at the control panel and began tapping away at a daunting array of buttons and switches spread out before him. In front of his panel was a large window which ran across the entire length of the room. He peered into the airlock as he ran through the relevant procedures, all while his fingers frantically worked away, almost without his knowledge.

On the other side of the glass the lights began to turn on, followed by another orange spinning light and an assortment of beeps and clicks. They revealed the empty airlock with its large outer doors still locked tight. Along the walls were rows of benches waiting for the crew to use.

"I do not see Stuart," L'Armin said.

"He'll be here soon." Nate watched the man at the control panel still chuckling to himself. "I really hated that guy."

For the next few minutes Nate and L'Armin were left waiting for Stuart to arrive. Each took a seat and tried their best not to get in the way of the crew that continued to work. After a few minutes the radio sputtered to life and Gemma began to speak again, much clearer this time.

"We're nearing the airlock now, Ryan. Any chance you could let us in? Over," she said.

Nate laughed to himself. She always had a way of making a sentence sound like a joke, when in fact it was not. He knew all too well that her *any chance you could let us in*, really meant *let me in now*. He could not count how many times he had been caught out by it during their marriage.

The man at the control panel sprang into action and again began to tap away at his switches and buttons. "Pressure reads ... zero. Opening airlock doors now. Over."

On the other side of the window the large doors slowly parted to reveal a figure floating outside. His grey and black space suit was bulky and cumbersome, but somehow he managed to ease himself into the airlock in one swift move.

81

Once stable and tethered to the inside, he began pulling the strap attached to his colleagues, in a hand over hand motion.

The door to the control room suddenly swished open behind Nate and L'Armin as they watched. Everyone quickly turned to see Stuart enter. In an instant the mood in the room became noticeably less jovial at his appearance.

Stuart walked over to the man at the control panel and stood behind in a supervisory manner. His hands slid slowly into the pockets of his overalls where they nervously twiddled with the contents. Each and every movement the man made was assessed by Stuart's watchful eye, making the poor man noticeably uncomfortable.

The last of the three floated into the airlock with absolutely no sense of direction, not even which way was up or down. He bumped occasionally into the side of the airlock as Gemma did her best to guide him to the floor. Nate's younger self was completely in her hands, something she clearly found hilarious.

Nate's memory of this went from amusing, as his helmet had filled with small bubbles of vomit that sometimes splashed onto his skin, to the most disturbingly vivid recollection of a layer of warm liquid slowly moving around inside his helmet. After expelling the liquid from his mouth, it had pooled around the back of his helmet and then gradually started to work its way back around his head.

He certainly had not seen the funny side of it at the time. The insides of his helmet had turned into a noxious hell that stung his eyes and threatened to drown him in his own vomit. Just thinking about it still caused him to gag slightly. He managed to hold it back this time.

"Did they complete the repairs?" was all Stuart said.

"Yes, sir."

"Good. I'll take it from here."

The man's eyebrows drooped. "Sir?"

"I said I'll finish up here. Alone. Everyone out."

"Yes, sir," the man said, flashing a confused look over to his colleagues.

The others quickly followed him in leaving their posts and scurrying out the door. They did not say a word. But their facial expressions showed their concern, with each displaying a sudden loss of composure. As the last person wandered out, the door swished shut again. A conversation erupted outside the door that was dampened by the metal between the rooms.

Nate jumped out of his chair and nearly followed them. He was instantly at odds with what he saw. Plus the conversation outside had him worried. What was going on? Nothing had happened that day, he would remember something if it had, he was sure. He suddenly realised, he had said the same earlier.

"Closing outer airlock door now," Stuart said. He watched through the window as the three returning crew finally settled down in the airlock.

Nate's double raised his thumbs in acknowledgement. "No rush," he said, which caused Gemma to clutch her stomach and silently roll about laughing.

Stuart's fingers darted about the control panel. "Pressurising. Activating artificial gravity plating … now."

The three in the airlock were gradually lowered to the floor. In one of the corners a violent—but inaudible—rush of white gas exploded into the room as the vacuum was filled. After a few seconds it was followed by a hissing noise that gradually grew in intensity and volume.

It did not take long to equalise the pressure in the room, which the three inside the airlock appeared to appreciate. Before Nate knew it they were gratefully removing their suits, now much heavier than before thanks to the artificial gravity pulling them down. They had to help each other de-robe, one at a time and starting with the younger, slightly soiled Nate.

With Stuart working away at the control panel, Nate took the seat next to him. The impressive speed at which he moved about the controls made it hard for Nate to keep up. His motion was smooth and his concentration unwavering, despite the comical scene playing out inside the airlock.

Even though his lack of a sense of humour was legendary, Nate was still surprised to see not even an ounce of amusement on Stuart's face. His mind was obviously distracted.

He had not realised Stuart had been so tense at the time either. His face appeared to be stuck halfway between a grimace and a frown. Something had him worried. This was made all the more obvious by his constant twitching and fiddling with switches and knobs. Was he nervous about making a mistake? Nate could not tell, so for the time being he allowed the scene to continue.

L'Armin stood behind Nate's chair and placed his arms on its back, reclining it slightly. "Does anything appear out of the ordinary here, Nathan?"

"Nothing so far. Although I hadn't realised Stuart relieved the others in here. I just assumed he had stepped in to cover Ryan. That happened a lot around here. Mainly when someone needed a piss."

Nate's double had begun the displeasure of removing the rest of his space suit. Their voices were muffled by the thick layer of reinforced glass that stood between them, but the laughter was obvious. Gemma and the third crew member—Nate remembered being nicknamed Bucky for some reason—were joking as he wiped his face clean.

The scene distracted Nate. It was not so much the embarrassment that he watched, but the interactions between himself and Gemma. The first flickers of something more, present in both of their eyes, was beginning to take shape. Fast forward Seven years and a proposal backlit by a supernova, no less, was on the cards.

Of course Nate did not appreciate the reminder. His own death had put paid to that particular memory now. Further recollections only served to exacerbate things.

It was not until he had noticed the clicks and taps had stopped, that he saw something was wrong. Stuart had frozen suddenly and was now entirely transfixed by one button. Nate looked over the controls and felt his heart nearly burst when he saw which one it was.

84

"What the fuck are you doing?" Nate shouted at Stuart, who heard nothing.

Stuart's left arm was back in his pocket and relentlessly rustling the keys inside, like some sort of nervous compulsion. But his right hand was now levitating just above, and dangerously close to, the Open Airlock button. His hand hung there open and with the palm facing downward, ready to slap the big, red button at an unknown moment of his choosing. He appeared to be considering something terrible, something Nate never thought Stuart ever could.

Nate turned to L'Armin in a panic. "He was going to kill the three of us."

The three in the airlock continued to chat casually as they removed their suits. They were utterly oblivious to the fact that at any moment the airlock doors could open and suck them back out. Only this time the vacuum would make light work of stripping their unprotected bodies of any heat and air they had recently accumulated.

Without thinking, Nate made a grab for Stuart's hand and attempted to move it away.

"You cannot change this, Nathan. It has already occurred," L'Armin said in vain.

However much Nate tried he just could not prevent Stuart's hand from moving ever closer to the *kill-switch*. He clenched his teeth so tight he was sure they would crack. Still he struggled, regardless of how little he could really do. He could not just sit and let it play out, even though the effort was making him sweat profusely. An unwanted element of moisture that was quickly loosening his grip on Stuart's cement-like muscles.

"But the killer changed things before," Nate said, refusing to be rational.

They remained locked in place, until they were suddenly disturbed by a click, followed by Gemma's voice over the internal comm. Thank God, he thought. But her question did not suggest any notion of threat or awareness of their possible demise.

"Can you tell this jackass, it's his round tonight?" she said. "He seems to think he can charm his way out of it."

Stuart did not reply. His hand stayed in position, with barely enough space for a hair to pass between it and the button. Nate could only watch it move closer as his own strength had dwindled. He was unable to do a thing about it. The Ring Beings certainly wanted him to see this.

"Yo, Stuart?" Gemma said. She stood at the communications panel next the internal doors, just out of sight of Stuart. When she was fed up with being ignored she then took to banging her fist against the glass. She leant over to see through the window.

Stuart suddenly snapped back to life. He was startled by Gemma's interruption, brought back from some awful pipe dream.

"Sorry. What?" he said. Realising his mistake he quickly fumbled for his microphone's transmit button. "Yes, er, what's up?"

"You OK? You look worse than, Nate," Gemma said.

"I heard that," Nate's double shouted in the background.

Stuart regained his usual stern demeanour before replying. "Yes, fine thank you. I'll open the inner airlock door and you can all go get yourselves something to eat. You must be famished."

Their lives had been spared by what Nate saw as nothing more than a cowardly loss of nerve. A vicious and vile hatred had boiled up inside Stuart, only to be gone again in a flash. Almost as if he had sweated it out. It would explain how his boiler suit had become so damp so quickly, the sweat had managed to seep right through.

What Nate had been forced to witness had left him with two possible conclusions: Stuart had either lost his mind, or his bottle? Regardless of the reason, the world had quickly returned to its default state. It was only a matter of time before it broke again. And then it hit Nate. He was unable to deny it any longer.

Stuart left the control room in a flustered state with patches of sweat discolouring his otherwise pristine overalls. Either fear, or guilt, or even perhaps the thrill of his undeniable power over life, in the moment he was deciding to wipe it out, had made his skin damp.

The air felt good as a light breeze was sent Nate's way by the sudden swoosh of the door. The relief was only fleeting, once more replaced with the stifling heat that his sudden exertion had caused.

L'Armin rested his hand on his friend's shoulder, imparting yet more heat to aching joints. "This is not yet finished, Nathan," he said, firmly squeezing the shoulder muscles underneath.

Nate fixed his sight solely on his counterpart, still sat trying to pry his oversized boots from his feet. He envied the ignorance of his double, a sentiment he afforded in more ways than one. Something inside him yearned to be back there, to be in charge of himself and no-one else. Certainly not the thousands of people that looked to him for guidance.

As the three left the airlock, Nate noticed how Gemma glanced repeatedly at the younger him. There was once love there, he saw. In a way it alleviated some of the rawness that was instilled in him after their marriage had failed. It did little to take him away from Stuart's obvious desire to see him dead, however. There was nothing, in his mind that could ever reduce the anger that was forming in his stomach over that.

"Nathan?" L'Armin had taken to shaking Nate's arm as he spoke. "There is still more to see."

"You're right, sorry."

"I suggest we follow Stuart again. He may yet lead us to the killer. His past actions have alerted the Beings of an involvement in this."

Nate mustered the effort to move and set a brisk pace toward the door. He knew he was in too deep to give up now, he had to follow it through once and for all.

This time, when the door swished open automatically, he was bathed once more by an overwhelming light. He was becoming so used to this sensation that he had already closed his eyes as he had stepped through. It was anyone's guess where they would end up this time.

Chapter 9

Glasses chimed, voices stirred, and the undeniable aroma of corporate people hit Nate as he entered the next realm: a pungent smell of aftershave, perfume and mouthwash, all mixed together. It was a recent memory, still easily accessed, and one that his sense of smell remembered well. Instantly he knew where and when he was, and knew exactly what to expect.

A vast and open hall with a high ceiling, two storeys or so above, appeared in front of him. Strip lights hung from metal support beams way above, while the floor was blackened by the many shadows cast by an uncomfortably dense crowd. Nate had to shove a woman out of his way just to find enough space to confer with his companion. He managed to find a place by a display cabinet with a small scale model of a competitors drilling rig inside.

"OK, now *this* I remember well," Nate said. He held L'Armin's upper arm to keep him close. "This was the big mining convention on Earth, only about six months ago."

"It is not a coincidence, Nathan. The Beings intend for you to learn something important. Can you recall where you should be?"

Nate stood on his toes, stretching the arches of his feet as far as he could, just to see above the crowd. The height he gained was barely enough to be considered an advantage, but something did catch his eye. He lowered back down and turned to L'Armin. "Come on, this way," he said.

They pushed their way through the shifting crowds and made a beeline for a makeshift bar to the side of the hall. He cut in where others slowed, elbowed indiscriminate people out of his way, and tried his best not to become boxed in by suddenly forming groups. The closer he got to the rudimentary bar—just a set of raised tables serving drinks—the better he could see who it was he had spotted.

From a distance, the man had a clean cut appearance. Up close, however, it was clear he was anything but, with two days old stubble and greasy skin that darkened his complexion. More importantly, his clothes carried the distinct aroma of alcohol. Either he had spilt his drink or the fumes had soaked in over time. For whatever reason, he stank of booze and those nearby were fully aware. He stood at the bar and ordered a drink. Nate hoped it would be an orange or a water.

"Vodka, straight," Cameron snapped at the smiling, twenty something girl tending bar. She wore a loosely buttoned shirt and a waistcoat that clung tightly to her busty figure. An enticing trap, Nate thought, typical for a corporate gathering full of middle-aged men.

Cameron, on the other hand, had not even noticed the woman. She was simply a drinks dispenser to him. A heavy emotional weight appeared to be pressing down on him from all sides and nothing was distracting him from it. Whatever it was, it had caused him to slowly sink into himself. He was resorting to alcohol to pick himself up again.

"He looks like shit," Nate said.

The girl delivered Cameron's drink, though with much less of a smile this time. He immediately poured it down his throat, giving the liquid barely enough time to touch his lips as it travelled from glass to mouth. As soon as it slid past his tongue, his back straightened suddenly before it once again returned to its default slumped position.

For a tiny moment, Nate could see the weight had been lifted, although the forlorn expression that remained on Cameron's face suggested it would require much more than one drink to release him from whatever troubled him.

The woman tending bar watched as Cameron made the contents of his glass magically vanish. Her smile had now completely disappeared, along with the vodka. She did not look away until someone more cheerful appeared behind, waiting to be served.

"What can I get *you*, sir," she said. Her smile reappeared like a sunbeam through dark clouds.

Nate barely had time to turn and see who she was talking to, before the man replied.

"Whatever he's having," a familiar voice said.

When he saw Stuart suddenly standing in front of him, he felt an urge to lash out. He wanted to grab him and not let go, or land one well-placed punch right in the centre of his bulbous gut, anything to get the anger out.

But Stuart was not glaring at him. His eyes were instead burning a hole into Cameron and threatening to set the air between them alight. He was in a foul looking mood too, without so much as a hint of a smile on his face. The cause was obvious.

Nate had to clench his fists, somehow managing to keep them by his side. His nails dug deep into his palms as he watched the two.

"What the *fuck* is your problem?" Stuart said.

At first Nate was sure the question had been aimed at him. In an instant his emotions had gone from immense rage to complete confusion.

"How can you ..." he began to say before he was cut short.

"It's only the one, sir, I promise," Cameron said.

Stuart placed one hand on the back of Cameron's neck and the other on the newly placed glass of vodka the barmaid had set down for him. But he did not lean in to speak to Cameron in a discreet manner, as expected. To make it clear who was in charge to those around, he spoke loud enough for them to hear.

"I don't give a flying *frig* how many, mister. You're on duty. That means no drinking. You got that?" He took the drink in one loud gulp and returned the glass heavily to the table.

Cameron pushed his own glass away, leaving one last sliver of a mouthful behind. He brushed himself down and reorganised his tie, head down like a naughty schoolboy, as Stuart continued to scold him.

"All you're here to do is watch, that's it. And I find you hitting the sauce instead. I swear this is your last fucking chance, Cameron. Get your shit together right now."

"Yessir," Cameron said. He tucked in a loose bit of shirt in one final attempt at looking dressed. "I won't do it again, sir, I promise. I've just had a lot on my mind, what with the missus' health bills and all."

"Not my problem," Stuart replied without an ounce of sympathy. He waved the barmaid over and pointed to his empty glass, completely unaware of the hypocrisy. She smiled and was soon pouring out another drink, before moving on once more. With his glass again in hand and full of a swirling clear liquid, he spun around to watch others rubbing shoulders nearby.

Cameron's whole body had slumped further than before with the added strain from Stuart's attack. It was clear he just wanted to finish the last few drops of his drink, but his hand fell short as the shaking started each time. To stop it he gripped his hand with the other, only to discover it was trembling just as badly.

Had Nate known any of this, he was certain he would have been less quick to judge. Everyone had written Cameron off as a useless drunk, and he had accepted it without a thought of why. It could not change how he saw Cameron now, after what had happened. He saw nothing else but the man who had stepped up when the need had arisen. If anything, he had performed better than anyone had given him credit for. Much better than Stuart had expected, at least.

"Wait," Nate said suddenly. "Why was Cameron chosen for this trip?"

L'Armin appeared behind the bar table, clearly misunderstanding its significance. He moved aside as the young barmaid rushed past with a tray.

"I do not follow your thought, Nathan."

"If Cameron was so unreliable six months ago, I'm pretty certain Stuart would have kicked him to the kerb. And if I know one thing for sure it's that he doesn't stand failure. So why choose him? Why not someone more reliable?"

"You assume Stuart had always intended on putting Cameron in harm's way, along with you?"

"Yes." Suddenly things were falling into place. "Was Cameron picked because Stuart expected him to fail? Maybe even to frame him? I don't know. Is that what the Ring Beings are trying to tell me?"

L'Armin took a glass from the table and gave it a sniff, immediately pulling it away afterwards. "I understand. Perhaps it is," he said, before moving on to the next abandoned glass and repeating his investigation.

The barmaid stopped and poured out a third drink for Stuart, which garnered a creepy wink from him. A curious L'Armin watched the exchange at an uncomfortably close distance like an unwelcome bystander on a news broadcast.

Again Stuart swallowed his drink in one greedy mouthful and then hammered the glass back onto the table. Each time he did so it sent a clear message to Cameron: do as I say, not as I do. The noise also startled Cameron, causing his back to straighten forcefully. The motion brought a grimace to his face that Nate felt himself mimic unintentionally.

"Shall I get back to guarding the door, sir?" Cameron managed to say all too feebly.

Stuart turned to walk away, and as if talking to someone else, he said, "If it's not too much to ask." He then rudely pushed past Cameron.

It was a shock for Nate to see a new side to both of the people before him. Stuart had an evil and angry side that he had never seen before. He was a bully. And as for Cameron, somehow Helen's warning did not quite live up to what he was seeing. The man was slowly imploding under the pressure of his home life. Yet a fate worse than that of losing his job appeared to have been on the cards for him; cards that were drawn from a deck stacked firmly in Stuart's favour.

Cameron finally found the energy to leave the bar. His eyes were glistening from the booze and Stuart's tactless reprimand as he skulked away, upset and ashamed.

Nate felt the sudden urge to follow him instead of Stuart, before he reminded himself that this was the past. If he could not help *this* Cameron, he sure as hell could help the man he now knew. After he had found his answers, he decided, he would do something about it. But they were so close to the truth that he was sure he could grab them out of the air.

"L'Armin, he's off," Nate said, but he could not see his companion anywhere.

"Of course," L'Armin replied.

Nate turned to find him nose deep in a glass with only a wisp of blue liquid remaining.

"Fascinating aroma."

"You should try drinking it next time. Come on," Nate said as he ushered L'Armin along.

They followed closely behind Stuart, who exchanged jovially with those he knew. Gone was the red-faced rage that had bubbled up earlier, gone was the look of disgust that Cameron's failings had elicited, and most noticeably, gone was the dismissive tone in his voice.

It was becoming abundantly clear to Nate that the Stuart he knew was nothing more than a veil of falsehood, created to conceal the evil underneath, one that always wanted something or sensed an opportunity. The realisation began to worry Nate.

Stuart continued to lead them to the high profile stand of Maddox Industries. On the way they had stuck close to him and had never strayed more than a few feet from his side. He had not spoken to anyone for long. A number of people had waved or smiled at him, but he had not stopped to speak with them, choosing instead to talk as he walked away. He was eager to get back to his company's stand, it seemed.

Once there, Nate could see that his stage was noticeably bigger than most of the others there. A large and spherical holographic display hung above, with red lettering spelling out the company's motto against a vivid blue background: "Bringing the richness of space to all." it said. What bollocks, Nate thought, as he watched the display spin around and start again, all in the flashiest way Maddox Industries could afford.

Underneath that was the stage, raised roughly three feet above the ground and littered with a myriad of display cabinets, each of which featured floating models of vessels from the Maddox family's ever increasing fleet. On the large temporary wall at the back, colourful and highly detailed plans of how their mining equipment operated in space had been hung up for all to see. A cross section of the first and largest Maddox mining ship—the Miner's Folly—was also on display.

Nate spotted himself pacing the stage, with a small microphone hugging his cheek that tucked neatly around the back of his ear. He nervously addressed those waiting for the Maddox Industries' presentation to continue. The speech had stopped abruptly, causing a few to whisper their irritated condemnations a little too loudly.

The Nate on stage regained his composure and put on his most compelling look of confidence. It was an awkward watch, as Nate saw himself quickly falter again. He had never enjoyed such events. Not like his father had. This was not an environment in which he flourished.

"Sorry. Our Graviton beams use the output from our highly efficient Gravitas propulsion drive." He waved his left arm over an image on the wall behind him. Unfortunately, he turned to see he had in fact gestured to a large picture of himself that had been stuck up. He quickly swapped his arms and pointed to the correct image to his right. The mistake caused a stifled laugh to break out among the audience.

"We break up the surface of the object, that we want to break up," he continued clumsily.

A wall of arms shot up at the front of the audience. Nate remembered how intimidating this had felt at the time. It had been even harder to decide who should question him next, with each having a particular bone they wanted to pick clean. It was not enough that they got the answers, they had to break him in the process too.

The Nate on stage stopped and, eventually, picked a questioner from the front row.

"Yes, thanks," a grey suited man said. "What does Gravitas mean in this context?"

An easy question, thankfully. "It stands for Graviton Augmentation and Stimulation. Gravitas," Nate answered more confidently this time.

"And how does it work?" the grey suited man continued.

"Well, er," Nate began. "It augments and stimulates Gravitons. It's complicated. It, erm …" He quickly pulled out a small card from his pocket and began to read it like a child giving a book report to the class. "It increases the output of Gravitons from a source by augmenting its density. This is then excited to a higher energy level before it is expelled, creating thrust, or releasing an energy beam."

The grey suited man immediately set about making notes. His fingers rushed about the glowing display that he wore like an armband. Nate knew, even at the time, that the man's notes almost certainly said nothing of his words and everything of his composure up on stage.

Still arms were waving for Nate's attention. It seemed that some flesh remained attached to the bone. Before continuing with his speech, he addressed another question, hoping it was not just to test him this time.

"Yes, the woman in the red top there." Nate pointed, ushering over a man with a microphone.

"Hi, Rita from the Interstellar Mining Journal," she said. "Is there any truth to the rumours that a merger between your company and the Mine-X group is imminent?"

Nate watched as his doppelganger lost it again. The woman's question had come from nowhere and slapped him sideways. He had only been in charge for a small amount of time and was still an amateur when it came to representing his family's company. And they all knew it. As the other Nate became hopelessly lost and stood staring mindlessly into the distance, the crowd once again grew restless.

When he finally began to speak, his voice had gone up by almost an octave. "A what? I haven't heard about that. Who told you that? I mean, I'd never agree to that." The panic was tangible, so obviously causing a conflict between his brain and mouth. "This isn't what I'm supposed to talk about."

The panic was getting to Nate all over again as he watched himself so badly fluff the responses. His hands had become clammy and itchy. Even though he told himself it was all behind him, he could not separate himself from it.

"It's just there's been a lot of talk about your company's financial struggles of late." Rita continued to pile on the pressure.

Just tell her to shut up or ignore her, Nate thought to himself. He was sure that if he had had the courage to do this at the time, he would have avoided the headlines the next day. They had savagely portrayed him as a weak leader, who lacked the temperament required to succeed in such a cut-throat business. It had taken him weeks to recover from that. Now his rule was with an iron fist, just like his father's had been.

"You appear to be disappointing these people," L'Armin said.

97

He could see his friend was right, yet however much it may have temporarily tarnished the company's image, he could not see the relevance. After a few seconds of watching people wander away from the stage, he had to ask a question he feared he already knew the answer to.

"Is this why Stuart wants me dead?" he said. "Because I'm not as confident a leader as my father?"

"I would suggest it is possible, Nathan. This Stuart is a troubling character."

L'Armin began to study Stuart, who stood next to them. He had caught something and was intent on investigating further. He leant his head in close to Stuart's chest. Nate was sure it was nothing important, until he too saw what L'Armin had spotted.

Stuart had begun to fidget relentlessly on the spot, like an itch that his entire body felt. He watched with both eyes locked firmly on the Nate standing on stage. There were no signs of anger on his face like before. But something else. His mouth threatened to break into a smile, possibly even allowing a chuckle through. Whatever thoughts had rattled around Stuart's head, they were ruining his cold and calculated appearance, making him look skittish and excited.

Before the other Nate could find a reply, a friendly face entered the stage from the left side and took to settling the issue.

"There are no such plans, thank you," Helen said with a stern look shot straight at Rita from Interstellar *whatever*. "Now please hold all questions until the presentation is over. Mr Maddox, would you like to continue?"

Nate caught the look his double sent to his saviour as a thanks. Her blue eyes met those of his double and replied with a wink. He remembered this moment well. It was one of the times he had seen more to Helen than just a colleague and a friend.

She stayed on stage to deter any more would-be character assassins, while he returned to his pre-written and partially memorised speech. Slowly the arms of the crowd diminished until only one stubborn limb remained.

Regardless of how determined Rita had remained to get an answer from him, with Helen as his protector she had not got one.

A low level ringing began emanating from Stuart's inside suit pocket. It was accompanied by a red flashing light that glowed against his shirt, Nate saw. He removed a small, transparent, screen from the pocket and tapped it lightly. Nate leant over and made out part of the message Stuart had received. Someone had requested a meeting, but he could not make out any more of the text. It was evidently urgent as Stuart took no time at all to quickly shuffle away.

Nate tugged at L'Armin's oversized and baggy sleeve. L'Armin followed, but reluctantly as the speech appeared to interest—or disturb—him greatly. Nate was not quite sure which. Once again L'Armin had begun to mumble under his breath as though he were having a conversation with himself. Nate regretted ever showing him his business.

"You appear to destroy for money, Nathan," L'Armin said after he had concluded his discussion.

Nate stopped, surprised by the tone of the question. "Well, I wouldn't say destroy. We mine."

L'Armin's face scrunched up as he appeared to not understand, or not like what he heard.

"We unlock the raw materials locked up in space rocks, asteroids, or comets and sell them to those who need it," Nate continued as he slowly set off in pursuit of Stuart.

"I see," L'Armin said with a hint of disapproval in his voice. "A somewhat messy activity, I sense."

They again followed Stuart. The sound from the Maddox Industries stage began to merge with similar presentations by the competition, all there to show off their services to potential new clients. Including, Nate saw, the Mine-X company that had been mentioned in rumours of a merger, now spreading across the industry like an infectious disease. Their stage appeared to rival his own in both size and popularity.

Past most of the noise they found large groups sat around circular tables. These served as the bases for the visiting parties. Some of the tables were also taken up by journalists, with their portable workstations and coffee fetching underlings—all Ritas in the making. Others had been reserved by smaller companies too small to afford a large stage of their own.

Stuart, however, was not the remotest bit interested in any of this. He was heading to a small room at the back of the large exhibition hall. Inside, Nate could see a pair of heavy set men guarding the door. He found it strange that no-one noticed or seemed to be paying the slightest bit of attention to this unusual set up. Certainly he had not seen it on the day.

"I'm here to see your boss," Stuart said to one of the guards. He puffed out his chest the best he could to show his authority. Nate held back a laugh at Stuart's pointless gesture, more of an over-zealous show of power than anything else. Nonetheless, one of the bulky men turned and walked away. He approached an elderly gentleman sat eating on his own at a table set aside, apparently just for him.

"I know that man," Nate said.

L'Armin was standing on his tip-toes again, just to see over Stuart's shoulder. "Why do you suppose Stuart is meeting this man in such a relatively private place?" he said.

"Good question."

The doorman leant down to the ear height of the elderly man and spoke softly—too softly for Nate to hear. He then pointed over to Stuart. The elderly man looked up, and after a few seconds considering Stuart's all too aggressive posture, he waved him over. His visit had been granted.

"I must admit, I'm surprised to see you again," the old man said.

Stuart took a seat at the other end of the table with Nate and L'Armin sat either side, like his very own entourage.

"Let's cut the crap and get down to it shall we?" Stuart said.

"Watch your tone. And please don't confuse my kindness with weakness, Stuart. I'm used to pissing in much bigger pools than you are, remember?" The old man raised a glass to his mouth and sipped slowly. The clear liquid inside sparkled as a ray of light passed through it. The effect matched his silvery, slicked back hair that shone under the hanging table light, like a glistening patch of icy snow.

It was obvious Stuart had found the old man's remark offensive as his chest heaved, his heart seemingly banging against his ribs and trying to escape. "I'll be a much bigger fish if your deal is still on the table."

The old man brought a cloth up from his lap and wiped it delicately across his thin lips. His eyes fixed onto Stuart's as a clear test of his composure. Nate felt a shiver race down his spine; he was sure the old man's glare could cut right through him.

"That was a one-time offer, Stuart," the old man finally said. "And if I remember right you spat it back in my face. May I ask what's changed?"

"Look, I have my reasons. But this is strictly business so they aren't relevant."

The old man threw his cloth onto the table. It landed in his half empty bowl of fish soup, spilling some onto the table cloth. "Not relevant. Don't be so naive, Stuart. Everything is relevant in this game. I'm not backing a horse without knowing its odds first. If we do this I need to know what you have against Nathan Maddox."

Nate nearly choked at the mention of his name. This was the concrete answer he had been looking for, but had tried so hard to deny. He watched with baited breath.

Stuart's face had reddened and he was allowing his hands to crease the table cloth. Whether or not he intended to was debatable. Although something strong was definitely peeking out of his normally distant expression. A tic, or a twitch, something Nate could see was being held back.

"I ... I don't have anything ..." But Stuart just could not find the words.

Nate had never seen him so dumbfounded.

101

"Come now, Stuart, this will finish him for good. I cannot believe it is simply for business sake."

"Listen," Stuart began, less forceful than before. "I've worked for his dad since the company started. And now the old man's gone, I'm expected to sit back and watch as his inept, shit of a son tears it apart? I can't do that."

"Son-of-a-bitch," Nate said.

Stuart reached for a jug of water in the centre of the table and poured himself a glass. With a noticeable shake that betrayed his increasing anguish. "I *won't* do that," he added.

"Jealousy is a useful emotion in this business, Stuart, highly underrated," the old man said. With one click of his fingers, he was handed a dark brown folder. He opened it by painstakingly unwinding a small length of string that had been wrapped around a brass fastener, sealing it tight. After a short rummage inside, he found the page he needed and scanned it.

Once satisfied he slid it and the folder across the table, making a scraping noise as his bejewelled hand rubbed against the cloth. "I trust the arrangement would be the same as before?" he said while rearranging the rings on his fingers.

"Exactly," Stuart replied, between sloppy sips of water.

"And you understand, for this to succeed, Nathan Maddox must be completely removed from the equation?"

This is it, Nate thought as Stuart picked up the folder and began to peruse it. The next sentence would seal it for him. Stuart's treachery was about to be revealed and his depraved accomplices along with it.

"He'll be removed completely and permanently, I assure you. I have something already in the works. Nathan's due a break in a few months time and I have my best person on the job."

The end of Stuart's sentence had Nate worried.

"Spare me the details, Stuart. Once he's out of the way and you convince the board to give you his job, you will announce the merger. I want to see both names on one sign before mine is on a tombstone."

"That's what he wants? A fucking merger, after I refused?" Nate said.

L'Armin was surprised by the increase in volume of Nate's voice and leant away in his chair, with a look of concern across his face.

"When it's done I'll have the money sent to an account in your name," the old man continued. "Until then there is to be no contact between us. Do you understand? None."

Stuart broke away from the folder and nodded in compliance. He extended his hand to shake the old man's, but his gesture was ignored, or not wanted. Nate assumed the latter was more likely.

"You appear to have disturbed Stuart's plans on many occasions, Nathan."

"I see that now, L'Armin. If I hadn't returned to work for my dad, he would have been the obvious successor. He's just too much of a coward to get rid of me himself," Nate said.

The old man lit a large cigar and began puffing away, clearly enjoying the tangible exhalations. He swung his chair away from Stuart and paid no attention to his guest's departure. There was no respect between them, only an ever expanding grey fog from the old man's decadently oversized cigar.

"So he hired some scum-bag to kill me. Just so he could take over the company?" Nate said.

L'Armin nodded, but watched as Stuart wandered past the two doormen. They stood with their arms tightly crossed, looking as formidable as ever. Their presence was enough to shoo Stuart away like an annoying gnat.

"But the guy screwed it up," Nate continued. "He won't let me leave this place if he knows, will he? So how do we find him? None of this answers that. I'm still sitting here with a target drawn across my face."

103

L'Armin stood and made his way to the door to see into the main hall. "I fear the answers are still with Stuart," he said with his back to Nate.

"How? I thought you said this is all from my memory? I saw Stuart only a handful of times after this, predominantly in meetings. There's nothing left in here …" Nate pressed a finger against his temple.

"We could continue to watch Stuart's movements. Yes, I know but..." L'Armin stopped halfway through his own sentence to Nate's surprise.

"L'Armin. You're not hearing me. I have nothing. In fact I'm not sure I had *this* much to begin with. How can we follow him?"

The smoke the old man sent around the room began to dry Nate's throat and sting his eyes, causing them to well up slightly. He left the table and stood next to L'Armin to get away from it. He welcomed the air from the main hall as they bordered the two rooms. It was not perfect either, but the breaths were scraping less at the back of his mouth now. He could think more clearly without the constant battering of warm, particulate air.

When he turned to L'Armin he saw that his guide had closed his eyes and was no longer watching Stuart.

"I am positive we will find him soon. A little more time is all we need," L'Armin said. "I am positive," he repeated.

Something about the way he spoke felt strange to Nate. It was similar to how he had mumbled to himself earlier, except now Nate could hear his words clearly.

"Hey. What's going on, L'Armin? What aren't you telling me?"

L'Armin ignored the question, choosing instead to continue mumbling as he wandered off. The regular chats he was having with himself were beginning to grind Nate's patience to dust.

Nate followed, but he was becoming increasingly impatient with his usually coherent companion. He was able to hear the conversation through the crowds, though what he heard was making no sense at all to him. Who was answering back?

"Can we stop for a second?" Nate asked, but again he was not acknowledged.

"We must continue. We must search further. No. I will, but not yet. I can help him further. Just let me explain."

Nate had had enough. He pulled L'Armin around by the arm. "Hey," he shouted.

Once facing each other, L'Armin's distant expression disappeared, replaced with one of surprise. "Please, Nathan. We must …"

"What's going on? Who are you talking to? Is it these Ring Beings?"

L'Armin wiggled out of Nate's grip and looked around sporadically. His eyes went everywhere but never met Nate's. If anything he was actively trying not to look at him.

He was becoming more and more distraught the further away Stuart was getting. He appeared to be contemplating something important, Nate had heard that much. But he hesitated to share what. What was clear was the need L'Armin had to stay close to Stuart.

"L'Armin, please. This is my life we're talking about. If you know something—"

"I cannot," L'Armin snapped as he again shifted his gaze. "They won't allow it."

Nate could feel a sense of panic run up from his stomach and to his head. It was getting hot all of a sudden and those around him were much too close.

Had he blindly put his faith in L'Armin? Was any of what he saw even true? He watched helplessly as his guide appeared to fall apart in front of him. He wished there was something, anything, he could do to bring his friend, his pillar of strength, back to him again.

"L'Armin?" he said. Somehow the crowd around them were even louder than before. He raised his voice once more just to overcome their incessant talking. "Talk to me. Who won't allow it?"

Finally L'Armin was back. He turned, revealing a tear resting in the corner of his right eye that Nate had not noticed before. It sparkled as it dithered, not quite ready to drop. The tear captured Nate and would not let him go. Like seeing a loved one cry for the first time, it took him aback. He had not considered whether L'Armin's species were even able *to* cry.

The voices again became louder.

"There is more that you do not know," L'Armin began. "Much you do not understand."

Nate was frozen in place. His head still felt uncomfortably hot. If only he could hush the voices around them.

"My words cannot leave this place, Nathan. We see good in you."

"What's going on? Did any of this happen?"

L'Armin reached out his hand and placed it on Nate's arm as a gesture of reassurance. "It did happen. But I have shown you more than I should have."

"You? What are you saying, L'Armin? Why is everything getting so damn loud in here?"

He did not answer. Instead he stumbled away, again heading in the direction Stuart had taken. Nate stayed in place, more confused than ever. He had no idea whether he needed to follow L'Armin or keep away, giving him some space to console himself.

Standing uneasily, and still surrounded by strangers, all far louder than they should be, Nate felt his ears begin to hurt. The never ending chatter had become far too loud for him to think clearly. It continued to build until the words began to merge and form only noises, echoing around him like a whirlwind of sound.

After a few seconds, he could not take it anymore, it had to stop. He raised his hands to his ears to block it out, but they did nothing to stop it. The noise was in his head as well, it had become inescapable.

"L'Armin," he shouted in pain. Up ahead he could see L'Armin standing deadly still with his eyes shut and his mouth moving quickly. He was speaking to someone unseen again.

For reasons Nate could not understand, his body was stuck in place. The sound was now so loud, and the vibrations so strong, that his sight began to shake like a pounding bass was running through his skull. He dropped to his knees and grasped his ears tightly. It was all he could do to reduce the intense pain.

With his eyes shut his world soon descended into a chaotic choir of hundreds of disembodied voices, all speaking at once.

"Stop, please," Nate screamed.

But by now the sounds were even managing to drown out his own voice. He slapped his head to try and clear the noises. Nothing was able to disrupt them as they invaded his once peaceful mind. With the voices smashing into each other he soon felt his head throb. Still the noise continued to increase uncontrollably, like a crescendo of voices. It threatened to split his head in two.

Until something suddenly cut through it all, bringing the world to near silence.

"Nathan," a distant voice said, just about loud enough for him to hear.

In an instant the noise of the crowd around him had stopped, only a high pitched ringing remained. The room had fallen a deathly quiet with everyone inside left rooted in place. Finally the voices were gone.

"Nathan. You are unharmed," L'Armin said.

Nate could hear him, but was reluctant to remove his hands in case the noise returned. He was surprised to hear how calm L'Armin had become in such a short amount of time. Had he even heard the noises?

"I am sorry, Nathan. I should not have left you like that. Your mind was not prepared to take the strain of this place."

When Nate opened his eyes and saw the still faces around him, he was completely and utterly lost for words. Some were stuck halfway between expressions, while others balanced on one leg after being frozen mid stride. All of them idly stared like waxwork models.

Somehow the world had been stopped dead in its tracks. Immediately after this the pressure in Nate's head was gone. He remained in place and forced a rhythm into his breathing—in through the nose, out through the mouth, then repeat, he thought. Slowly he was returning to a much calmer state. He continued the same process until he could feel his pulse begin to ease.

"Please forgive our dishonesty," L'Armin said. "It was a necessary deception."

"You can control the Beings, can't you?" Nate said through a nervous flutter in his voice. He leant back on his legs and peered up to his friend. The light above forced his eyes to wince. "That's who you've been talking to isn't it?"

L'Armin carefully pulled Nate to his feet. "No Nathan," he said, steadying his companion. "There are no Beings."

Chapter 10

Seconds after returning to his feet, Nate was again unbalanced and found himself stepping backward into one of the unmoving figures. He bashed into a woman's elbow, which stuck in his spine and caused him to flinch. The world around him may have frozen, but what he had just heard was far more shocking. Inevitably, his bruised back was pushed to the bottom of his list of concerns.

"What? I don't understand. Who were you talking to if not the Ring Beings?" he said.

The sudden realisation that the Beings were fake had shattered his preconceptions into billions of tiny pieces. He tried to keep his breaths as regular as possible while he dealt with this new piece of information. If they did not exist, then who was responsible for the re-creations?

"My people," L'Armin began, "have been in contact since the attempt on your life. They agreed that I should help you. But we are able to do more."

Nate rubbed his fingers against his temples in a circular motion. Creases of skin formed like bow waves at the tips of his fingers, before they were smoothed out again. The massage did little to dissipate the heat in his head, but he continued regardless.

"This is crazy. How is all of *this* possible, then?" Nate waved his left arm around the room. He continued to caress his temple with the other.

"It is my race. *We*, and not the Beings, are responsible for creating this from your memories, Nathan. You and I are connected. More deeply than we usually allow."

"So, can you read my mind?" Nate said with a worried tone to his voice.

"I cannot hear your inner voice, no. I can, however, see fragments of your past. And, as you have seen, we can experience them again."

"But there's things here I'm sure I'd forgotten. And what about the meeting we just saw? I didn't witness that. I'm over by the stage, still giving my speech. Explain that."

"We are able to see more. This can be considered a second viewing. Or a repeat of time, if you will," L'Armin said. "As long as the event happened within this bubble of time, we can see it. Venture too far away from your other selves and the memory will collapse. This is what nearly happened a moment ago."

"The noises," Nate said, excitedly. Finally he could understand something.

"Indeed. The discussion to help you further had intensified, and I had become distracted. Our connection was nearly broken, leaving you alone with the burden. Your mind could not cope. I am truly sorry," L'Armin said, while bowing.

"My head felt like it was about to explode. But I don't understand why you hid all of this?"

"You must understand, we do so for our own safety." L'Armin turned away as he spoke, leaving only the left side of his face still visible. "Many generations ago we came here to escape enslavement. My people were abused and threatened because of this ability. It cannot happen again."

Nate watched as a small tear formed and trickled down L'Armin's face. It followed the path left by an earlier drop, hesitating at the peak of each wrinkle it surmounted. Eventually, it nestled just above his lip, precariously close to falling to the floor. A tear from the other side slowly followed and ran down to join it. There the engorged tear hung on for dear life.

"So what's with the festival and these Ring Beings? Why make all of that up?"

L'Armin turned back and smiled. "We can share our gift without revealing it."

"A cover story? Clever, if not a bit over the top."

"We do like a spectacle." L'Armin let out a breath followed by the faintest whiff of a chuckle. "We have learnt to appreciate our gift through sharing in this way." He wiped the tear away.

"And this?" Nate pushed against one of the frozen bodies standing next to him. The material of the man's shirt was soft and his skin, underneath, as fleshy as it should be. He removed his finger and found that everything bounced back as usual too. The man was there, but the lights were well and truly out.

"I may have the ability, Nathan, but you are guiding our steps. We were linked the moment we entered the rift together."

"But you're able to control it?" Nate said as he nervously studied the crowd.

"To some degree, yes. I can stop it, as you can see."

Nate turned suddenly to face L'Armin. "So why didn't you stop it when that guy tried to kill me?"

"He was real, Nathan. I can only do certain things in here."

"Can't you re-create it like you did these places then? We could find the killer—"

"I cannot," L'Armin interrupted. "Memories can only be re-created once. They are too unstable after that. Memories, new and old, become permanently intertwined. The mind cannot survive such a thing."

"Is this where it ends, then, with Stuart? We still haven't found the assassin."

"No, Nathan, it is not. I have shown you things you had not seen before. The ability allows us to see things that happened within the proximity of the memory holder. This is why we were able to hear Stuart's conversation in that room." He pointed back to the smoke filled room, only now the cloud appeared solid above the old man's head.

"Well, where do we go from here?"

L'Armin turned and slowly shuffled away. "Come," he said.

Nate followed closely behind, weaving in and out of frozen bodies. His progress was slower than L'Armin's, who was able to manoeuvre through them much quicker due to his lesser height. He now appeared a changed man and one as determined and enthusiastic as ever. The pressure of keeping his race's abilities a secret no longer held him back.

They made their way through the crowd until L'Armin stopped abruptly. Nate was struggling to keep up and nearly did not see. When he did he felt a brief moment of dizziness nearly overwhelm his balance as he was forced to halt on the spot. His head was still full of static and fuzz from before. He steadied himself against another unknown figure. They were proving handy.

"This is where we go next," L'Armin said, pointing to one of the frozen people. He had a broad smile across his face that surprised Nate.

The man he pointed at was the unmoving statue of Stuart. Nate could see he had been paused while walking, with one foot left hovering above the squeaky floor. He found it hard to resist shoving him to the ground like a school bully and demanding he hand over his lunch money.

"How can we get more from Stuart?" he said.

L'Armin shook his head. "I do not mean Stuart." He waved his hand over the dark brown folder still in Stuart's hand. "This will lead us to his accomplices."

Finally Nate was starting to understand just how much L'Armin had been holding back. All the time he thought he had had some kind of mental link to the Ring Beings, he had in fact been connected to the man right next to him. L'Armin had made all of this possible, not a group of ethereal beings living in space dust.

He watched as L'Armin placed his hands together and closed his eyes. Gradually the people around them became

112

animated once more. Like a video being sped up, their movements appeared to wind up, until they were moving at normal speed again. Nate was amazed by the spectacle and nearly did not notice a charging Stuart pushing right past him.

The automatic response to follow took over both of them. They soon found themselves heading toward the large exit of the hall. Stuart was in a hurry to catch up with someone he had spotted heading out. His feet moved much too quickly for his gait to keep up with, making every other step almost a skip.

Once Stuart reached the door, he whistled loudly. When the person ahead did not turn, he called their name instead. "Helen," he shouted.

This was nothing out of the ordinary, Nate considered. Helen was after all Stuart's assistant. But their exchange made his heart sink just a little.

"Helen," Stuart said as he pulled up next to her.

The sudden stop caused a build-up of disgruntled people behind, who tried their best to traverse a gap made half as big by an all too inconsiderate Stuart. Nate had to force his way through to stand next to them.

"Hi, Stuart. I was just heading out for a smoke," Helen said.

"Yes, yes. You know that side project we spoke about?"

Helen nodded as she searched her bag for something. She held an open pack of *lite* cigarettes in her hand with one pinched, but unlit, between her fingers.

"About Mr. Maddox?" she said, placing the unlit stick in her mouth. With both hands free she proceeded to delve deeper into her bag. The further she rummaged the more determined she became to find the lost item.

"Yes. I'd like you to go ahead and organise things. Remember what I said, though, pick somewhere convenient. You will need to make time to meet my contact beforehand," Stuart said.

113

Finally Helen produced a lighter, exactly what she had been looking for in her large bag. She quickly lit the cigarette—red coloured to denote its high nicotine supplement content—and began to puff away. She inhaled loudly, held it in for a few seconds and then exhaled, before sending a look of concern to Stuart.

"Your contact?" she said, the smoke flowing gracefully out of her mouth between syllables.

Stuart waved a hand in front of his face in a disapproving manner. "Yes, and I need you to give him the details of the contract."

"Right. I'll get straight on it, sir." She moved the lit cigarette to her side in response to Stuart's gesture. Out of sight, out of mind, it seemed.

When she went to walk away, Stuart grabbed her by the arm suddenly. She first looked to his hand in shock as he gripped her a little too tightly, and then moved up to his eyes. Nate swore he had seen a degree of disgust in her face at the touch of his skin.

"After you do this, I promise you'll be on your way up the company ladder. In fact I guarantee it," Stuart said.

Nate stood next to Helen, studying her face intently. He watched her eyes crease ever so slightly as Stuart continued to man-handle her. She clearly did not approve of the overly tactile way he was dealing with her. Except she did not move away. Nate just could not interpret what he was seeing. Her eyebrows had dipped at the mention of the unknown contact, but now her face beamed with delight at the promise of a promotion. Was this the way Stuart always treated her?

"Really? Great, thank you sir," she said.

How much she knew about Stuart's plot still remained a mystery. Nate contemplated the question of her innocence while he watched on. She was no doubt one of Stuart's accomplices, that much was certain. However, what was not clear was whether she had been willingly or not.

She had arranged everything. Had she booked the killer as well? He feared the answer might not sit well with him. It

114

became difficult for him not to imagine her laughing as a trained killer took aim. The only thing he *was* sure of was that she had not pulled the trigger.

Still standing and blocking the doorway, Stuart looked ahead with an ecstatic grin that painted his bright white teeth across the width of his face. Nate was disturbed to see such a joyous look on his colleague's face. He had never seen him so happy.

L'Armin was the other side of Stuart, his expression a complete contradiction to the latter's. He had interlocked his fingers and was watching contemplatively. The conversation had not revealed enough to suggest where they went from there. For the moment the three of them simply stood in silence, though with one thinking much darker thoughts than they let on.

"I don't know what to believe right now, L'Armin. If she organised this whole thing for Stuart, then I know nothing for sure anymore," Nate said. He ran a sweaty hand through his hair before continuing. "How could I be so blind?"

"We are blind to what we do not want to see," L'Armin replied.

As Helen walked away, the outside world appeared to dissolve into her. It seeped through her image until she was gone, entirely replaced by the night. Only the outside appeared more sparse and featureless than Nate was used to. He could not make out anything but a blur of shapes and an eerie, encroaching darkness.

He watched, mesmerised, as the edge of the bubble L'Armin had told him about cut a line through his world. Whatever had happened beyond this point was out of his reach. So too was Helen, it appeared.

Stuart took in a deep breath and let it out slowly, noticeably pleased with himself. He fiddled with his watch, sliding it around his wrist in delight. He could see what Nate and L'Armin could not, including everything outside the bubble. Was he staring at Helen, or the night-time scene that spread out before him? Whatever it was it satisfied him, which only angered Nate further.

Once his lungs had been filled with fresh evening air, Stuart swung around and sped off, back into the crowded hall. In keeping with his obnoxious nature, he never once apologise to those whose paths he had previously hindered.

A sudden quiet swept across Nate as the area cleared. Finally the voices around had become low enough for him to hear his thoughts again. One in particular screamed louder than any other inside his head. He had to know how deep Helen's involvement went. The voice he heard was angry, but confused at the same time. How could she? The voice said, over and over again.

However much he wanted to reserve judgement, the voice inside him would not listen. It had already moved on to sentencing.

"Can we see what Helen has done since we arrived?" he said.

L'Armin became deeply locked in thought as he pondered Nate's question. He searched the dark distance outside the large hall, like a night-time predator fixed on its unbeknownst prey.

After a few thankfully peaceful seconds he squinted and then unlocked his fingers. "There is one memory that could work," he said, holding up a single finger excitedly.

"Is this how it worked before? I didn't really do anything did I?"

"I'm afraid not, Nathan." L'Armin held his hands out in a confessional manner. "It is a necessary deception. In truth we find the memory you are focusing on."

"So can you see all of my memories?"

"No. Your mind is understandably fixated on your own demise. In your case, I have been searching for anything from your past that your mind deems important in this situation. And there is one we can use." He reached out and up, placing a hand on each side of Nate's head, and peered deeply into his eyes.

A strange sensation, spreading out from L'Armin's fingertips, ran across Nate's entire head. It carried with it a comforting warmth that permeated his skull and the grey matter contained within. There was undoubtedly another presence rummaging around in his head, peeking in dark corners he had rather not share.

Pieces of past memories flashed at the forefront of his mind. But they were gone equally as fast. The usually ordered state he kept his mind in had being overrun by a messy intruder, who refused to tidy up after himself. The entire close encounter was making him uncomfortable, but somehow he remained intrigued.

"There," L'Armin said, his fingertips unintentionally squeezing Nate's temples as he proclaimed excitedly.

L'Armin had an amazing talent that he had been forced to keep locked up. The holiday experiences that—until now—had been the only things he was permitted to create, were unfocused and made with a blunt tool. Things had since changed. He had been set free and could go on to sculpt with the finest tools at his disposal. He was clearly revelling in the chance to use it as well, his excitement had begun to make him fidget on the spot.

Nate doubted he would have had the strength to keep such a gift a secret himself. L'Armin's people had their reasons and he respected that. He still could not imagine ever possessing such restraint, certainly it did not seem something he would ever have to do. The benefit of such a high profile job was in its openness. He could not keep anything from the many that competed against his company, even if he wanted to.

L'Armin closed his eyes and pressed his hands even tighter against Nate's head. His thumbs dug in gently just above the eyes. "You must concentrate on that memory, Nathan. It is recent and not fully formed in your memory. This will be challenging to re-create."

"Why does that worry me? OK, which mem—" Nate began.

Before he had a chance to finish the sentence, his mind's eye swept across a vast vista of past events, all laid out like a tapestry of his life. They had been sorted but not by him. Someone had guided his thoughts each time. He now knew it had always been L'Armin at the helm, not ethereal beings he had let in during the festival. This was a much more comforting revelation for Nate. He trusted his new friend.

Eventually L'Armin's guiding hand made him mentally settle on one picture, that of the large pyramid from the festival at the beginning of the night.

"Wow," Nate said. "How are you—"

"Focus, Nathan. Close your eyes and see yourself. Where are you?"

Nate closed his eyes to bring the scene into full view. The sounds from the hall and all of those inside disappeared, their presence no longer required. He concentrated harder and found that somehow he was able to move around the new place he saw. It was familiar but still hazy. It was not until he could see the back of himself standing outside his hotel room that he could tell exactly where he was.

"I'm on the balcony," he said as it finally drifted into full view. "I'm in the hotel."

"Good, good. Now we must enter. Move to the door."

Without even trying, Nate did as he was told and moved his floating consciousness toward the door of his hotel room. He opened it and stepped through, not once hesitating.

Suddenly the images vanished, leaving him in complete darkness. He realised that he could only feel the pressure of L'Armin's grip against the left side of his head. When he opened his eyes he saw that the other was held out and opened wide. The fingers were splayed out broadly, revealing their thinness.

With a flicker of light and a tiny web of visible static, a glowing shape began to form. Nate thought he had become immune to the impressive sight of the rifts, until he saw one form from L'Armin's own hand. A new appreciation of what he was seeing, of how it worked, made him inhale in awe.

"Shall we?" Nate said. He gestured to the glowing shape like a concierge ushering a guest through.

L'Armin opened his eyes and smiled. "It is your memory, Nathan," he said. "You should proceed first."

Nate was more than happy to oblige. He wanted to leave the convention hall way behind him. And Stuart along with it.

Chapter 11

Unlike before, Nate's vision was completely comfortable with the sudden shift in brightness as he walked through another rift. He assumed his eyes were somehow becoming accustomed to it. It was not until he was on the other side that he realised the real reason. The area he was entering was dark, much darker than he had expected.

A light breeze brushed past him, bringing a tingle to his skin. It swished his clothes playfully as it continued on. The hot and uncomfortable air of before was now a distant memory.

He breathed in greedily, feeling the colder air rushing down and into his chest. In the background he could make out the faint sound of trickling water. It took him a little while to figure out where they were. They had not appeared in his hotel room as expected, but somewhere else entirely.

To his left was the hotel swimming pool, its water slow but still moving. Beyond that he found the source of the trickling water sound; the small fountain he had spotted L'Armin sat beside, on the first day of his visit.

It felt good to be back, like nothing had ever happened. He thought about continuing his vacation in here instead of going back. The temptation to just pull up a chair, stretch out his tired legs and let the world carry on without him, was almost too much to resist. Someone else could look for the assassin while he sipped unknown alien cocktails.

Without meaning to, L'Armin broke Nate's concentration and simultaneously shattered his hopes of relaxation with a misjudged entrance. When they collided, Nate could saw how unsteady his friend had become. He felt compelled to offer an arm in support, which L'Armin took to leaning heavily against.

After a second or two he regained his strength and straightened up, his back slightly arched as he stretched. He then looked around to see what Nate had already seen. There was no surprise on his face, he had no doubt expected to arrive by the pool.

"You OK?" Nate said.

L'Armin looked up and nodded. "As I predicted, that was very much a challenge. I have not used my abilities in such a focused way for many years. It is more tiresome than I remembered." He laughed between breaths.

Above them hung the familiar sight of sparkling icy rings, cutting through the sky like a mesmerising glitter trail. It bathed the dark side of the moon in a comforting light. Its luminosity was still low enough to afford a sense of anonymity to its guests.

Nate took a few steps around the pool to see up to his own balcony, after first making sure his companion was sturdy enough to stand alone. Small lights around the pool guided him away from its edge as he snuck about. As expected there stood a mirror image of himself, wearing the clothes he had arrived in. But even dressed differently the sight was odd; a mirror image that was not mirroring him. Nate pointed to himself on the balcony.

"There, see," he said.

L'Armin leant against one of the pool side loungers for support. "Interesting. You appear to be alone."

"I am, I mean I was. Helen had just left, so I had a drink while watching the festival being set up."

They followed the direction the Nate up on the balcony was looking in, and saw the same process playing out in the distance. The busy workers dashed about intently, striving to meet whatever deadline drove them on. Behind them the large raised platform was slowly taking shape, with tiny sections waiting to be positioned correctly. It still looked like an unfinished pyramid—and would do even when it had been completed.

Although the area was a mess, it was gradually becoming the spectacle Nate had been impressed by. He could now see just how much planning had been done to make the festival work. And as with any rehearsed play, not one of those involved had missed their cue to perform. It had all been an illusion after all, just not quite the one he had expected.

For a minute they calmly watched, until the sound of a door detracted their attention. Nate looked up and saw that his double had closed the balcony door and disappeared inside. The night was quiet, refreshingly so. He could not help but feel envious of his double and the night of undisturbed sleep he was about to enjoy.

"Weird," Nate began, "I don't get why this is important."

"I felt a relevance. I did not see specifics, Nathan. There is something here."

As if spurred on by his obvious doubt, Nate heard a rustling noise from behind. He searched for the cause of the noise, but at first only saw shadows. All he could make out was a line of weird and wonderfully exotic potted plants surrounding the pool area, nothing else.

Only when a sudden flicker of light reflected off the pool, did he make out a mysterious figure standing behind the plants. A second later and the intermittent light was gone, returning the man to darkness. It was not just the guests who benefited from the low light level, it seemed.

"Did you see that?" Nate said.

"Indeed I did."

They approached the man, still seemingly hidden in the background. Upon closer inspection it became clear this was his intention. He did not want to be seen at all and was good at remaining so. The question was why?

The man's entire body was covered by one long and baggy robe. It appeared to be a shade of blue, in the little amount of light that was permitted to touch it. A large hood at the top concealed the face from view. It did not matter how far Nate peered into it, the darkness only peered back at him. He was not absolutely sure there was even a face inside.

"Any idea who this could be?" Nate asked.

L'Armin leant in, but his face remained the same. He shook his head rigorously, almost like Nate had accused him of something.

Nate moved in closer himself. "Me neither." He reached out slowly until he could gently touch the man. The hood felt rough in his hands, like made from strands of rough rope, or a sack. He continued to pull the material away, intent on revealing the face beyond. Gradually it slid back.

He took care not to disturb the man. Whether or not it was possible for the man to see him, he decided to choose caution over speed. His eyes squinted as he concentrated on this one act. But just when he thought he could make out skin of some kind, the man turned his head suddenly. Nate jumped back in shock, regaining his balance just inches short of the pool.

Another person was approaching from the direction of the hotel. This second person, however, did not move stealthily like the hidden man. But instead walked noisily and with little concern of who could hear. The footsteps were odd sounding too. Each step made a double clicking noise as the foot landed on the tiled floor. It took him a second or two to place why it was familiar. It sounded like a heel, toe, heel, toe kind of motion. Helen, he suddenly thought.

There she stood, her high heels having already given away her dainty figure. Nate immediately felt a sense of impending doom. What was about to play out had him worried. For now she waited patiently with her right arm held across her body, holding her left arm protectively.

Hanging from her left hand, down by her waist, was the dark brown folder. She had brought it with her on the journey, Nate soon remembered. But what did it contain? He had not considered before, but now it wanted his attention. He now knew it was important and that it was something linking back to Stuart, though he could not be sure of anything else. Whatever was contained within, he had to see it.

After leaving Helen standing and waiting for a minute or two, the man finally exited the darkness just enough for her to see. He had been studying her from the safety of shadows and was now evidently confident she had not been followed.

"Oh," Helen barked. "I didn't see you there."

The man did not speak, he just slid gradually back into cover. But in those few moments Nate had caught a glimpse of the man's leathery purple skin. He was not human, that much was certain.

Helen waited nervously for a reply. After an uncomfortably quiet few seconds had past, she pushed on regardless. "I was told to give you something. I have it here somewhere." She ruffled through the folder, passing page after page from right to left as she searched.

The man moved through the darkness toward her, his head cocked to one side. Nate did not like what he was seeing at all.

"I swear I'd lose my head …" She trailed off, unaware the man had moved.

It was hard for Nate not to feel protective. He moved with the man, keeping Helen closely behind him. Something inside told him the strange man was looking for more than just paperwork.

"Ah, there you are," Helen said.

Nate turned to see she was talking about her missing paper and still had not noticed how much closer the stranger was. The man's hood drooped for a second before slowly returning to its original position. He knew exactly what the man was doing. He could just imagine a pair of threatening eyes scanning up and down Helen's body, lingering at times.

Every curve of her was available to be silently caressed by the man's eyes, and she had no idea. But Nate did. He had the man's intentions clear in his mind and was stood, poised and ready to attack.

"I really don't like the look of this prick," he said, with an emphasis on the 'K'.

"My suspicions tell me we have found the killer, Nathan."

"Come on Helen." Nate looked straight into her eyes, but they peered beyond his. "Leave and go back to your room. Please."

She held out the piece of paper. "There you go."

"Don't do this please," Nate continued to plead with her.

The man rudely snatched the paper from her. Instinctively, she leapt back in surprise, sending loose paper flying out of the folder. A couple of them landed in the pool, where they bobbed about on the surface. They taunted her as they became more and more sodden. She fidgeted, clearly eager to retrieve them, but the man was acting odd and making her nervous. He was doing the same to Nate as well.

She took one small step away as the man appeared to sniff the paper she had handed him. Sensing he was too engrossed in its contents to notice, she aimed for the pool to retrieve her ruined paperwork. She managed to fish out one at the edge, but could only watch as the rest defiantly sailed away on the breeze.

Nate watched, thankful that as she had created some distance between her and the man. He was happy enough that she would not come to any harm while she tried to reach the paperwork. It looked like it was going to take her some time too as pieces continued to venture further into the middle of the pool. The man's actions were strange, but they did not appear as threatening as they had originally.

125

Still the man sniffed at the paper he held. If he drew in any more air Nate was sure the words would fly off the paper and into him. He let the image expand automatically in his mind until it reached a point of absurdity. He saw the words flow through the man's mouth and down into his chest, like a breath of air full of letters. Their meanings were drawn out and into his lungs, where they were absorbed into him, perhaps racing around his bloodstream until it reached his brain.

Maybe there was something more to it than just an overly active imagination at play. Maybe he *was* taking from it more than what was written. But what?

For the moment Nate left Helen to recover her things and stood next to the man. He peeked at the paper through the bony fingers that held it, and made out a few of the lines. What he saw was puzzling. It was no more than a printed memo to his own internal staff. This was not the proof of deadly intentions he had expected, only a note on overtime allocation.

He waved L'Armin over. "This is bullshit," he said, pointing at the sheet. "She gave him nothing."

As the man continued to study the sheet, moving it up and down, L'Armin pulled down the top corner and caught what little he could of the words. But there was no confusion on his face at all. He appeared undeterred by the seemingly unrelated nature of the information it contained. Unlike Nate, he was focused and watchful.

"What do you see?" Nate said after returning his contorted face back to normal.

L'Armin let go of the paper and waited until he saw the clue again. "There," he announced.

Nate jumped forward when he saw it. The man was not randomly smelling the paper, his movements were following a pattern. His first hunch had been right. The man was moving the sheet up and down, and then an inch or so to the right each time he reached the bottom. He was reading it, though Nate had never seen it done quite like this before. He was breathing it in, both literally and figuratively, it seemed.

"What's he getting from it?" he said.

L'Armin began to wag his finger, indicating to the paper. "I believe I have seen this before. We have visitors from many different worlds during The Passing, and I have witnessed those able to communicate through pheromones."

"Can you see, I mean smell, what it says then?"

"Unfortunately not," L'Armin said as he took a sniff of the paper. He quickly moved his nose away soon after. "There is a strong odour emanating from this. I cannot differentiate between the scents. How strong is your sense of smell?"

Nate leant in and did the same. It had a musky smell, one that punished his nasal passage within seconds of drawing in an all too enthusiastic breath. How any being could find meaning from such a heady mix of scents was beyond him. And yet the man moved it up and down his face, like a printer building a picture one line at a time.

"Not good enough. So we can't see what it says? Great," he said.

"I am afraid so. But whatever it contains it is assuredly concerning you, Nathan."

"Jesus," Nate said, prolonging the last 'S' longer than really necessary. "It could be a bloody picture of me and we'd have no way of proving it. The guy would have thrown it away after he read it. God-dammit."

In frustration, Nate threw his arms up in the air and turned away temporarily, he then let them slap back down against his sides. So close to the answers and yet once again they were just out of reach. There was only one question he really wanted answered and he still did not know how to. What Helen had done was inconclusive. She had handed over paperwork she could not possibly have read herself. It was just not quite enough to prove she was totally innocent.

"I've got to see Helen," he said. "No more memories."

He returned to watching Helen floundering about the pool for the last of her paperwork. Occasionally she stopped to check the man was still there; his odd behaviour had not gone unnoticed by her. She rushed the last two pieces into her hands, choosing to scrunch them up in one big, wet handful rather than file them away carefully.

The clenched fists at Nate's side began to warm up in their centre. He had not even realised he *was* squeezing them, let alone far too tightly.

"I have to know if she's involved," he said. "None of this will answer that."

"I understand, Nathan," L'Armin replied.

By now the man had gotten everything he needed from the paper and had begun to fold it in a slow and considered manner. Once finished, he tucked it away in his pocket and then took one last lingering look at Helen, his head cocked to one side again. Nate could see a silvery shine to the eyes that hid beneath the man's hood. There was a dangerous curiosity in them. Under different circumstances he might have been a threat to Helen. Maybe he still was, Nate considered.

As Helen left and headed back into the hotel, so did the man. They used different entrances, with the man using an emergency exit, to the side of the hotel. Once it clicked shut, the night became peaceful once more. Only the noise of the fountain and distant footsteps remained. Yet it was anything but peaceful for Nate.

A thousand different thoughts vied for his attention, all at once, with a new more worrying addition at the forefront. No longer was it only the risk to his own life that concerned him, but now the risk to Helen's too. All of the time he had spent inside his own memories, Helen had been alone. If the killer still wanted her, he could have her and Nate could do nothing about it.

"I have to get out of here. Now," he said, after quickly coming to realise that it may already be too late.

Chapter 12

Nate became agitated at the thought of Helen being harmed, and was getting more so the longer he stayed within the memory. He had found no peace by the pool, only more questions. Worse still, the killer's face had completely eluded him, with only a partial description obtained. It was not much to go on at all.

The strange man may have left, but his image still hovered at the front of Nate's consciousness; it had become like a bothersome and incessantly buzzing fly inside his head. He tried to swat it away by planning his escape from the memory rifts. But it proved a fruitless endeavour, as each time he tried, it quickly returned. Nothing else concerned him anymore. He had to find the man.

"We must return through each rift in turn, Nathan. You must try to relax before we do," L'Armin said.

"Relax? That may be a bit hard at the moment."

Without even considering being cautious, Nate trudged off to the still glowing orb they had entered through. He had had enough, the novelty had worn off. There was nothing left for him in these memories anymore.

As he approached the exit, with the glow becoming stronger, he felt someone touch his arm from behind. It had only been faint, like L'Armin had made a grab for him and only just missed. He chose to ignore it and instead attributed it to the breeze upon his skin. Dismissing the notion that his friend had tried to stop him allowed his mind to focus only on getting out. He had no time to hang about any longer.

He continued until the glow had replaced all signs of his surroundings. The only remnant of before was the echo of L'Armin asking him to wait. What was there for him to wait for? The quicker he could escape the rifts the better, he decided.

Once through he found himself back in the exhibition hall. Nothing much had changed, it was still far too busy to be comfortable. As he marched a speedy pace through the hall, he was grateful to see most of the people were moving out of his way. He had no issue with forcing those aside who did not leave him room. They were not real anyway, he considered, only obstacles in his path.

Pushing through the hall was much easier this time, now that he knew exactly where to go. He raced past the old man and his ever expanding cloud of smoke, past the bar he had found Cameron slumped over, past his own presentation and the horde of rude journalists still surrounding it; everything that had been important before he quickly left behind. He waited for nothing. Not even L'Armin, who he had completely lost track of behind him somewhere.

Almost at the exit, he was surprised to see a small build-up of people in front of the rift. He thought nothing of it at first and continued on, still moving at a confidently brisk pace. But the closer he got, the more people near to it appeared to join in. It no longer looked to be a random build-up of people anymore, but rather a wall of organised bodies with an unknown intent.

He took the last few metres in his stride, until only the group remained between him and the exit. Even though his pace had slowed, the group were still there and they continued to appear as impenetrable as ever. He had expected a gap to have formed at some point to allow him to gracefully slide through. But no such space was created. If anything the group had become even denser.

They did not move an inch. At least not until Nate crashed straight into them, forcing the front few bodies to the side. When the second row began to take up the slack, it became clear they were all *trying* to stop him. It was not simply an obstruction, the group had the collective desire to keep him there against his will. They said nothing and showed no emotion at all as their arms flapped about, all trying to grab him and hold him back.

Parts of Nate's clothing were being tugged nearly to the point of ripping while he fought them off. He was sure he was just starting to make some progress in getting past them, when they switched to a new tactic. Suddenly a huge amount of weight was being piled on top of him, in an obvious attempt to bring him to the floor. It was working too, as he quickly found himself lurching downward under the weight of the bodies now pushing against him.

His frustration soon began to turn to anger as his limbs became increasingly entangled. In the chaos, some of the people had tumbled to the floor already and were covering the ground beneath him. He could feel a mass of hands gripping him tightly from all sides now—even from those stuck at the bottom of the pile. They were all much stronger than he expected and were making light work of holding him in place.

During the struggle Nate could hear a voice in the background, telling him repeatedly to stop. He had no interest in the person's pleas. Escaping a world that was quickly turning against him was all that mattered at that moment.

"Get the hell off me," he shouted.

They held onto him tighter and tighter. They had become a writhing mass of limbs that acted like sinking sand as he thrashed about. The more he struggled the stronger they gripped the tiny bit of him each of them held onto. Soon he could feel himself being dragged further toward the floor. If they succeeded in pinning him down he knew he would be trapped.

He lashed out at a few of the unknown faces, in a complete state of panic. His strikes were solid but his victims were unmoved, not once flinching with pain. It would take every ounce of effort to get them off. Realising this he began to feel an immense rage bubbling up inside him, overtaking the milder feeling of anger from before. It caused a froth of spittle to form at the sides of his mouth. Yet despite this he could still feel the hands scratching and squeezing parts of him.

He barely acknowledged the continual pleas from L'Armin behind. The words were there, though no longer registering with him. They were being drowned out by something. A noise, accompanied by a dull ache in his temple.

It was happening again, the voices were becoming too loud. It quickly sent a surge up through his body, forcing him forward. His intention was now to get out before it reached the intensity it had earlier. The searing pain of before would have to catch him this time.

A tiny part of him knew the sensible thing to do was to stop and try to calm down. Maybe even perform another breathing exercise. His connection to L'Armin was being stretched too far and was at risk of breaking. He needed to stop. But the thought found little company at the back of Nate's mind.

The more he panicked the more he pushed and threatened to sever the link entirely. He had no idea what would happen at that point. Maybe he would break with it. There was no time to explore the thought fully. It did not occur to him that he may be about to do himself some serious harm either, as he blindly carried on.

Ploughing through the last of the crowd was as difficult as he had expected, though with enough kicks and elbow blows to the few people still on their feet, he was getting somewhere at last. Soon enough he was again entering the rift, which only moments earlier had felt completely beyond his reach. They would have to follow him through if they wanted him now.

This time the sensation of the world disappearing around him was followed by a sudden increase in momentum. Someone had stubbornly held on and not let go until the last possible moment, propelling him forward head first. His unhindered motion sent him tumbling through unexpectedly. Although it was pleasingly quicker than it would have otherwise been.

The joy brought about by his release was short lived, as a reflective surface appeared in front of his face. He landed heavily with his arms clumsily splayed out in front of him, just stopping his face a few inches from the ground. He may have saved his face, but he had forced his knees into the metal plating, like stone grinding against a much more brittle stone.

To stay in position on his hands and knees was not an option. The final exit was much further ahead and he wanted desperately to get to it. So regardless of how much he knew it would hurt, he returned to his feet and pushed forward. He would just shake off the inevitable bruises along the way, he decided. Either that or let the head splitting noises catch up with him and bring him to his knees once more.

Again he was heading through like an out of control bulldozer. His knees were stiff and a few dark splotches on his trousers suggested he had grazed them, drawing a small amount of blood, though he was hardly going to slow down to tend to such minor injuries.

The rift had spat him out by the door of the forward airlock, on the Miner's Folly. By now his double had moved on, leaving only strangers littering the hallways. He tried to ignore the people who suddenly stopped and stared at him as he swept through the ship he knew so well. For some reason they were interested in him now. They watched like spectres of a forgotten world.

He made his way through the bowels of his father's ship, retracing his steps from earlier. All the while he was followed by the distant clicking sound of sandals. He had completely forgotten about L'Armin. The poor man had

133

been left to fend off the same crowds. Somehow he had made it through and was now running for all his life's worth, just to catch up.

Nate decided, reluctantly, to carry on and head for the next rift by himself. If he stopped and allowed L'Armin to reach him, he was sure the pain would eventually get him. Not once did he consider that he may be the one making things worse. To him the world had suddenly decided to turn against him. He had fended them off once and assumed he would have to again at some point soon.

He continued at a slightly slower pace. At this speed he was able to watch the flurry of activity that played out for no-one but him to enjoy. It was like any ordinary day aboard the Miner's Folly, with everyone going about their everyday business. Except occasionally when they were compelled to glare at him. All of the familiar faces he passed looked back at him with obvious mistrust.

His knees felt raw against the material of his trousers as he walked on. For a few minutes he chose to pay no attention at all to the people around him and concentrated on nothing but the slight stinging pain instead. It was working until he realised something was missing. The noise was no longer building around him. He could not place when it had dissipated, but it was definitely gone. Had he finally outrun it?

To test this he decided to stop and allow his breathing to catch up. Within seconds he began to feel the blood pumping through his limbs. The sound was not catching him, he was spared the pain this time. With the wall behind, he leant his back against it and bent forward, placing his hands on his shins. The muscles stretched, but the tension remained.

A regular pattern of clicks accompanied L'Armin's footsteps as he raced through the ship, still trying his best to keep up—sandals were proving a bad choice to run in. It brought Nate's attention back to his immediate surroundings and away from his body's bad reaction to the sudden sprint. For whatever reason things had become deceptively quiet around him, though those nearby were still far too interested in him.

As the sound of his friend became louder, Nate found it hard not to think over what he had seen Helen do. Again and again, he let it play out in his head. Yet each time he was left wanting more answers. He began to wonder if he could simply ignore what he had seen and carry on where he and Helen had left off. Would it go away if he tried hard enough to forget it? He would not have to find out whether she was guilty or not then.

But to his annoyance, his thoughts swiftly moved on to a conclusion that he wanted desperately not to be true, one which was becoming harder and harder to avoid. Helen was involved from the beginning, she must have known something.

L'Armin eventually arrived with a sweaty sheen to his skin and wheezing heavily. In the last few steps he had managed to lose his right sandal, only adding to his flustered appearance. He laboriously retrieved it and hobbled over. "Please," he managed to say before gulping down a lung-full of air.

Nate returned to an upright position, but kept his back against the wall. "I'm sorry, L'Armin. I just have to get out of here."

"I understand"—another large breath—"but we must be careful." L'Armin lent against Nate and slipped his sandal back on. "Your anger is disrupting the connection between us. If we proceed too quickly we may destabilise it."

It was soon painfully obvious to Nate that this was why the inhabitants were acting so odd toward him, where they had been completely disinterested before. His anger had caused the bundle of people in the exhibition hall. It had been his fault all along. The closer they had come to breaking the connection, the more the world around them had reacted. Thankfully, L'Armin had caught up with him just in time to prevent it from happening, this time. Finally, the tiny part of him that had suspected as much was allowed free rein of his mind.

135

In his now much calmer state, he could see how manic he had previously been. He had thrashed around like some kind of rabies infested animal, attacking anything that moved. The realisation brought with it the familiar feeling that he was not in control. If anything he was actually making things harder for those who were. The memories may have been his, but he was merely lending them to L'Armin to re-create. It all felt much more alien to him than before.

"I need to get back to Helen, *now.*"

L'Armin nodded. "One memory at a time," he said, setting off in front.

Although still weary of what lay ahead, Nate followed closely behind. He was annoyed at losing himself so quickly to his own anger. He took a few moments of silence to consolidate his thoughts into one coherent voice. The sudden calm had at least quietened the others enough to allow him to think clearly.

They found the exit hovering in the middle of the corridor, exactly where they had left it. One at a time they stepped through, L'Armin first this time.

The boardroom was now empty. Only the hectic traffic whizzing past the large window at the rear showed how alive and active the world still was. All other signs of life had since moved on. The affluent remains of a corporate gathering were all that had been left behind: empty champagne glasses, trays with the leftovers of exquisitely prepared snacks still sitting on them, even a handful of discarded wrappers from celebratory smokes—that had evidently been handed out, though only between the top ranks—littered the room.

They headed straight for the exit and left the room behind, choosing to head onwards to the ship once more rather than stay and admire the scene. Nate was confident they had gleant everything they could have from this place anyway. To stay would only make his impatience worse.

Again Nate noted the differences between the two memories of the Miner's Folly, as they returned to the first.

This time its corridors had the sparkle and shine like that of a much younger and less *lived-in* vessel. The outside scene of space was impressive too, with the entire length of the corridor displaying it through its many windows. Those working in the deeper parts of the ship, as he had, were rarely allowed such a grandiose view. He could remember many occasions—often weeks at a time—when he had seen nothing but corridors and walls.

His attention rapidly returned to more immediate concerns, once they had arrived at the next rift. The scene that existed beyond was not one he particularly wanted to return to. It was the last hurdle to overcome. After that he had one last stroll through his childhood memory of the park and then on to freedom.

It appeared L'Armin shared the same feeling of trepidation. He paused just at the edge of the rift and looked to Nate. The silence had become more noticeable than ever between them. Neither of them had wanted to disrupt the quiet as they found the courage to enter the next area. This time Nate chose to go first.

The moment he exited the rift he looked around the edge of the room. The image of his death could not affect him if he kept the evidence dancing on the edge of his vision. At least that was his intention. He tried not to notice the obvious blood stains still spread out on the floor, however much they haunted his peripheral vision.

Mercifully, the body of his double had escaped the room during L'Armin's earlier demonstration. Still he chose not to look out the hole that used to be the pressurised and strengthened window, just in case his remains were floating around in full view. The last thing he wanted to see was his own body after being shot *and* sent into the void. Yet he could not help but imagine what it would look like. The idea of his own blood boiling while it streamed out of a large gunshot wound, as rapid de-pressurisation wrought havoc to his remains, made him gag.

The killer had caused a major deviation from the original memory, one that had continued to evolve on its

137

own. So too had the damage to the room, which was so much more extensive than it had been before they had left—with most of it now appearing to be outside. What continued to play out bore more resemblance to a disaster movie than it did to what had really happened.

Thankfully, Nate's concentration was needed to push through the debris that was hovering in front of him. As a demonstration of just how realistic the re-creations were, the gravity plating had failed since their last visit. He had not even noticed his feet were an inch or so off of the floor. He had been so focused on avoiding any glimpse of his dead double that everything else had faded into insignificance.

Pieces were sent flying away at the slightest touch as he slowly waded through. He moved by, passing one hand over the other and dragging his body along the side wall. The years of working in zero gravity made it easy for his limbs to adapt. The same could not be said of his stomach, which quickly twisted uneasily.

L'Armin copied as well as he could manage. It was not as instinctive a transition for him as it was for Nate. The uneasy movements he was making often sent him flapping about in the wrong direction. It was taking all of his effort just to stay upright.

Soon, bits were moving all about them, compounded by the ripple effect their movements were causing. Nate knew from experience that the problem would quickly become dangerous, yet he was in no mood to care. Between the increasing tightness of his bowels, the pain in his knees and the overwhelming desire to return to reality, he had little interest in worrying about his own mortality any longer.

At the exit he stopped and waved L'Armin through. Behind he could see the room was beginning to come alive with sharp swarms of moving debris. He wished the pieces would tear the place apart and wipe it out of existence like it had his own treasured memory of the place. It was lost to him anyway. His memory of proposing to Gemma had been damaged beyond repair.

All the anger from before returned as he soon realised his loss. Why relive such a personal memory when one change could ruin it so easily? Time may distort recollections of past events, but it rarely destroyed them in such a violent way. These things were fragile, like dry forests. Without meaning to they had wandered through as though pouring petrol wherever they stepped. The killer had merely ignited their trail, turning it all to ash and forever robbing him of a once special moment.

He thanked whichever God may have resided over him that the killer had not struck during one of his younger memories. Otherwise there would have been no confusion over which Nate was real and he would have died for certain. Though he knew this was worth noting, it gave him only a second of peace before the bitterness returned.

He pushed himself through the rift without so much as a *goodbye*, or even a *good riddance*. It was behind him and that was all that mattered. As he ventured further into the light he was softly returned to the ground.

On the other side he was greeted by the warm embrace of sunshine from his childhood. The entire front of his body became pleasingly tingly, while the hairs on his arms began to stand up and dance amid the rays. Stood there waiting for him was L'Armin, who watched as the sun gradually washed Nate's pain from the previous area away.

The young child version of Nate was still running around the park, but now chased a friend he had since forgotten the name of; a little girl roughly the same age. The sight diluted his anger instantly as he watched a tiny version of himself playing without a care in the world. He would give anything for just a second more of such freedom.

"Sir? Everything OK?" Cameron said. "And where the hell you been all this time..?"

It shocked Nate to see Cameron standing in front of him. For a moment he thought he had slipped back into the convention hall and was once again watching a broken man drinking his pain away. Thankfully, he lacked the smell of alcohol on his clothes and breath that had stung Nate's nose earlier. It was the same man, but with a new lick of varnish applied to a cracking veneer.

Obviously he had managed to change his ways, or at least had learnt to conceal his addiction better. Whatever the reason, he was back to normal and was performing above and beyond everyone's expectations, even Nate's. The vodka fuelled man destined to fail in his duty protecting his boss had come good and done the complete opposite. Nate found comfort in the thought that Stuart's plans had been scuppered by this one miscalculation.

"Have you seen or heard anything?" Nate said.

"Nothing I'm afraid, sir. Nobody has come in or out since you were … Er," Cameron replied, stopping short of mentioning the untimely demise of Nate's double.

"Good. I have to find Helen right away. Follow me."

Nate set off before Cameron had time to ask any questions. A quizzical finger was raised that suggested something had come to mind, but he had no interest in explaining anything just yet. His quest continued and the need for closure was ever increasing. Cameron would have to go along with him for now, he decided. Even L'Armin had become intent on avoiding the inevitable explanation by following closely behind and leaving Cameron to catch up.

The three of them set a quick pace out of the last rift. The comforting warmth of Nate's youth was soon behind them, figuratively and literally. Once outside they found themselves back among the groups attending the Passing. The ceremony was still in full swing, with the beam of light continuing to shine just as bright as before.

In stark contrast to his own group, which headed away with obvious urgency, those that remained appeared calm and relaxed. Though Nate counted fewer of the glowing orbs as he hurtled past, with most of them having since closed. Having seen all they intended to see, they had evidently retired for the rest of the evening. Their absence created obvious voids where once a group had been standing.

The remaining visitors, however, were still enjoying themselves and had been so while he had been digging through his past. They no doubt visited memories of happy times surrounded by loved ones or even lost loves. All the things Nate had been expecting. But *murder?* Did they witness such things as they watched themselves? He hoped not, and yet at the same time felt envious that they did not.

Within a short amount of time Nate had lead the group back to the hotel pool. There a few of the groups from the festival relaxed peacefully under the dim light of the rings. With no humans in sight he found it hard not to stare at the mixture of beings all sat around, *holidaying*, like any human would. Despite his more immediate concerns he allowed himself to be swept away by his curiosity.

Most were recognisably humanoid, with only the slightest noticeable differences in skin colour, texture, or even number of limbs. All except for a strange pair that conversed enthusiastically underneath the water. They were exceptionally unusual in comparison. He had no idea what to make of them with their six—or seven, he struggled to count—tentacle like limbs bobbing about in the water.

If this had been an ordinary vacation, he would have found it hard not to be curious. He knew he may have even managed a few sales pitches to beings he normally would not have met. That was the point anyway, he thought, to broaden his horizons whichever planet they may reside on. The opportunities were there for the taking and he almost certainly would have taken them.

The long list he had of things he had missed out on during his visit was beginning to distract him more than he liked. He knew he should be concerned with the assassin, not this. The comparisons of his real and intended vacations were only annoying him. He had something much more worrying to focus on than how crappy his holiday had been so far.

He shook it off as much as he could and decided to move his eyes away from the two underwater beings, who no doubt were slightly miffed by his unmoving glare—not that he could really tell. Instead he turned his attention to locating Helen. Except nowhere in the surrounding area could he see any hints of her. In fact there was not anything to suggest any humans were there at all.

It occurred to him that he had no idea what she had been doing while he was busy. She had left to catch up on work or something, he could not remember. Perhaps she sat back in her room with a glass of bubbly as she planned how she would celebrate her ill-gotten gain? Surely she could not be so cold? His mind was so fuzzy that as he checked around the pool for her, he simply could not answer it himself.

"Sir?" Cameron said.

When Nate turned he was surprised at the expression on Cameron's face. His eyes were deeply focused and searching for something. Whatever he had seen, it was on Nate's shirt. He investigated until his eyes were unable to reveal any more. At which point he was suddenly no longer content with looking and began to pull at it instead.

"It's gone," he said. "The blood, it's all gone."

He was right, every drop of it had vanished. Nate had tried his best to ignore the dark patches that had slowly dried into his shirt and caused it to feel coarse against his skin. Now he needn't worry as all that remained were the creases he had made while trying to rub the blood away. His shirt had somehow become as clean as it had been at the start of the evening.

"Where's it gone?" Nate asked L'Armin.

"The blood was not real, Nathan. Nothing inside the memories can escape into this world," he replied.

At any other time in Nate's life, L'Armin's words would have seemed like that of a madman to him. Yet he had no trouble at all accepting the explanation. He had much more of an open mind than he had first thought. Either that or the weirdness of the situation just had not hit him fully. One thing he could be certain of was that he trusted L'Armin and was just thankful an explanation existed at all—even if he did not entirely understand it.

He nodded to confirm he had understood and continued to look around for Helen. The vanishing blood was a bonus, but his main goal was still to be achieved. Again, though, he was unsuccessful, and becoming more irritated with every second that passed.

Cameron did the same and searched the immediate area, then made his failure unnecessarily clear to the rest of the group. "She's not here," he said, stating the abundantly obvious.

"What's her room number?" Nate looked up to the balconies above in case, by a remarkable stroke of luck, she was taking in the view from her room. To his disappointment, all but two were occupied and it was clear none of them were occupied by Helen—or Humans.

He turned to his companions for an answer. Cameron had a blank look on his face that he decided to top off with an exaggerated shrug of his shoulders. L'Armin on the other hand copied Cameron's expression exactly, unintentionally mocking him.

The impatience was unbearably frustrating for Nate and the empty looks from his friends did not help. A list of questions spiralled endlessly around the inside of his head like the contents of a blender at full speed. He had no idea how to form them into coherent sentences, with only snippets of emotions available. It soon dawned on him that he was sending the exact same blank expression back to Cameron and L'Armin. He was unintentionally mocking the both of them.

"She didn't give me any contact details. Otherwise I would have spoken with her earlier," Cameron said.

Nate thought over his last few encounters with Helen. For someone so obsessed with being organised, she had been short on information with him too. There were things he had not listened to, though he still remembered roughly what the subject matters were, and her room number was not one of them. He was positive. So had she just forgotten to mention it? Or was there more to it than that? Perhaps she was harbouring the killer there?

143

He became angry with himself for ever thinking such a thing. There was no evidence to suggest she had ever been willingly involved. Yet his mind insisted on conjuring up images of her betrayal. In reality it came down to the toss of a coin, and until he found her it would remain so.

L'Armin ran a hand across the top of his head, pulling some of the ruffled skin back as he removed a build-up of sweat. "I believe we keep all room information in the central computer. Visitor records are stored there," he finally said.

"Then I guess we'll start with that," Nate replied, waving ahead. It was not much, but it was enough for them to focus on for the time being.

They continued into the hotel, through the door Helen had used after meeting with the killer. Nate had used it himself before. Except what had happened since then made it feel like a lifetime ago. It was as unfamiliar to him now as it had been the first time he had used it.

Through the door was a large bar area that served various selections of brightly coloured beverages, all lined up behind. It housed a row of booths at the back, separated by shoulder high walls that served as private areas for the more serious drinkers. The small tables that filled the gap between the booths at the back and the bar at the front were all empty, except for a few used glasses.

The lighting was dim, creating a more intimate atmosphere than that by the pool. Still only the private areas were in use. Whichever corner of the galaxy those currently frequenting the bar were from, it seemed they still preferred to drink in much the same way as Nate: isolated, with nothing but a bottle and a glass for company.

Behind the bar stood the proud choice of well-lit bottles Nate had noticed upon entering. Beverages of all colours and viscosities were on display, hailing from all reaches of known space. His attention was immediately drawn to them in much the same way it had with the two underwater creatures at the pool. They were unlike anything he had seen before. Some were even moving of their own accord, not something he would expect in a Human bar.

Unfortunately, the same could not be said of the autonomous drinks dispenser on wheels that purported to be the barkeep. He was very much used to these bar room abominations. Cheap labourers they may well be, but they just could not hold a candle to a real person. A sentiment compounded by the fact that only one of the two *could* actually hold a candle. And this one was no exception. It served drinks by standing next to the person ordering with its serving hatch open. No attempts at working limbs had been made.

As Nate made his way through the canyon of tables that stood in his way, he kept a curious eye on the bar area. For some reason it had him curious. It was unusual for him to focus on such an unrelated detail, especially now that something so much more important was going on.

It was not until a figure skulking at the far corner of the bar blocked his view, that he realised what had really caught his attention. Colourful drinks and irritating autonomous bar staff aside, he had seen something. A familiar face, he just could not tell whose. When the man turned slightly and downed the rest of his drink, he was sure. It was him. The killer was at the bar.

"Sir?" Cameron said.

Nate gave no reply as he stopped suddenly and stared. His attention was solely on the man who now searched his pockets for a means of payment, completely oblivious to the danger coming his way.

Something inside told him to approach slowly, to sneak up on the serpentine bastard while he rummaged for change and take him by surprise. Unfortunately, a much louder voice screamed at him to attack fast and hard, and unleash a well-timed left hook at the same time.

Without any warning to Cameron he leapt into action and charged at the man as fast as his legs allowed. Within seconds he found himself engulfed by a wave of tables as he hurtled forward, scattering everything in his path across the floor in one tremendous crash. It happened so much quicker than he had planned. Before he knew it, he had a handful of the man's clothing crumpled up in his fists, with no idea what to do next.

"Who the fuck *are* you," he growled into his victim's greasy and blue tinted face.

The man replied with a gurgle, his eyes bulging with panic. Not at all the reaction Nate was expecting. There were no retaliatory swings of fists or opportunistic kicks to the shins. Just fear.

"Who paid you to kill me?" Nate continued, ignoring the obvious signs that this was not the man he first thought.

An overwhelming wave of frustration forced his balled-up fist back, coiled and ready to strike. The reaction had him stymied and with a growing pressure in his arm that had nowhere to go. He was barely seconds away from letting it loose on the man's, not at all scaly skinned face, when he noticed someone was holding it back.

All he could think about doing was landing his knuckles into the man's angled and leathery chin, but he could not. The similarities had gradually faded, leaving him angry and with nowhere to aim it. He fought the person holding him back and quickly found there was strength there that *he* did not possess, and just could not overcome.

"Sir," Cameron shouted.

Nate suddenly snapped out of his rage and looked to Cameron, who tightly gripped his forearm, suspending the fist in the air. If not for his companion's quick reaction, it would have continued on its mindless quest for vengeance and harmed an innocent man.

"It's him," he said.

"Who?" Cameron replied with a perplexed look on his face.

"The killer."

The unwelcome sense of doubt that had appeared only strengthened as Nate ran the man's smooth textured clothing through his fingers. It was not at all rough and rope like as he had been expecting.

He had been certain a moment ago that this was the same man he had seen with Helen. But that moment had since passed, along with his confidence. Now he found himself raising an innocent man almost off of his feet, after very nearly launching him across the room. He dared not look at the man now that his anger had subsided.

"I thought he was …" Nate tried to finish his sentence but could not. Instead it caught in his throat and refused to come out.

"Maybe you should let him go, sir."

L'Armin stood behind Cameron with a hand raised to his mouth in shock. "Mr Cameron is right, Nathan. That man has committed no crimes against you. I saw the man you seek. This is not him."

Nate met the man's frightened and confused eyes and immediately let go, which prompted Cameron to do the same with Nate's arm. The man landed awkwardly on a barstool and nearly slid straight off before eventually steadying himself. His eyes locked onto his attacker's, but the intensity faltered only seconds later, prompting him to quickly look away.

When Nate tried to pat the man's clothing down flat, his arms leapt up to his chest in defence. He was clearly confused and was looking to each of them in turn for an explanation. None of them had one and any attempts to set him straight only served to upset him further.

"I'm sorry. I didn't …" Nate said, facing away in shame.

The man hurriedly dusted himself off, before scurrying away with a cautious look back every few steps. While he wandered off he continued to murmur in his own language, still sounding like a person gargling mouthwash.

Even though the words were unintelligible, their meanings were still easy to interpret. No translator was required to work out the man was probably saying something offensive. Nate did not mind that as much as not having a chance to explain himself. The temper that had burst out of him surprised him as much as everyone else.

As soon as the man was out of sight Nate slumped down onto a barstool, his body hunched over the bar for support, causing the railing to dig into his chest. After all of the adrenaline had flushed away, it left him feeling weak and shaking. His fingers pulsed as they tightly gripped the sticky surface of the bar counter in front of him. He could feel the layers of dried drink adhere to his fingertips as they rested there.

What was wrong with him? The last few minutes had come out of nowhere. He was not a violent man, normally. Yet as he stared at his reflection in the coloured bottles, he was surprised to see a dangerous rage in the face that looked back. He was then disturbed by how familiar it seemed.

Cameron took the stool next to him and asked the talking drinks machine for a glass of water. It replied in a synthetic voice that contained not even an ounce of acknowledgement of what had just occurred in its bar.

"Human. English language. Water. Acknowledged," it said through a tiny speaker in its gleaming metal face. After its pre-programmed responses had been entirely ignored by Cameron and Nate, it continued to process the order. A series of mechanical clunking noises from its internal workings then followed, until it served the glass through the infamous serving hatch in its midriff.

Cameron took the drink and set it down gently on the bar. He then watched as Nate immediately picked it up and began to slurp the water gratefully—but in no way gracefully. Then, rather than following with a blitz of questions, he waited patiently for Nate to talk first.

"I swear it looked just like him." A tiny trail of water zigzagged down Nate's chin as he spoke.

Cameron's left eyebrow raised suddenly, almost as though it were trying to reach for the ceiling. "You—"

"Can I interest you in a cocktail?" the *Bar-bot* interrupted.

"Do you mind," Cameron snapped back at its lifeless face. "You two saw him in there didn't you?" he finished, as the barkeep returned to its default standby mode.

Nate sent a quick glance over to L'Armin, who nodded his approval. "Yes," Nate said. "But there's more to it than that. We saw who we think could be behind it all as well."

Cameron's face widened. "You're shitting me."

"No. And if we find Helen, I think we can do something about it."

"Then I'll find her for you, sir. Give me half an hour. Stay here and don't attack anyone for a bit." Cameron leapt up from his barstool and sped off out of the bar, surprising Nate and L'Armin with the energy he appeared to have stored up in his body. He was a completely new man and one with a mission he was not going to fail at.

The same was not quite as certain for Nate, who was struggling to stay as professional as he wanted—as proven by his outburst. His anger had appeared suddenly once again. It bobbed about just below the surface, ready and waiting to jump out. The next time it did, he was not so sure he or Cameron would be able to stop it.

Although with Helen stood in front of him, he suspected his reaction might be the complete opposite. Whichever way it went he certainly would not be able to control it. His emotions were roaming free. If she was in fact in on the whole thing, could he trust himself not to break down right there and then in front of her? Only time would tell and he knew it was not going to be long before he would find out.

Chapter 13

The bar was now empty and Nate's water had become much warmer than he liked. He continued to take frugal sips of it anyway, just to keep his mouth from drying out completely. It was always too much to expect things to be exactly as he wanted, and no ice was the least of his problems. Something much more troubling was only minutes away.

He slowly wiped his forehead with the palm of his hand. A stowaway drop of water from his drink was smeared across his skin, leaving a pleasing layer of dampness behind. It lasted a short while before evaporating away.

It had been almost twenty-five minutes since Cameron had disembarked on his solo quest to find Helen. He would make light work of scouring the hotel for her, Nate was sure. Convincing her to follow him, on the other hand, would be an altogether much trickier affair. She would quickly come to dislike him more if he pushed her too much.

L'Armin watched Nate curiously, though not very discreetly, while nurturing his own drink. When Nate had occasionally looked to the bar entrance to see if Cameron had returned, he had quickly turned away and concentrated on his glass. He was unaware he had been caught each time.

Since Cameron had left they had waited in almost unbroken silence, allowing Nate the time to fully consider what L'Armin had told him. He still found it hard to believe that the Ring Beings were nothing more than a cover story; all one huge lie to conceal the ability L'Armin's race possessed. It was such a monumental achievement to have kept it going for so long. So why take such a huge risk by revealing it to someone only visiting for the weekend?

Even though telling him was surely a sign of trust, Nate had grown concerned with how he had found out. Had he pushed L'Armin into revealing the truth? If so would there be repercussions for his friend for telling him? Part of him wished he had simply gone along with it and not questioned things at all. If he had they would be in the same position, except the secret would still be locked away under L'Armin's watchful eye.

Only now was Nate beginning to grasp the severity of what he knew. The blindfold that had hidden the reality of the Ring Beings from him had been removed and he could finally see them for what they really were. But in doing so L'Armin had revealed his people's vulnerabilities. He had given up so much more than originally intended during their time together.

The one reassuring aspect of it all was the unspoken trust they shared. There was no doubt in Nate's mind that L'Armin and his people were his friends and they would do him no harm. His discretion was all they wanted in return. Knowing the truth meant he would have to tread carefully from now on. No-one else needed to find out, especially from him.

"Can I ask you something?" Nate said to break the silence, which was quickly becoming uncomfortable.

"Of course."

"Why did you tell me the truth about the Ring Beings? I mean, I'm grateful for your help and all, but why tell me?"

L'Armin wriggled in his seat. Either he had become uncomfortable or Nate's question had surprised him. He looked beyond the bar and became still. After a short wait he nodded his head to no-one and then turned in his chair

151

to face Nate head on. It was obvious he had been silently communicating with others of his race again.

"I shouldn't have," he replied. "My intention was only to help you find the killer. We are a peaceful people and have been for centuries. But I saw a way in which we could help you. A way in which our ability could be used properly."

"Does anyone else know?"

"They do not. My people were afraid to tell you. They were afraid to help you as well, at first."

"So what changed their minds?"

"I did," L'Armin said. "I showed them the goodness in your memories. Apart from the destructive nature of your work, that is."

Nate put his hands up to acknowledge the disapproving tone in L'Armin's voice.

"We trust that you will not reveal our secret because your past experiences tell us so. Our gift was once used solely to help others." L'Armin paused for a moment before continuing. "Something many of us miss."

Nate was about to reply with another question when a voice interrupted. "Nate," someone called out from the other side of the room.

They both soon spotted Helen heading toward them, with Cameron in tow and a concerned look on her face. She weaved a complex path through the tables and chairs—some of which lay upside down after Nate's earlier rampage—as she raced forward. When she finally reached them she threw her arms around Nate and nearly knocked him off the chair. Her body smacked into his, sending a rush of heat through his centre. She then proceeded to grip him far too tightly.

"What's going on?" she said. "Cameron said something bad happened to you during the festival. I was really worried. Are you OK?"

Nate did not know where to start. Even if he did the words could not form on his tongue with it stuck to the bridge of his mouth. The dryness had returned yet none of the anger had. What appeared instead surprised him, at first.

It felt good to rest his head against her, if only for a second or two. Having her there with him was a tremendous relief. Soon it was all he cared about. Nothing else interested him anymore, he just wanted to stay there. He enjoyed the moment of peace in her arms more than he thought he ever could.

But before he knew it, it was over and he was suddenly expected to say something. When she moved away and held him at arm's length his mind refocused. It all came flooding back, and with more force than before.

"What have you been doing since we got here?" he said.

Helen let go and stepped back. The question had caught her by surprise. "I don't understand. Why?" She looked to Cameron and L'Armin helplessly, immediately making Nate regret his choice of tone.

"I just need to know. What did Stuart ask you to do here?"

Her arms flopped down, like the air had been let out of her. "He told me to look after you. What's going on? What's this all about?"

"Tell me why you met with a stranger by the pool the other night?"

"How do you know about that?" she said, raising her voice slightly.

"Just tell me."

She did not speak, she just stared back at him. The longer she did the more Nate could see tiny creases forming in the corners of her eyes. Was she trying to detect a crack in his demeanour? Perhaps even trying to break his confidence? For whatever reason, it made him feel as nauseated as zero-gravity did. He knew he had to get the truth out of her whatever. But the sight of angry lines across her face as she glared at him was something he never wanted to see again.

153

His accusing tone had turned the conversation on its head. It now ventured into unknown territory for the both of them. The closest they had ever come to a confrontation before was during an argument about which action holo-movie was the best. He had conceded defeat on that occasion.

Finally she made a move and crossed her arms in a brazen act of defiance. It was a confrontational pose that Nate had no idea how to interpret. Was it out of a feeling of guilt, or because of being accused of something? Even though he had not directly accused her of anything yet. Whichever it was she had picked up on his accusing tone and was poised, ready to fight—even if he was not.

"I don't see why that's any of your business, Nathan," she said.

Nathan. Only his mother had said his name in such a way when she had chided him for being naughty as a young boy. He was not the one on trial, regardless of how he was being made to feel. His confidence began to turn inside out as it imploded in a frenzy of panic and worry.

"Please Helen, it's important," he said, less adversarial than before.

"Fine," she replied.

Nate was sure he would never want to be up against her in business. She showed an admirable ruthlessness, which in the face of his accusing tone had hunkered down for the coming storm. She was not giving anything away.

"Stuart asked me to give the guy some paperwork. What on Earth is so interesting about that? And why is it so bloody important to you?" she said.

The sides of Nate's head began to throb. He could feel his temples pulsating from a sudden rush of blood. Without thinking he opened his mouth wide and let whatever words he could find just bellow out of him. The floodgates no longer held back the torrent.

"Because that guy tried to *fucking* kill me," he said.

Helen froze on the spot, unable to react while the sentence slowly sunk in. After a second or two she raised

154

her right hand to cover her mouth. Yet there was no angry stare or defensive posture this time, only a blank face that had lost its colour. No armour remained, it seemed he had stripped her of it entirely.

As soon as the words had left Nate's mouth, he had regretted them. He had wanted to break it to her gently, not shout it at her in a blind temper. He was having a hard enough time sustaining his own confidence, the last thing he needed was to shatter hers.

"No," she said, as her eyes began to well up. "That's not true."

"I'm afraid it is," L'Armin said, having sensed the tension had built up a little too much. "We each saw it happen." He gestured to Cameron.

"Why would he do that? Why would anyone try to hurt you?" Helen said, still half covering her mouth.

Nate could not take his eyes off of her. Her entire body had been rocked by his words and no longer stood as straight as before. He could see that her hands had begun to shake ever so slightly too.

Again his anger had burst through unexpectedly. It had required all of his remaining energy this time to prevent it from escaping entirely. He only wished he could lock it away deep inside of himself and never let it see the light of day again. The stress he had suffered had allowed his emotions far too much freedom of late.

Still his outburst had at least served its purpose, however unplanned it had been. The reaction he watched was exactly what he needed to see and to hear from her. There was obvious pain in her words, she did not want to see him dead after all.

"The guy just strolled in and then, *bang*." Cameron slapped his hands together to reinforce his point. His tactless description appeared to shoot through Helen like a shock-wave. She jumped on the spot, then raised her left hand to her mouth to join the other.

"Jesus, Nate, are you OK?" The words were slightly muffled by her hands again, as they hovered in front.

"I'm fine," he replied.

"I don't understand. Did he miss?"

Nate moved his sweaty hands off of his knees and revealed two damp patches where they had rested on his trousers. He rubbed them against his temple in an attempt to ease a pressure which refused to dissipate.

What he really wanted to dull it with was locked behind the mobile bartender that wiped down the bar; a fruitless attempt at looking like it belonged there. Any of the glowing bottles would have sufficed. He could lock himself away and drink the entire day out of existence, replacing it with nothing but darkness. Much like the assassin had done to his once treasured memory.

Cameron decided to answer Helen's question, seeing as Nate was finding solace in the prospect of destroying half his brain cells with alcohol.

"There was another Nate—" He looked at Nate before correcting himself. "Mr. Maddox I mean. He shot the wrong one."

"Thank God," Helen said. "Did you catch this man?" She shot a scornful look at Cameron. "You are supposed to be a body guard, right?"

"Yes ma'am. But no I—"

"You let him get away? You really are useless, do you know that?" Helen snapped, cutting Cameron off mid-sentence. "I think you should start looking for another job when we get back."

Nate could not listen any more, he wanted to tell her to leave Cameron alone. But he could not shake off the feeling that she had deliberately steered the questioning away from herself.

"Did you know about any of this or not?" he said, almost without thinking this time.

Cameron immediately dropped his attempt at defending himself, even though his now reddened face suggested he severely wanted to continue. Instead the room settled into an uncomfortable quiet as the question hung in the air.

This was surely it for their relationship, Nate told himself as he tried in vain to breathe calmly. She would never forgive him for asking the question. But it had to be asked. He had to hear her say that she was not involved, even if it cost him dearly. Only his heart seemed to disagree as he felt it begin almost jumping around inside his chest. He was certain he could hear it too.

"What? How could you … I would never …" Helen said, moving closer once more.

With no more than half a metre between them, Nate could see the toll his question had taken on her. Her cheeks drooped at the sides as she wrestled with the obvious turmoil that beset her entire body. The longer she took to process Nate's question, the more he could see himself reflected in her tear filled eyes.

"We saw you hand the guy a piece of paper. Did you know what it said?" Nate continued softly for fear of shattering her into a million pieces. His own eyes began to feel damp at the idea of hurting her.

"No. It said nothing, just numbers. Nothing important."

He could tell by the way her voice wavered that she was desperately holding the rest of the tears back. They lay in wait behind a crumbling wall that he was dismantling one brick at a time, with each word he said. If he pulled out the right brick, the rest would collapse.

"Did Stuart tell you anything?" he said.

Her tears subsided for a second. "Stuart? What's he got to do with it?"

Nate turned to Cameron and L'Armin who both watched with an intense interest. Neither of them said a word. He was on his own this time.

"He's the lying, cheating bastard behind all of this," he said.

"Holy shit," Cameron exclaimed.

"I saw it with my own eyes. He's wanted me out of the way for years," Nate continued. He chose to ignore Cameron's interruption and focus only on Helen.

157

"You're lying." She began to shake her head as the words came out.

"I'm not. He planned the whole thing so he could take control of the company. Helen, just listen to me."

"I won't listen, I won't. He wouldn't do such a thing," she said, refusing to look at him. While still shaking her head she covered her ears and closed her eyes. She then began to repeat the same words over and over again: "He wouldn't," she said. The wall was rebuilding each time she refused to listen.

Nate grabbed her by the arms. "Helen. Stop it, please," he said.

She did not respond. He pulled her arms down and away from her ears. But she immediately yanked them out of his grip and clamped them back into place, blocking everything out again. It was no good, she had become determined to wipe out any signs of his presence.

Finally he decided to reach for her and pull her into him. He wanted to console her and doubted he could get through by using words alone anymore. She was wound up tight and ready to snap. He just was not expecting her to snap so suddenly.

Once close enough she instinctively unleashed her right hand, which made contact with his face soon after. Before he could determine what happened, the noise from her slap had already echoed around half the room, and his head. He placed his hand over the point of impact, which began to sting sharply with a building heat.

Helen breathed in quick successions, while resting her hand in the other and cradling it like an injured animal. It had clearly hurt her palm as much as it had Nate's face. Still she looked immensely angry with lines on her face where before there had been none. The energy she had suddenly expended appeared to have lessened the intensity only slightly.

She had surprised Nate with the amount of force she had managed to put into the slap. He had no idea she possessed such strength, mentally as well as physically. It had totally shocked him. But somehow it was also a comfort to know she could keep herself safe when needed. The killer was not as much of a threat to her as he initially thought.

As they stood tending their wounds a thought struck Nate, thankfully much less painfully than Helen had. He realised that there remained only one way of proving what he had seen. They needed to catch the killer.

"I know it's hard to believe," he began.

"You're damn right it is." Helen wiped the lingering layer of moisture from her eyes. "How could y—"

"But I can show you," he just managed to say before she could continue.

Nate's comment had struck a curious chord in her. Suddenly her posture snapped back up to attention. The prospect of evidence ignited something in her that instantly retracted her claws and eased her tears. Proof was obtainable and more importantly, undeniable. It was the only way of convincing her, once and for all.

In his mind a plan was forming that he thought simple enough. For it to work, however, he would need her complete trust, which was something he knew he would have a hard time earning back. "Just hear me out, OK?" He spoke as softly as he could.

Helen squinted and then looked down at the floor. She stared at the carpet in silence. Either she had found a new—and badly timed—interest in décor or she was considering her options.

Nate took a few moments to do the same. He ran through them in his head as best as he could. If he knew her as well as he thought then the options would come down to only three.

The first would be to leave and put it all down to something like substance abuse, and move on without Nate in her life. If only it were that simple, he thought. He was acutely aware that *he* could never live with this choice, let alone her. The second would be to go along with him until a chance arrived for her to contact Stuart and tell him about Nate's paranoid delusions.

The third on the other hand—the one he knew she would surely take—was to see it through and decide after the evidence had been presented. Unfortunately, he would not find out for sure which of the last two options she had chosen until it was already too late. In this instance the plan would be as dead as his double.

"OK," she finally said. "But if it isn't concrete proof, then I'm leaving."

"Great." Nate tried to put his hand on her shoulder but she quickly moved away. "Look, I'm sorry for asking you if—"

"No," she barked, surprising Nate. "You don't get to just apologise. I hate you for thinking I'd be involved in this … Live with it."

Before he had a chance to continue, Helen walked off toward the exit. Her involvement in his little scheme was clearly going to happen on her terms. No rank, title or superiority mattered a damn now. It was all about the proof, everything else was on hold.

The dynamics of their relationship had changed faster than most of Nate's recent ones had lasted. And yet this was the one he held most dear and the one he wanted desperately to cling onto. The prospect of losing her left him empty, just like during his divorce. He quickly realised there was more at stake than he liked to admit.

Cameron swivelled in his chair to face Nate. He leant in to speak, with his arm outstretched across the bar. "Stuart's behind this?"

Nate nodded with a look of guilt on his face. "I'm sorry I didn't tell you first."

"No worries," Cameron said. "Sir," he hastened to add.

"We're going to get the killer and Stuart, if my idea works. I know you'll want to help me after the way he's been with you."

"Damn right. I'd love to nail that prick." Cameron stopped suddenly. "Hang on."

"Do not be concerned Cameron," L'Armin said. "We have seen the disrespectful way in which Stuart has treated you."

"And I will make sure he doesn't in future. To anyone," Nate added.

"How did ... You know what, I'll take your word on that," Cameron said as he waved his arms, disregarding the obvious question he really wanted to ask. "So what's your idea?"

"First -" Nate pointed to the exit Helen had disappeared through. "- we need Helen back."

Cameron rocketed out of his seat and stood to attention, ready for action. "I'm on it, boss," he said before speeding away and quickly vanishing once again.

The first request was easy. Nate's second, however, would require far more from the person he needed to ask. He reluctantly turned to L'Armin and, after a few seconds considering how best to word his request, he spoke.

"I'm going to need another favour I'm afraid," he said.

L'Armin raised his eyebrows higher than humanly possible. It sent a wave of extra ruffles through the skin atop his head that stopped just out of sight, somewhere around the back. He stayed like this as he listened.

Nate continued to explain his plan as carefully as he could. It was risky, but it was the best he had been able to conjure up in such a short amount of time. Yet with enough luck, he was sure they could pull it off.

Chapter 14

A glass smashed as it landed against the concrete floor at the back of the bar. The yellow-eyed man who had been drinking from it a second earlier stood, pushed his shoulders back and lifted his chin as high as he could to the large, greasy skinned creature that had chosen to knock over the drink. The latter towered above the yellow-eyed man with a snarling mouth half open, revealing a row of sharp, shark like teeth.

The two stood locked in a stare until the smaller man decided to make the first move. He pulled away, narrowly avoiding a lumbering swing of hammer like fists from his foe. As he did he appeared to remove something shiny from his side with an enviable speed.

In one fluid and unbroken movement the smaller man spun around 180 degrees, slashing his blade across the larger man's belly, and then finished off with a violent backwards thrust, sending his weapon straight into his enemy's exposed chest.

The large man fell heavily onto his knees, his face aghast at what had just befallen him. He clutched the protruding blade as he flopped onto his side. Then with one last escaping breath to bid the world farewell, he was gone. The argument had been settled before it had even started.

The smaller man removed his dagger and wiped it on his enemy's sleeveless and unbuttoned utility jacket. Their quarrel had been settled the only way that mattered in this place: with violence. Soon after, the smaller man was ordering another drink. He hardly looked phased at all by what he had just done. Simply another day at the office it seemed.

"What a shit-hole," Cameron said. He stared down at the body, now surrounded by a pool of orange liquid that threatened to stain his shoes. "I definitely prefer your other memories to this one, sir. So why would you have come here of all places?"

The question was not one Nate particularly fancied answering. He was not even sure he could, at least not without them seeing him differently afterwards. This was a chapter in his life that was never pleasant for him to recall. So recreating this memory and entering it through another rift was something he had done reluctantly.

He looked around the room at surroundings that were both familiar and threatening to him. He thought he had managed to wipe this time from his memory, and never thought he would end up revisiting it on purpose. Except this memory appeared the perfect place to carry out his plan. At least it had earlier when L'Armin had entered his head and found it.

The walls told a million stories similar to the one they had just witnessed. Stains of God knows what ran up and down them in streaks and dried blotches. This bar was light-years away from the one in his hotel, both in distance and appearance.

Each visiting patron carried significant mental baggage that undoubtedly had driven them on from one place to another, before finally dumping them in this most unwelcoming of establishments. It was not much of a stretch of the imagination to assume they were all fairly dangerous, too. This was not a place people *chose* to drink in but one they *found* themselves drinking in. A place where no order prevailed but that of self-preservation and the survival of the most aggressive.

"I have to agree with Mr Cameron, this place is indeed displeasing." L'Armin stuck closely to Cameron.

"This was a bad time for me," Nate said, as if that were enough.

The three of them stood unwilling to touch or even approach a table, for fear of catching something ungodly. The same could not be said for those who sat at them. They appeared quite happy to cavort in the depravity of what passed as the bar area. Nate could see a weapon hanging from most of the occupants' belts or tucked into their trousers. He was amazed he had not died in one of these places.

Past the bar area, the room opened up into three rows of large glass cubes with two seats bolted down in front of each. Some were engulfed by groups of cheering spectators: a rag tag selection of different species, not one of which were human. The others sat idle, except for bright displays above that beckoned to anyone willing to lose their cash. Nate remembered these machines well, he had lost enough money on them himself.

"So what's the plan again, sir?" Cameron asked, with one hand never more than an inch or two from his side-arm. If the three of them were actually there, it was certain they would have drawn more attention than was safe.

Nate searched the area past the bar but could not locate his younger self anywhere. His memory was being tested well in this place, he could not remember where he would be at all.

There were two incidents in this place that cowered in the naughty corner of his subconscious. But which was this? Was it the first where he had been kicked to the floor and mugged for looking at someone in a *funny* way? Or was this the second, where he had caused a little trouble with the management?

It was important to establish which, because the latter had left him with much more than a scarred memory. He rubbed his side while remembering a knife being dragged across his flesh. All he could hope for was that this turned out to be the first of the two incidents. He had no real desire to see either of them, but at least he had received only a mild beating in that one.

He quickly shook off the feeling before addressing Cameron's question. "We're setting a trap in here."

"Yeah, you said before. But how exactly," Cameron replied.

"Right, so Helen should now be explaining to Stuart that my visit has been a little odd. She'll then tell him I had a strange experience during the festival."

"The guy trying to kill you?"

"Yes. But she'll make it sound like we thought it wasn't real and that we're trying again. Stuart should make contact with the killer and tell *him* to try again too, seeing as no-one suspects anything."

"And we'll be ready to catch the bastard when he tries," Cameron said.

"Exactly. That does mean one thing, though."

Cameron's premature excitement vanished suddenly as he waited for Nate to continue.

"This guy will be hidden until he tries to kill me. So you need to be vigilant. I mean really vigilant. I don't want to go through this, only to find out we've only made his job easier. OK?" Nate said.

"Are you positive you have judged Miss Helen correctly," L'Armin said, as someone much larger unceremoniously pushed him aside.

"We can trust her." Except Nate was not as sure as he wanted to be. Their relationship had stalled and there was nothing he could do to restart it. Until he had some kind of proof in his hands, their friendship was left waiting for a tow.

A group from one of the glass cube machines finished their game with a roar and set about barging their way to the bar. L'Armin was nearly lost in their superior numbers and height. They failed to spot him at all as they almost trampled him underfoot.

The three of them regained their composure and relocated to a quieter spot near an empty machine. They were finally now far enough away from the rowdy group, who had entirely commandeered the bar area, to stand unhindered. There they were granted a better view of the machines and the holographic fighters that were entombed inside the glass cubes, awaiting their next battle.

"Woah, this thing's neat," Cameron said, as he fiddled with the control system. The fighters ignored his input, but a line of strange looking letters scrolled above them, floating in mid-air.

"They need credits to work." Nate tapped a slot on the side of the machine.

Cameron's face suddenly broke into a smirk. "You've used one of these?" His expression suggested he was impressed.

"Unfortunately yes. For a few weeks this place was where I chose to make my money. On these machines. Not something I'm proud of."

"Why were not you working for your father?"

"Because, Cameron, at 18 I thought I knew better than my father and went in search of a dream. Only that dream went south pretty quickly as I found out the galaxy did not work the way I thought it did. This was one of the delightful establishments I ended up in, with some very questionable people. Thankfully I eventually crawled back to the family business, where I stayed put."

"I'm not sure you really need me here then, sir. Sounds like you can handle yourself pretty well," Cameron said. His mouth widened even further, pushing his cheeks up slightly.

Nate replied with a small and momentary smile.

The lights above them flickered for a few seconds as the power fluctuated, another sign of the buildings dilapidated state. No doubt the power was being syphoned from another business anyway, Nate surmised. He knew he had never belonged in such a place.

The noise in the room had built up since the group had taken residence around the bar area. The three of them were by all accounts trapped with no clear eye-line to the rift entrance. Nate suddenly felt worried that the killer had

166

already entered without them seeing him. It called for a second relocation, this time to a raised area where a couple of drunks were arguing in some unknown and aggressive tongue.

"This is perfect," he said.

With his unbroken view of the rift restored, Nate relaxed a little. The plan was beginning to come together in his mind. The raised area would be perfect to display himself to anyone that entered. The killer would spot him straight away and try to get to him. But Cameron and L'Armin would be hidden in plain sight among the drinking crowds.

Excellent, he thought as he padded his pockets. Cameron had been kind enough to arm him earlier and he was well aware that this was his real back-up. Despite the weapons rather minuscule size, it was powerful enough to make up for the seconds it would take for Cameron to act. Seconds in which it could all be over.

"Shit," Nate suddenly shouted. His calmness had proven all too temporary.

Cameron instinctively burst to life, ready to take down the nearest person. He raised his arms but had nothing to attack. The people around were no threat. After a quick scan of the area he dropped his fists and looked to Nate.

From the beginning they had agreed upon one thing that was never to be changed. Helen was to be left out until the killer had been apprehended, not before. He had made this perfectly clear. And yet here she was walking among the worst beings the galaxy had managed to shit out, a stubborn flower beset by a post-apocalyptic backdrop. She wandered around searching. When she spotted their group, she immediately changed direction to meet them.

This was the last thing he wanted to see. Nate's heart raced as he made the necessary changes to the plan, quickly deciding she would have to be hidden with L'Armin. They had to be out of sight. He had to concentrate on not getting himself killed first and foremost. With Helen now in the mix, he knew it could prove a dangerous distraction.

167

"What the hell are you doing here?" Nate demanded.

"I need to see this," she replied. "I told Stuart what you said. Now I want to see for myself what comes of it."

"Fine. You can watch with L'Armin, from over there." Nate pointed to the far wall, as far away from the raised area as possible.

"No way—".

"Listen, Helen." Nate broke her sentence in half like a thin twig between his fingers. "This guy is going to try to kill me. I'm not letting you anywhere near him."

After a few seconds deliberating, she replied. "OK. So what is this place anyway?" she asked, tactfully shifting the conversation.

"It's not important right now. I'll tell you about it another time. Now this is what's going to happen."

Thankfully for Nate, she took his tone as the sign to stop talking he had meant it to be. She stood waiting for instructions as the plan was put into action.

"Cameron, I want you standing with these people." Nate tapped the arm of a man in a small group at the steps of the raised area. "The killer needs to think you're part of the illusion or he'll make a run for it."

"Right. He'll know I'm real when I shove *this* in his face." Cameron pulled his pistol out of the holster and waved it about like a gun-toting cowboy. Thankfully he had stopped short of firing a few shots into the ceiling as well. They all stared at him, temporarily bemused by his over-enthusiasm.

"Great, just don't shoot him unless you think he's about to fire," Nate felt compelled to say.

Cameron nodded and dropped his gun to his side, as if disappointed.

"So now what?" Helen asked.

Nate looked to the rift entrance. "We wait," he said, knowing full well his world could end the next time it was used.

***

The next two hours were the worst Nate had ever experienced, as he waited for his would-be killer to arrive. He had watched as a large crowd formed over by the glass cube machines. They had taken up so much of his time in the past that he still remembered every single noise they made as people and aliens bet their credits away. He quite enjoyed hearing the cheers and boos from those using them too.

Small disagreements were still occurring between the scourges that occupied the bar, kicking up the level of noise every few minutes. But each was quickly settled one way or another. The tension was high, as it had always been. He knew well that within a heartbeat the room could descend into anarchy, only to return to normality before the next.

All of this was happening as his younger self bet his only money away on the machines. He had spotted the long, dirty haired stick of a man he had once been, scurrying about under people's noses earlier. It had proven too hard for him not to watch himself dicing with death. Like tiny scavengers, he and his accomplices moved among much larger creatures that could squash them under their thumbs if they became too much of a nuisance.

Nate sat at a small round table in the raised area he had chosen, no more than three steps up from the rest of the room. He tried not to look over to the rift entrance in an obvious way. The plan would be for nothing if the killer entered and saw him staring straight back. But, paradoxically, it was also crucial that Nate saw him first.

The agreed signal would then be given to Cameron, who stood with a drink in hand as he reacted to people that were not real. To show he meant business, he had also decided at some point during the course of the last hour to put his black glasses back on. Such a small addition, and yet he now appeared as formidable as ever. Nothing would get past him.

Helen thankfully had agreed to stay back with L'Armin, albeit after multiple attempts at getting Nate to change his

169

mind. They were also keeping a close eye on the rift and were set to give their own signal if they saw someone enter. So far the plan was going well, it just lacked the one ingredient that any murder plot required: the murderer.

As Nate surveyed his surroundings once more he spotted his younger self take a seat at another one of the glass cube machines. He tapped away at the controls with a noticeable degree of swiftness and finesse. Nate watched himself, impressed with how rapidly his fingers fluttered between buttons as he laid waste to his opponent's holographic counterpart.

All that talent, and I used it to cheat others out of their money. He laughed to himself at the thought. Most of them appeared to take the beating in their stride, but slowly the suspicions were building. Soon his opponents would discover the device hidden under his shirt that he had been using to hack the machines. Idiot, Nate thought, as he reminisced of the chaos that had ensued. He had since realised which of the two incidents this was, and he had not been happy with the answer.

The room was now somehow calm, a rarity considering the occupants. His thoughts were allowed a brief moment to escape the fear that was present like a stone weight tied around his body. It required all of his strength to resist giving into it. These few moments to clear his thoughts had taken some of the tension away, but it had also taken his attention away from the rift.

He had been distracted for a mere second or two, yet it had been enough to miss something important. In the corner of his eye he spotted movement, not from the rift, but from Helen and L'Armin. Still confused, he looked to the rift for a split second before returning his gaze to the two waving frantically at him from the far side of the room.

His concentration had slipped temporarily, allowing someone to enter through the rift. He sent a panicked nod to Cameron, who appeared shocked and a little fazed by the sudden announcement. Worryingly, the killer had already disappeared within the crowd before Nate had even seen him.

"The bastards already inside," he said to himself, slapping his palm against the table.

All the planning leading up to this moment now seemed but a blueprint written in crayons. It had faded to the point of being unreadable. He scanned the faces around the room, trying to remember the killer's features.

He could picture the leathery skin and how the man had resembled a lizard. Or was it a snake? Which was it? No matter, he reminded himself. The guy would be pretty obvious to him soon enough. It was time to let the trap play out. There was nothing more he could do anyway. Except sweat.

They waited patiently for a sign of someone who did not belong. Unfortunately, the location was one that hid the killer's kind well. It was they who clearly did not fit in. He could appear right in front of them and they would not know, just another apparition to be ignored. Only this one was capable of killing.

Another short-lived scuffle interrupted the tension, drawing Nate's gaze. When he quickly turned back his eyes locked on to the empty spot where Cameron had once been standing. His missing presence was a stabbing reminder of how close to disaster he was treading.

At any moment the killer could strike, and where was his protector, his shield? Maybe he had been taken out by the killer? He looked around frantically. The calm appearance he had been forcing to the surface was no longer on show, having sunk suddenly to the murky depths.

"You dirty, cheating human," someone shouted from behind.

Nate jumped, startled and too afraid to turn. He did not recognise the voice, but it had to be talking to him. It had come from no more than a few metres away, who else could it be talking to? He considered his perilous situation and what he could do to escape it. But within seconds it hit him, he had heard it before.

171

"Please, I didn't do anything," came the reply, in a voice Nate knew well. It had become more forceful and refined over the years but it was unmistakably his own.

He tried to ignore the commotion as he left the relative safety of the table to search the immediate area, where Cameron had once been standing. There was no sign of him. His drink had been placed carefully on the ground and the group he had been hiding among was still in the same place, each chatting away. Yet he had gone.

The intact glass hinted to him that Cameron had not been dragged away by force. So he had left his spot intentionally? This was much worse. Was he staying out of the killer's way to protect himself?

The argument began to draw nearer as Nate took tiny steps through the crowd. He kept a look out for any obvious signs of a scuffle where Cameron had been. But however much he tried he just could not see anything there. Cameron had indeed left of his own accord.

He had also now lost eye contact with Helen and L'Armin. The plan had completely disintegrated. The only thing that gave him comfort was the weapon sitting peacefully in his pocket.

Still, the disagreement between his young double and a much larger creature could be heard in the background. The young Nate pleaded as he was pinned down by one of the creature's unnaturally long arms. "I'm sorry," he yelped helplessly.

Nate could see it happening in the corner of his vision. The same frustration and desperation was building in his muscles as a sensation of being trapped began to take over. He just could not ignore the perilous situation his younger self was facing, however irrelevant it may have been. It was playing out exactly as he remembered, leading to one awful outcome that he could never forget.

As he pushed strangers aside to find any hints of Cameron's whereabouts, it became impossible for him to resist stiffening his muscles in anticipation of a blade being drawn once again.

"No. Please," the young Nate screamed.

The unmistakable sound of a metal blade being released from its sheath sent a shiver down Nate's much older spine. Even though it could not possibly cause him harm again, it continued to disturb him regardless.

When the young Nate saw the blade he froze. The moment had come to leave and never return—or so he thought at the time. In one rapid and desperate show of strength he kicked out at the large man, somehow managing to force enough space between them to break free of the man's crushing grip. But freedom was still on the other side of the bar. He bolted without looking back.

"Come here, little man," the large man called to him joyfully, while swinging his three bladed knife in the air, from side to side.

Nate watched as a worryingly thin version of himself ran in panic and began knocking into other large beings. It had not gone unnoticed by those around that the scavengers were starting to make a nuisance of themselves.

The scene began to follow the same pattern as that of the floating debris from earlier. Pieces had started flying off and hitting others, with the disorder growing exponentially after each impact. Now the young Nate had caused enough of a disruption to be considered a pest that needed removing. It was only a matter of time before he was punished for his wrongdoings.

For the time being, Nate decided to concentrate on what he *could* change and let his younger version face what he had already. With the crowd surrounding him becoming much denser as he made his way through, he slowed his pace. His feet moved only inches at a time. As fast as he dared.

It was quickly turning into one of his nightmares, where he became lost amid a sea of strangers' faces. This place wanted him. It tested his confidence, like Rita from the exhibition. He was sure that if he stopped he would become trapped forever. *Just breathe*, he told himself. But even this proved difficult as he drowned in endless and

173

empty eyes that only saw what they were allowed. He wanted out, and back to the real world again.

His steady footing became the first casualty of his descent into panic. He could feel the room begin to spin and had no choice but to reach out for something to right himself. Thankfully a sleeved arm was available. It was rough to the touch, like old rope.

As he gripped it tightly it reacted suddenly as if surprised. Then, weirdly, the arm pushed back and forced him away. The first thing that entered his mind was that he had somehow stumbled into Cameron. But his sleeve was certainly smoother than this.

"Don't move." The person spoke from behind Nate, with an odd emphasis on the 'T'.

At the same time he felt something being pushed into his back. It touched against his spine causing him to flinch. It was definitely something metal, possibly hollow and almost positively deadly. Blade or gun? He just could not tell. Whatever it was it stayed in place and had become the only thing that concerned him. Even his younger version's fate was of little consequence to him now.

"Clearly my earlier mistake went unnoticed," the man continued, his voice now coming from directly over Nate's shoulder. He was close. So close in fact that Nate could feel the faintest sensation of air flowing across his ear as the man spoke.

The assassin had found him.

Chapter 15

Nate raised his arms. He did not know what to do, no-one had informed him of the correct procedure for meeting one's maker. He could feel his face reddening as blood rushed to his head, partly due to his imminent demise and partly because of a degree of embarrassment at having handed himself straight over to the killer.

He knew all too well that things had gone utterly wrong, as he felt the implement of his death tucked neatly into the groove of his back. He had severely underestimated his enemy.

The killer lingered on every 'S' and 'T' as he spoke— exactly as Nate had come to expect. "Your scent is unmistakable. I won't make the same mistake again. Turn around," he said, followed by a jab with his weapon.

Nate did as he was told. Face to face the man looked thinner than before. But the skin was as scaly and purple as he remembered. Only now in the light he could make out every line and intersecting angle that decorated the assassin's snake like face.

He had the same empty look as the soulless people around them, with eyes the darkest black Nate had ever witnessed. Whatever presence lay hidden beyond was staying put and giving no indication of its existence. The only human thing Nate could find was his own reflection, shining back from the piercing abyss' that stared at *him*.

"I'll double whatever Stuart is paying you," Nate said, his voice portraying more confidence than he felt. It was the first thing that came to mind, and yet the last thing he thought he would say.

The man stared back, his mouth twitching as he scanned Nate up and down. After a few seconds a grin swept across his face. "I am intrigued, how do you know Stuart is behind this," he said.

"Does it matter?"

"I suppose not. However, do not think I can be swayed by merely money, Mr. Maddox."

This is it then, Nate thought while he studied the shiny metal casing of the pistol, now aimed squarely at the centre of his chest. The room was loud but the sound of the shot would easily drown it all out. Cameron and the others would hear it and maybe they could still catch the killer. His death would not be completely in vain, he considered. It was at least something.

"This will be quick and quiet, I assure you," the assassin said, instantly putting to bed Nate's hopes of ultimately getting retribution.

Quiet, shit, Nate thought. As the gun was raised to his head, he found it impossible to do anything but stare into its barrel: a black hole that waited, eager to suck him in, stretch him out like spaghetti and dismantle him atom by atom.

He thought about making a grab for the gun and perhaps forcing it away. But he saw two problems with that idea. The first was his own speed and strength. Could he be that quick? The second was what to do next. He was not so sure he could overpower the killer once his hand was on the pistol.

It quickly dawned on him that it did not really matter if it was worth a try or not, he did not want to die. Not like this.

The killer spoke softly as he held the weapon, without as much as a wobble. His aim was perfect and unflinching. "This time I will not miss," he said.

As the assassin began to pull the trigger the world seemed to slow to a crawl. Nate could only watch as pressure was applied to the firing mechanism as if in slow motion. He assumed this was what people meant when they said their lives flashed before their eyes, in near death experiences. He closed his eyes and waited for either the flash of the shot, or a white tunnel to head through.

Inevitably the shot rang out. It sent a sharp pain through Nate's right ear as the sound reverberated around his head like an earthquake. An explosion of intense red laser-light invaded his black world, despite having involuntarily clamped his eyes tightly shut. With it came a scalding heat across his face, like a cup of lava had been thrown at him.

He spun away from the assassin, hunched over in agony and frantically wiped his face. Death certainly felt more painful than he thought it would be, and not at all the peaceful release he expected.

"You're mine shit-bag," someone to the side of him suddenly said. The voice was just about loud enough for Nate to hear in his left ear. He could not hear a thing with his right, the shot had temporarily deafened it.

When he finally realised his miraculous survival was indeed real, he quickly turned his attention to the painful heat that threatened to sear his entire face off. He scraped at his own skin. But there was nothing on it. Only a line of sharp tenderness across the right side of his face and a smell of burnt hair proved anything had happened at all. But how?

He eventually managed to open his eyes and was shocked to see Cameron on top of the killer. The two were on the floor with Cameron pinning the other to the ground. He had a tight grip of his enemy.

There was nowhere for the killer to go, except further in the direction of the floor. After a few seconds of struggling, Cameron had the killer face down and was pulling his arms out from under him. Neither of them were going anywhere for the time being, with Cameron appearing to have gotten the upper hand. For now.

"I've got him. You'd better get help. This guy's feisty," Cameron said.

Nate's slight deafness lead him to unintentionally shout his reply. "Jesus, Cameron. I thought he'd got me."

"You were never out of my sight, sir." His teeth remained clamped shut as he spoke.

The killer hissed as he struggled; a futile attempt at breaking free that was met with a swift knee to the side. He doubled over as the wind was forced out of his chest. He could do nothing but watch as his weapon escaped his grip. As his arms were then roughly bent backward, immediately incapacitating them, he ceased struggling. He had been caught. His captor was in control and happy to demonstrate it.

Now, finally, Nate could make out the being behind the dead eyes. He was not scared or panicked at all, just incredibly angry. A great deal of that rage was probably reserved just for Cameron, though the rest was definitely for him.

The pistol had come to rest only metres away, having slid over the smooth ground. Nate made a quick lunge for it, but was left empty handed as it quickly became swamped by a moving crowd. It slid even further away as busy feet kicked it unintentionally out of sight.

He was sure it did not particularly matter, only it would have made him feel more at ease. He would have certainly enjoyed aiming it between the killer's eyes, just to see his reaction. Give the son-of-a-bitch a taste of his own medicine, maybe the taste of his own energy weapon. That would have to wait for later, he decided. The stalemate was not guaranteed to last forever.

"I need to get L'Armin. You OK to hold him until then?" Nate asked, with a concerned look to the disturbingly quiet man in Cameron's grasp.

"Sure, be quick about it though." Cameron flicked his head to the side and immediately back again. "Wait, watch—" he tried to warn as Nate took two steps backward, straight into someone else's fight.

The argument Nate's younger self had caused had continued to spill over, engulfing everything in its path. He had mindlessly wandered right into the middle of it, having forgotten about it entirely. The chaos he had been responsible for so many years before now threatened his future as well.

Without Nate and Cameron even noticing, the entire bar had slowly been dragged into the row, while the three of them played out their separate disagreement. Now a good proportion of the bar's occupants were fighting or shouting as loud as their lungs allowed. The pistol was long gone as well, and quickly so were the killer and Cameron.

All he could see after being violently forced to the floor, was the large grey man holding up his younger self like a cat by the scruff of the neck. He hopelessly watched as the man sent one of his enormous fists into the angled jaw of the young Nate. Followed by the knife, which was dragged with great deliberation, across his side in one diagonal motion.

The pain was obvious. The young Nate's eyes were sealed tight, scrunched up and hidden away behind a growing film of tears. He hung for all the world to see like a disobedient pet, kicking and screeching.

All was not lost, Nate reminded himself, despite not being able to look away. The scene would play out the same way it had the first time. His accomplices had been ready and waiting to pull him to safety before the large man could do more serious harm. He may have been left battered and bruised, and with a nasty, bloodied, gouge to his side, but he had survived.

The large man's blade had tasted its last drop of blood on that day. Revenge was not normally in his nature, but he had vowed to get it on this occasion. The next day his friends had ambushed, and remorselessly ended, the man's existence. As the killer was once more free to do to him. The one consolation was that the assassin had almost certainly been caught up in the fighting as well.

179

As he lay flat on the ground, too afraid to stand in case the killer spotted him, he scanned the legs that surrounded him. Most appeared to be moving away from the large grey man, who was still displaying his catch of the day. Only a few were static.

Thoughts of the young him had now completely vacated his mind. He would have plenty of time to repent for this part of his life if he finished today alive. But the situation threatened to become far more dangerous as he tried to get his bearings.

"Cameron," he called out.

There was no answer. It became hard to make out anyone's voice but his own as the bar descended further into chaos. He quickly found himself having to dodge groups engaged in the fighting. A tide of bodies, all trying to avoid a violent encounter, began to move toward the exit. Fists were flying in all directions, even chairs were being used by a few of the particularly troubled individuals.

But still he could find no signs of either the assassin or Cameron. He was about to lose all hope of finding them again, when he caught a brief glimpse of someone through an opening in the fighting. A hand stretched out on the floor, bouncing about as those around trampled it. Straight away he knew it was Cameron unconscious on the floor and in severe danger of being crushed.

Nate slide across the ground and took a scruff of Cameron's black suit in his sweaty palms. The killer had hit him hard, smashing his black sunglasses to bits. The frame still rested on his nose but both eyepieces had been shattered. To top it off, a large reddish mark on the side of his head had begun to trickle blood. Whatever the killer had used to knock him out with, it had been solid but relatively small. Still, it had definitely been more than simply a fist.

He dragged Cameron's limp mass slowly toward the raised area a few metres away. His fingers were crushed each time he misjudged his movements, squashed under feet that did not care.

Once there he struggled to heave Cameron up the three small steps. Each time he tried he let out a frustrated groan that prompted a quick check behind. A growing paranoia was urging him onwards, back to relative safety. Once at the top he slumped down under the weight. He was not as strong as he needed to be. Too much time spent pushing paper around, he thought.

"Someone help," he shouted, but the noise in the room reduced his voice to a tiny squeal.

Cameron was still breathing, with regular but shallow intakes of air. For the time being Nate was sure they were safe. It was not how he had seen any of this playing out in his mind. He had relied so much on Cameron for the plan to work. Had it been an unreasonable thing to put on one man?

"Cameron? Come on buddy, wake up," Nate said with a gentle pat on the arm.

The blood on Cameron's head had at least stopped and was now no more than a crimson smudge. He was well and truly out for the count, but seemingly stable for now. With no real medical knowledge of any kind, Nate knew his bodyguard needed help. Except he had no idea where L'Armin or Helen were. For all he knew they had not seen a thing.

As he looked around to the ongoing chaos, he realised the time had come to clean up his own mess. He had caused this after all. His plan, his responsibility. It was only right he finished things once and for all, for Cameron as much as himself. Besides, he was the only one left. The fighting may have hidden the killer, but it had not yet allowed him to escape. There was still time to do something about it. But what?

He jumped up, adrenaline fuelled and ready to act. First he checked the area where Helen and L'Armin should have been hiding. The spot had been completed vacated. He then surveyed the pushing and shoving masses that stood between him and the rift. His eyes shot about the place, excitedly checking each face as the urge to burst into action began to take over.

It did not take long to see something: a shape frantically weaving in and out of the rioting crowd and heading straight for the exit. The assassin was taking a zigzag path to the rift and getting closer by the second. This was his only chance. With the killer having obviously cut his losses and deciding to run, the time for him to act had arrived.

"Got-cha," he said, springing into action. Without thinking he pulled the modestly proportioned weapon out of his pocket and threw himself forward. *Aim, fire, one shot, down; simple*, he thought. Except he was not entirely sure he was even holding the thing the right way up.

An entire body's worth of tension was suddenly released in one giant leap into the crowd. The closer to the rift he got the more excited he became. It was building with every step he took, spurring him on. He could feel strength forming in his fists. They each wanted an equal amount of the action and he was more than willing to oblige.

Was revenge once again rearing its ugly head? It had again snuck out of the dark corner he had been keeping it in. Untapped, he knew it would only continue to bubble beneath the surface until finally smashing through. It led him to one conclusion: he did not just want proof, he wanted the assassin dead. If by his own hands or not, he wanted to end another's existence. In exactly the same way he had wanted with the large grey man years before.

An odd amalgamation of the two formed in his mind with grey, scaly skin, but with the same dead eyes as the killer. What he pictured represented all of the unbridled hatred he felt, and it was quickly approaching the exit.

He found it hard to keep up the momentum as he neared the bar area. Most of the intense fighting had moved there, with quite a few stand-offs now blocking his path. The entire area had broken up into different factions, each deciding whether the enemy of their enemy was their friend, or if everyone was their enemy. Each side waved their weapons as threateningly as they could muster. It was hopeless.

Ahead the killer had taken to throwing tables to the side, making his own much more direct path. It was no good, he was escaping and Nate could do nothing about it.

The excitement turned to fear as he watched his plan finally self-destruct in front of him. After only two or more steps the killer would be but a fleeting memory. Perhaps one to revisit with L'Armin's help? He did not find the thought very funny.

With one last push he dug his heels in and forced his way forward. He refused to give up until every single cell contained within his body could do no more. His head drooped as he put more effort in, watching as one foot defiantly landed in front of the other.

Within a few steps it was beginning to pay off, bringing him ever closer to his target. At the peak of his strides the crowd began to part until the route ahead was soon clear. Finally he could see the assassin just ahead of him, no more than spitting distance away.

But something was not right. By now Nate was certain the guy should have disappeared through the rift, and yet there he was. The path to the rift was blocked and the killer's only chance of escaping had somehow passed. Nate was amazed to see his chances of catching the killer had suddenly increased dramatically.

The rift entrance hung only a few feet in front of the assassin. It taunted him for being so close and yet, strangely, he appeared unable to reach it. His arms thrashed about as he appeared to be trying to release himself from something.

Nate watched with a twisted glee as the killer tried to find what was holding him back. Eventually he spotted a corner of his overcoat caught under someone's foot. But however much he struggled it would not come loose. The killer had become entangled among a small group of people now stood lifeless and frozen in front of him.

In fact the entire room had stopped sometime during Nate's last desperate push for the rift. He had been so

183

focused on reaching the killer that he had not noticed. Some were paused mid punch or still in the process of taking a hit from another. The world had stopped, just like he had seen it do before. The only things moving now were the killer and him.

The time to worry about who had frozen the room would come after he had the assassin in his arms. He was well aware that someone had granted him a second chance, it had not simply been a serendipitous event.

He wasted no time and raced blindly forward. His new plan was simple: launch himself at the killer, using any available part of his anatomy to stop the bastard from escaping.

So with only a metre or so to go, Nate put his plan into action. At the same time the killer had decided to hastily remove his overcoat entirely, ripping it at the seams in the process. When their eyes met the killer automatically raised his arms to block Nate's clumsy punches.

After a round of hits that barely did a thing, Nate quickly realised he had already used most of his energy. The only remaining strategy was to keep swinging regardless. He could at least prevent the killer from getting a real chance at striking back. He dared not use his weapon, however much he wanted to. He needed the killer alive.

Within seconds though, he could feel the speed of his attacks diminishing. Soon the assassin would surely retaliate and end it. He considered using his weapon now.

But their impromptu battle was brought to an end by one well-timed retaliation. The killer sent a swift and solid kick into the middle of Nate's left leg. It sent him reeling away in agony as it buckled under the strain. He was sure something had snapped, either a tendon or a bone. All he could do was fall back onto his right leg, but soon it too gave way.

The floor was his next stop. All the while Nate could see the killer beaming a broad smile back at him. As he crashed to the ground he could make out the obvious pleasure across his enemy's face, no doubt brought about by his pain.

He could not think of anything he could possibly do to stop the killer from casually strolling out, never to be seen again. He could not even imagine being able to stand again with the splintered pain that ran through his leg.

The backup plan was now his only hope. He pointed his pen-sized weapon at the killer and pulled the trigger. Having been the first time he had ever fired a weapon in anger, however, his shot was inevitably off by inches. Not much, but enough to miss entirely. The narrow beam of blue laser light was sent bouncing around the room. It made contact with several of the frozen fighting patrons, yet only appeared to do superficial damage.

The assassin took his time in making his first step into the rift. His leg lingered for a moment before it moved into the light and disappeared. Then slowly the rest of him began to follow. He had not even noticed the badly timed shot. Nate was now certain it was too late.

The light progressed further up the assassin's leg until it met his hip, at which point he pushed his hand through. The rift had the killer worried, leading him to act more cautiously than expected. A sign of weakness, at last, if not slightly too late.

Or was it? Just as the killer was about to overcome his sudden nervousness, he stopped. Something held him back, something strong. Nate assumed Cameron had regained consciousness and had grabbed the killer at the last minute. But the arm that was forcing the killer to yield was not Cameron's, or human for that matter.

"L'Armin," Nate called at the top of his voice.

L'Armin turned to face him. The sight of his injury appeared to have ignited something within; a strength that tensed L'Armin's entire body as he dug his fingers deep into the killer's shoulders. His eyes were deeply focused as he pulled his victim down to kneel before him.

The strength he demonstrated must have come from somewhere other than his muscles, somewhere beyond the physical. His grip caused the killer to shake involuntarily, like violent electrical shocks were shooting from his fingers and then on through the killer's entire body.

Nate watched for the few seconds the two were connected, with no idea of what he could do to help. Once again L'Armin had surprised him. But before he could decide, something changed.

Suddenly the concentration vanished from L'Armin's face. He let go and collapsed to the floor, sending the killer in the other direction. They landed in an entangled heap, with their legs jutting out from under them. Whatever L'Armin had done to the killer it had taken its toll on his own body as well.

Nate was compelled to get to his friend quickly. But his misjudged attempt to stand only resulted in his injured leg twisting underneath him again. "Shit," he cried out.

"Nate. Are you all right?" Helen said, appearing through the stationary crowd behind him.

"I think the bastard broke my leg."

"Let me help you up," she said, grabbing his arm.

Nate gratefully accepted the assistance. He pulled her arm unintentionally hard, nearly dragging her to the floor beside him. Eventually he managed to struggle to his feet, although his injured leg refused to take any of the weight. Once up he leant on a frozen person next to him. "Thanks buddy," he said to his unmoving helper.

"Where's Cameron?" Helen asked.

"I left him over there." Nate pointed to the raised area. "The killer knocked him out. Can you check he's OK? I need to get to L'Armin."

Helen did not argue. She headed off quickly in the direction Nate had gestured, leaving him to balance on his own. Things may have gone badly wrong but somehow they had stopped the assassin from escaping. And with Helen now cooperating to the fullest of her abilities and tending to Cameron, it seemed the end was finally in sight.

But it proved too difficult for him to move. A familiar pain was beginning to build in his head that kept him on the spot. He knew instantly it would continue to do so, until eventually overtaking the pain in his leg. L'Armin had explained the cause of it to him before. It was only a matter of time before it became too much once more.

"L'Armin?" he called, but heard nothing in return.

He forced himself to move and hopped a few feet to the next resting point—really just another statuesque patron, frozen on the spot. With each movement the pain in his head was increasing, until a loud static-like hiss perturbed the silence like a pick-axe through his skull.

All of a sudden the sight of L'Armin sprawled out on the floor began to bounce around his field of view. His head had begun to shake. He had no choice but to stop and clutch the sides of his ears, which had become dangerously hot.

Unlike before, he was sure he could hold on, at least for longer. He had gotten through it the last time after all. If he held on long enough to reach L'Armin, he knew he would be able to bring him back around just in time. If he did not he was not sure what would happen.

L'Armin had explained that when he was not able to keep the rifts open, it would revert to the memory holder. This meant Nate was now the only thing stopping the entire re-creation from collapsing around them. It did not help that one sentence played over and over inside his head: your mind was not prepared to take the strain of this place, L'Armin had said.

He was about to land another foot closer to L'Armin when the pain was again turned up. He had no idea how much more he could take. Just keeping L'Armin in view became a herculean task.

"Nate?" Helen called from behind him.

He could not turn to face her, the noise and searing pain had debilitated him. All he could manage in acknowledgement was a heavy exhalation of air that vibrated his lips, causing them to slap against each other. Sweat now entirely covered his face and body, which made holding onto anything nearly impossible.

187

Helen appeared again in front of him. She spoke in an extremely animated fashion, but Nate quickly realised he could no longer hear a word she was saying. Her mouth was moving, but all he heard was a sound akin to a million tons of thunderous and gushing water. His body just could not take any more.

In one last attempt at regaining control he leant against another of the motionless characters next to him. He grabbed at the man's arms, but the sweat inevitably caused him to lose his grip. The sensation of weightlessness suddenly overwhelmed him as he lost his balance and lurched forwards.

The ground was an unforgiving mattress of solid stone that punished his face as he landed against it. There was little he could do to stop himself. The pain had cut off any signals his brain sent to his extremities. To Helen he would have appeared to fall like a felled tree.

Strangely the injury he knew had befallen him upon contact with the ground, carried with it little feeling. He lay with his head to the side and nothing but Helen's shoes in focus. Everything slowly faded, until the only colour he could see was that of a small fleck of blood—that had emanated from his own nose, he assumed—on the side of Helen's left shoe.

And then the world was gone.

Chapter 16

Consciousness came and went in waves. One moment Nate was riding the tide toward a state of awareness, and the next he was being dragged back down to the black depths. The darkness always ended up winning in the end, however much he tried to fight against it.

Although brief, the few seconds he was awake between blackouts had at least allowed him to catch tiny snippets of dialogue.

"Nate? Can you hear me? It's Helen. Please wake up. Jesus, what do I do."

Helen's words became distant and muffled again. When her voice returned it was joined by someone else's. Time was passing much faster than Nate could grasp.

"What happened?" A Male voice. It was Cameron.

"I don't know. He told me to check on you. But then I saw him stop suddenly, so I went back," Helen replied.

"Did he just collapse?"

"Yes, I tried to get him up but he's too heavy. What do we do?"

"Just calm down and—"

Blackness again. Nate had no idea what he had missed each time he resurfaced. There was no time to find out before he was once again ripped away.

The next voice he heard was one he did not recognise at all. It was not Cameron or L'Armin speaking, though it was definitely a male voice. Whoever it was he could tell the person was within a short distance of him. Everything else remained too distant to be heard clearly.

Much more time had passed than before. But the veil of darkness that blocked out the world around him each time he lost consciousness did not arrive. He had expected the world to disappear, only for it to then reappear moments later, once again leaving him guessing the length of time that had passed him by. When this did not happen, Nate knew he was finally waking up properly.

A tiny point of light appeared suddenly for him to focus on. Slowly something was coming forward through the emptiness. It took him a little while to realise his eyes were slightly open and were allowing a sliver of light to pass through. The world had returned and with it a tingly feeling began to spread throughout his whole body.

He no longer lay on his front, face down in the dirt— the ground was not pressing against his nose or cheek, so he was confident about this at least. He assumed Helen or Cameron had flipped him over, no doubt while trying to wake him. As for the rest of him, he was still too numb to determine his overall condition.

His limbs felt distant, almost like they had become detached from his body and were floating around somewhere nearby. When he tried to rub his eyes—as he always did when awakening from a bad dream—he lost control of his arm, with no idea where it was heading. It soon made contact with something unexpectedly, possibly the floor to his side, he could not tell. The disorientation had destroyed his sense of self.

After three failed attempts at opening his eyes, he gave it one last try, though with a disturbing amount of effort. Once he had managed to separate the lids, he opened his eyes wide and was immediately disappointed by the distorted and blurry scene he saw.

The light was trying desperately to shine through a film of sleep that coated his eyes, but not enough could get through. It took a couple of quick blinks to clean up the image completely. Then, with his sight restored, he surveyed the world around him and noticed how much dimmer it was than expected.

Again he could hear a voice in the background that he did not recognise. He could make out a rhythm to the words the person used—but not the language—and it sounded to him like some sort of a chant. It was repeated over and over again, without a gap in between. It was strange, but he found the quietness around him even stranger.

"Hello?" Nate said with a croak.

A ruffled noise to the side of him momentarily broke the flow of the chanting, though the person continued soon afterwards. Someone else was there and they were responding to his call. He could hear their footsteps approaching him.

"Cameron quick," Helen said. "He's awake."

Seconds later, Nate looked up and saw two faces staring back down at him. The blurriness had gone completely so he recognised his friends straight away, along with their worried expressions. Cameron was still garnishing a nasty bruise to the side of his head. Helen, however, was as beautiful as ever. She had tied her blond hair back into a pony tail at some point during his comatose state.

"Sir?" Cameron said. "Can you hear me?"

"I can hear you. What happened?"

"You collapsed right in front of me. Scared the shit out of me," Helen said.

"Sorry about that. Where's L'Armin?"

Both Cameron and Helen looked away and then to each other. Despite feeling slightly hazy, Nate could still interpret their hesitation to answer. Something was making them appear on edge and it was obvious L'Armin was involved. Neither of them appeared willing to reveal a thing to him.

"Best you see for yourself, sir," Cameron said.

Nate tried to sit up by himself, but only made it halfway. He let out a grunt as the exhaustion set in again and began slowly pushing him back down. Cameron had to

191

pull him the rest of the way, until eventually Nate was sitting up on his own.

He took a moment to locate his limbs, once and for all, before finally rubbing away the muck from his vision. At this point he noticed the sky above and immediately became enthralled by it.

"Where the hell are we?" he said, staring nervously at a red sky decorated with even redder clouds. They were a long way away from the likes of his memories of the bar. This was something he had never seen before, he was certain of that.

"We've no idea," Helen began. Again she turned and looked to the side as she spoke. "But we think he caused it."

Once he could bring himself to look away from the unusual sky overhead, Nate reluctantly peered over to where the chanting still continued. To his surprise, L'Armin had been joined by another member of his race. The man was dressed similarly, with loosely fitted clothing and an equally wrinkled complexion—a shared feature of his race after all. The chanting appeared to be another of their people's rituals.

The man sat on the floor with his hands hovering a few inches above L'Armin's. His eyes remained closed as the words flowed out of his mouth almost automatically. Over and over again the lines were repeated, with barely enough time to take a breath, before they started again.

Nate's heart sunk. He watched, fearful that his friend lying motionless on the cold, rocky floor had been lost. Was the ritual the other man performed for the death of a loved one? Nate desperately hoped not. It was not until he saw a deep breath enter L'Armin's body, that the sudden and growing feeling of loss was stunted.

"He's OK," Helen said, sensing his concern.

"Thanks. So did he just appear?" Nate arched his head in the direction of the stranger.

"Yes, then the bar disappeared and we found ourselves here. Wherever here is."

192

The bar had indeed vanished along with all signs of the drunken beings, who Nate was sure he had been among only seconds before. What had replaced it was far more threatening, with a red sky above offset by a dark purple and rocky landscape below.

In the distance, Nate could make out huge cavernous gouges throughout the scene, as well as large towering spire-like mountain ranges. Wherever they had been transported, it was a harsh and unforgiving place.

A dry and particulate wind lashed at his bare skin, stinging slightly as it sped past. The air lacked any moisture too and made light work of removing what little he had had in his mouth. Within minutes he could feel small cracks on his lips, as well as tiny grains of black sand sticking to his face.

"I've never seen a place like this before," he said, removing a small piece of grit from his tongue.

"I doubt any of us have, sir," Cameron said. "All we've been able to ascertain is that we're on some kind of rocky plateau."

Only ten or so metres ahead, Nate could see where it ended sharply. Beyond this were other raised areas, similar to theirs, stretching out for many miles around them. They appeared to be roughly in the middle of a large group of plateaus, each many tens of square metres in area. It was a precarious position to be in and one he was not about to risk exploring alone in his unsteady state.

Separating each raised platform were dark areas of almost black sand that looked like veins against the brighter rocks above. The continual gusts of wind were kicking up the sand in some areas and creating clouds of black material. Although short lived, they were capable of travelling quite far, as proven by the light dusting of dark sand across the top of each plateau.

"Can you help me up?" Nate asked, feebly. He had seen all he wanted of the surrounding geology.

Both Helen and Cameron made a clumsy grab for the same arm. Helen quickly let go and moved around to the

193

other side to take Nate's right arm instead. Gradually they hauled him to his feet and then held him in place. He shifted the weight from his left leg as soon as he felt the pain return. Though not as bad as before, it remained enough to cause him to hop on the spot until his other leg had taken the added strain.

"Any idea what we do now?" Helen said. "This was your plan after all."

The plan, of course, Nate suddenly remembered. The killer had to be there, but where? After a quick survey of the surrounding area he spotted the body of the assassin. It was in the same place as earlier. They had left it alone and still in an awkward position, like it had been dumped there with little thought.

"Has the killer moved at all?" Nate said.

"No. He's been like that since you collapsed. Our friend here moved L'Armin away so we left him." Cameron squinted, appearing slightly confused. "I don't understand what we can do, he's out for the count."

"I haven't quite figured that out yet," Nate said. "The plan ended once we caught him. I need to talk to L'Armin. Any idea how he's doing?"

"None, sir. He hasn't moved much."

The man seeing to L'Armin stood and finished one more verse of his chant. With the ritual coming to an end, he began to wrap up any loose ends by checking his friend over one more time. He straightened out L'Armin's loose clothing, in a show of dedication and respect. Once this had been completed he turned and made a beeline for Nate. It stopped their conversation dead in its tracks.

"In-coming," Cameron said.

During his determined march toward them, the man locked his sights solely on Nate. It was obvious he was intending to speak with them and that the matter was urgent—as made evident by his quick pace.

"Please accompany me, Nathan Maddox," he said.

Before Nate could reply the man had already wandered off toward the sharp drop at the edge of their plateau. It may have only been a few metres away, but the distance was still far enough to cause considerable difficulty to Nate. He hopped a few steps until his balance once again failed, sending him lurching into the supportive arms of Cameron.

"I'm fine," Nate said, knowing he was not really. "Can you both keep an eye on L'Armin for me?"

Helen nodded and then pulled Cameron gently by the arm. They walked slowly away, with a look back every now and then. Neither of them spoke as they left Nate to hobble away on his damaged limb.

There was an aura of authority to the person Nate cautiously approached, which distilled an uneasiness in him. The man's stance was straight like an upright pencil, with his arms tightly crossed. He was the polar opposite to L'Armin, who had always been courteous and joyful, like a kind old gentleman. It appeared to be a personality trait not shared by all of their race.

Eventually, Nate pulled up level and was about to lean against the man when he suddenly thought better of it. The caring nature L'Armin had showed was not guaranteed to be present in this fellow. It was awkward, though Nate was able to balance with his left leg just about touching the ground; more like a bike stabiliser than a full working wheel.

After a moment of silence, the man spoke. "I allowed this to go too far," he said.

Nate did not know what to say. Perhaps things had gone too far. After all, he and L'Armin could have been severely hurt, or killed. And for what? As far as he could tell the plan had failed miserably and the evidence was no closer than before. Without it the killer was still a free man.

Thankfully Nate was not expected to speak, only to listen.

"My name is L'Eshran." The man stared out across the endless and desolate vista that stretched out before them. He did not face Nate at all, as he continued, "I have been watching. It was wrong of me to listen to L'Armin, he was not able to control this as he had promised. He is a fool, but he is the oldest and wisest fool of all of us." He paused for a moment, then turned just enough for Nate to see the rest of his face. "Do you know where we are, Nathan Maddox?"

The stern look on L'Eshran's face told Nate not to answer. Instead he chose a spot of the landscape, at random, and stared at it. Almost as though the answers were hidden between the dark ridges he gazed upon, scattered as far as the eye could see.

"This is my race's only memory of the Dark Times. L'Armin's memory."

The two just did not match. How L'Armin's gentle nature could have survived in such a hellish place without any signs of wear at all, eluded Nate. He could not understand how a place could even exist, let alone how anyone managed to live there. Only a nightmare could be compared with it.

"L'Armin was once here?" Nate said. The urge to know more had taken over.

"Yes. He is older than you know. This was centuries ago, before we escaped. I was born many years later, as was everyone else here. L'Armin is the last of those who left our home-world, so long ago."

"To escape what?"

"Enslavement. L'Armin told you this. Our ability was abused for others' gain."

Nate felt a sudden pang of guilt.

"This was our home." L'Eshran waved his arm from right to left, sweeping across their view of the rocky and foreboding landscape ahead. "But that was our past." He pointed down, gesturing to something below.

A growing cloud of dust and black sand was moving along the ground between their plateau and the one nearest. At first Nate thought it was just the wind stirring up the loose ground material again. But it was moving, rather unexpectedly, at a steady pace and in a straight line.

"What's that?" Nate asked.

L'Eshran did not speak. He stood with his finger extended as straight as possible, forming an unbroken line that ran from his shoulder to his fingertip, and then down to the dust cloud below. He said nothing as the scene played out by itself.

As the air began to clear, Nate could make out a familiar face. It was L'Armin and his clothing was no longer the loose and casual type he usually wore. Instead, they appeared ragged and torn, with dark, dirty patches on the knees and elbows that suggested he had been crawling at some point. More worrying, however, was the collection of scars across his chest and face. They did not appear to have completely healed either.

He was surrounded by odd looking creatures, each sat atop a saddled four-legged beast that snarled and grunted with its one large, downward facing tusk proudly on display. They were seething with anger at something L'Armin had evidently done. In frustration the riders began slapped their chests like gorillas, while managing to project as much spit as hatred, although they looked more like humanoid crustaceans than anything else.

The five huge beasts they rode, were each eyeing L'Armin up like an impromptu snack. He cowered on the spot, visibly shrinking as he crossed his beaten and bruised arms. To these creatures he had have served as no more than a plaything, if they were allowed to have him.

Nate tried to listen to the conversation. But their language was unlike any he had ever heard before, with lots of speedy clicks and snorts. He had no idea what they were saying, though it was certain the person next to him did. Without even realising he was doing it, L'Eshran had begun to copy the words under his breath.

"This was my people's way of life," L'Eshran said once the shouting had ceased below them. "It can never happen again. Do you understand why I am showing you this, Nathan?"

Nate thought for a moment before giving an answer he was sure was correct. "You have my word, I will never reveal your secret to anyone."

L'Eshran spun around to look at Nate directly. The obvious and sudden annoyance had pulled his face inwards, temporarily introducing a number of extra ruffles to his skin. Nate's ignorance was not at all appreciated, or tolerated.

"That is not why," he said. "L'Armin is the only living record of my people's past. With him gone the lesson we learnt so many years ago, will lose its impetus. We brought the abuse onto ourselves by helping those who did not deserve it. Now we simply do not help, even if we can. L'Armin wanted to show us it was time to change that."

Finally Nate was beginning to understand what L'Eshran was telling him. They were content to trust him with their secret, so long as it did not put L'Armin at risk. The small snippets of information he had been given were all he had needed to know at the time. L'Armin had been holding back the rest, including anything that revealed the danger he may have been putting himself in.

So with L'Armin out cold it had fallen to L'Eshran to limit the damage, which he did by taking the opportunity to make the potential risks as clear as possible. The scene that continued below them was unarguably the best demonstration of what was at stake. In the grand scheme of things, it was obvious that Nate's problem was inconsequential in comparison to their own.

"I had no idea …" Nate began.

"It was as much my decision as his to proceed. No, the blame is with me."

By now the L'Armin far below them had been threatened to within an inch of his life. The next minute or so they watched as he was forcibly ushered into a small metallic cage. His captors showed little, if any, concern for L'Armin's wellbeing. At every opportunity they kicked him, slapped him and poked him with implements of punishment.

Within a relatively short amount of time, the entire group was racing away and once again kicking up a growing cloud of black sand. They headed back in the direction they had taken while chasing their escapee. Although the dust surrounding them was thickening, it was still fine enough for the image of L'Armin clutching his cage bars, to shine through. An image that was instantly burnt into Nate's permanent memory.

"You have the killer, yes?" L'Eshran said, finally breaking the sudden silence that had followed the scene below.

"Yes, but—"

"Then you are finished."

"Well no, you see—"

"We cannot help you any further, Nathan. I have shown you what will come of helping others. This must stop now."

L'Eshran turned away before Nate could continue his attempt to explain the original plan. He walked back to the others, leaving Nate with nothing more than the rough textured wind for company. It was no good, the matter had been settled and the motion passed. Whatever evidence existed, it was still just beyond his reach.

Cameron left Helen, who had not moved from L'Armin's side, and walked over. He avoided eye contact with L'Eshran as they passed each other. "What did he say?" he asked.

Nate did not know where to start. So much had happened in the few minutes he and L'Eshran had spoken, that he could not remember what Cameron already knew and what he did not. He had completely lost track himself.

"Well, he told me that L'Armin is older than we thought," Nate said. It was all he could say for certain as he mentally grappled with the rest.

"Really? Huh. Looks good for his age."

All Nate could do was chuckle at the ease with which Cameron made light of things. Whether appropriate or not, he could not care less. It simply felt good to laugh, if only for a brief moment.

"I think we're done here, too," Nate said, instantly resetting the mood to neutral. "They can't help us anymore."

"So what about him?" Cameron pointed to the assassin.

"I have no idea. I'm not sure we can prove any of this actually happened. I guess we could search him at least."

"I suppose. But it's unlikely he'll have any—"

"Nate," Helen called. "L'Armin is waking up."

With a quick nod to Cameron they were soon on their way. The three legged gait they adopted proved difficult to maintain without forcing Nate's injured leg down every other step. It shot a pain up the entire length of his back each time it touched the ground. Even so, he could feel that it was easing ever so slightly. Either that or the joy of hearing L'Armin had come around was temporarily masking it.

"L'Armin, can you hear me?" L'Eshran said, as he pulled his friend up into a seated position.

Cameron helped Nate down to the floor beside L'Armin the moment they arrived. It was too early to get any response from him. His eyes stared at the sky and still seemed empty of all life. If it were not for L'Eshran holding him up, Nate was sure L'Armin would have fallen back down again by now. The only clear proof of life was his shallow breathing. Which by itself had everyone watching nervously.

Two more large breaths later and L'Armin was finally beginning to come around fully. Slowly an, undoubtedly confused, consciousness was appearing behind his eyes. They focused and immediately dilated in response to the dim surroundings.

Nate hovered in front, waiting eagerly to greet his friend. He and L'Eshran were already well within L'Armin's field of view, yet they moved in further regardless. The moment L'Armin settled his gaze upon him, Nate felt a wealth of emotions suddenly hit. At the forefront was an immense feeling of relief.

"Nathan?" L'Armin finally said, with a smile creeping through.

"Christ. You scared me there," Nate replied. "What happened?"

Gradually L'Armin sat forward. He placed a hand across his forehead and held it there as he looked around. A perplexed expression stretched across his face that drew his forehead and his lower jaw down an inch or two. Nate could see he was trying to work out why he was sat on the floor.

His gaze moved about the ground in front of him as he visibly grappled with the answer. He then noticed the footprints left in the dirt all around him and began to follow them. They trailed away from his position and continued all the way back to the killer's body, a few metres away. His left eyebrow raised the moment he spotted it.

L'Eshran moved purposefully, until he was directly in front of L'Armin and blocking out everyone else. When their eyes met, the mood quickly changed. The small grin that had begun to form on L'Armin's face disappeared. The sight of L'Eshran had removed it completely.

"Hello my friend," L'Eshran said.

L'Armin opened his mouth, ready to speak, when he noticed the world around him. Whatever he was about to say was no longer relevant. Something else much more devastating had now taken his attention away.

"No," he began. "Why … why did you bring them here? You had no right."

"It's over." L'Eshran took L'Armin by the shoulders to make sure what he said next was completely understood. "We're finished helping these people."

Nate had not known L'Armin to be aggressive at any point during their time together. But that was about to change. Being ordered to stop had caused cracks to form in his friendly disposition. He chose to make his disagreement abundantly clear by moving his head away and dismissing L'Eshran's words entirely.

"It is not over," he said.

"Have you forgotten what it cost us before?"

201

"Forgotten?" L'Armin suddenly refocused. "I remember exactly how much it cost. Your family were nearly among those that were lost, or have *you* forgotten *that*." He pierced the air between them with an accusing finger.

"And of course I am eternally grateful for that, but please look at yourself, L'Armin. I beg of you, end this now. Before we lose you, like we almost have before."

"I am not as frail as you all think. I may be the oldest and I may miss the times when we were brave enough to help others. But I am not frail. I can and will help these people."

L'Eshran stood and carefully stepped back. The frustration from having failed to get through to his elder brought about a loud sigh as he then turned away. His audible disappointment marked the end of their short but heartfelt argument.

Nate wanted to help in some way, but he was worried he had only made matters worse by wading in. Then again, the suggestion that it was not the first time the situation had occurred had him leaning toward a decision that would end the discussion completely. Stopping was the only real choice they had left. The problem was convincing L'Armin.

"You've done enough for me, L'Armin. Please, I think it's best we stop," Nate said to the surprise of Cameron and Helen. He was on L'Armin's side, but even *he* could see how unwise it was to continue. L'Eshran's concerns had become too hard to deny.

For a moment L'Armin appeared surprised by Nate's decision, too. But a slight grin once again creased his face, soon after.

"That will not be necessary, Nathan. I have what you require," he said calmly.

Everyone stopped on the spot. The curiosity was now airborne and highly infectious. Nate was not alone in his suffering either, with the whole group having caught the bug. They turned to one another with blank looks, until each came to the same conclusion: L'Armin had done more than simply stop the killer from escaping.

Each began to celebrate with smiles of varying wideness. Cameron even went as far as slapping L'Armin on the back, his excitement was once again flowing all too freely. L'Eshran, however, lowered his head and placed both hands on his waist. He wanted nothing more to do with it.

"What do you mean? What did you do to him?" Nate pointed to the killer as he spoke.

"I think I may have pushed myself a little too hard. His mind was strong. He resisted me much longer than I'd expected."

"Did you find something in there?" Nate said, aware that Helen and Cameron were watching with interest. If they had not known something important was being withheld before, they surely did now.

Helen fidgeted excitedly next to L'Armin. She had figured something out and was fast becoming like a rolling and unmanned train, barrelling dangerously ahead without the self-restraint to pull the breaks on her inquisition. It was coming and when it eventually hit, Nate knew she would be unstoppable.

Cameron on the other hand appeared happy enough to let it go. He hardly noticed the odd conversation Nate and L'Armin were having. Instead, he continued to watch with a blank look on his face that suggested he thought it all above his pay grade.

"I did. A memory that serves your purpose well," L'Armin said.

Helen gently placed her hand on Nate's shoulder to draw his attention. He ignored her and desperately attempted to avoid the inevitable, at least for the moment. Too much had been discussed in front of her to keep it a secret any longer. For the time being he chose rudeness over honesty.

"Can you show us? I mean, is it safe for you to show us?" Nate continued, while keeping his eye contact with Helen to a minimum.

This time she pulled at his arm and with much more force than before. She was becoming impatient with every word he and L'Armin exchanged.

"I believe so. The memory is now shared between myself and the killer. We must be quick though, it will not last long. I will need some help to open the rift, too. I fear I may be slightly weak," L'Armin finally admitted.

"Got it. And thank you," Nate said.

The patience had now run out for Helen. She pulled Nate's arm back so hard that it tugged uncomfortably at the shoulder socket. It forced him to face her.

"What's going on?" she said, with a scornful expression painted across her face.

Nate turned away. He shared an unspoken exchange with L'Armin, who returned his answer by shaking his head. It was all Nate needed to see. L'Armin was understandably reluctant to tell Helen, or anyone else, the truth. The risk to his people was already too high. It highlighted just how much trust they had placed in Nate by telling him.

"It's the rings, like you told me," Nate said.

Helen did not buy it for a second and instead pushed again for a proper answer. "But it's more than that isn't it?"

"I don't know."

"Bullshit," she snapped.

"It's complicated OK? These Ring Beings are able to do some weird shit. Look, there's something more pressing that we need to do."

Nate turned away again, using his shoulder as a temporary barrier between them this time. L'Armin sent him a smile. His discretion had been noted.

"Are you absolutely sure you want to do this, L'Armin?" Nate asked.

"Yes. We must finish what we started."

"But what about what L'Eshran said?"

"I appreciate your concern, Nathan. But we have come too far to give up. L'Eshran worries for me because I am the oldest. He does not understand the ability our people have, as I do. It was meant to be used in this way."

"I've seen what you went through in this place, though. I have to say, I kind of agree with him. Is it worth the risk to carry on? We can find the evidence another way, surely."

"This is the best way. The assassin has many secrets and he has kept them for a very long time. He will not tell you anything. What I have found will show you exactly what you need. You will have little time to find it, however. Even with L'Eshran's help, we must hurry."

"Really?"

"Yes, time is limited."

"In that case, let's do it. I promise we'll be quick as well." Nate turned back to Helen, but she spoke before he had the chance to.

"We?" she said, surprised.

Nate smiled with excitement. "You said you wanted to see proof. Well, this is it."

Finally Helen's fidgeting had stopped.

Chapter 17

Nate's leg still throbbed as Helen helped him struggle to his feet. It took some of the weight, although he had little confidence in its support. He could feel the muscles twitch while a shooting pain ran up and down it. If he remained still, it settled. Unfortunately, staying still was the last thing he wanted to do.

He knew he was lucky to have come away with only a few injuries. His younger self had sustained much more damage and he had survived that. This is nothing, he thought, just an inconvenience. His confidence lasted until another bout of pain spread through him.

Nate looked across to Cameron, who tended his own bruises with spit and a folded handkerchief. He was looking slightly unsteady on his feet as he dabbed his head. That he could manage to stand at all was a testament to the dedication he had to the job. Considering someone almost half his size had knocked him clean out. Which Nate suspected had hurt much more than any physical injuries.

The memory he and Helen were about to witness had a very real chance of placing Cameron in the roll of the intended fall-guy. He did not deserve that, he had already been through enough in Nate's eyes. Still, Stuart framing Cameron as the killer had an unavoidable logic to it that he resented being privy to.

All he could do for now was hope. The answers were only moments away.

"You ready?" Nate said to Helen, who nervously bit her bottom lip.

"I still don't understand how you're going to show me. If these Ring Beings are responsible, then what did L'Armin do?" she said, once again pushing for answers he did not want to give.

"Just trust me OK?" he replied, followed by a hop.

She helped him move by placing an arm around his back and tucking her head neatly under his other arm, before then pushing up. Nate was immediately pleased to feel a portion of his weight disappear. He still tried his best not to lean on her too much. He did not want to test her strength to breaking point.

As they were about to head over to L'Eshran, Cameron stopped them. "Can I just say something, sir," he said with a disheartened look on his face.

Helen spoke before Nate had a chance. "Make it quick," she said.

"Sure. I want to apologise for failing you earlier. I should have had this under control. I didn't, and I'm sorry for that."

Nate just about managed to hold back his anger. He was furious. How could Cameron think he had done anything wrong? The truth was the complete opposite and he needed to know it. If not for his own poor balance, Nate would have grabbed Cameron by the arms and shaken him vigorously, until he agreed he had done exactly the right thing. Thinking anything else was just absurd.

"*None* of this is your fault, Cameron, none of it. You saved my life. I'm standing here now because of you. So you've nothing to apologise for, especially to me. OK?" he said.

"Yes, sir," Cameron replied. His unwillingness to look directly at Nate suggested he was agreeing reluctantly.

"Now, the killer is still out cold. I need you to tie him up or something, keep him secure until we're back."

"No problem. He'll be sleeping for a while, I'll make sure this time," Cameron said while rubbing the discoloured side of his face again with his handkerchief. The attention he had lavished on his wound appeared to have reddened it further.

"Look after L'Armin as well. He's a little dazed, I think," Nate said.

"Will do."

Cameron trundled over to the killer at a laboured pace that implied he still thought he had let the group down. Nate knew otherwise. He was certain all of the blame should be placed at his own feet. No-one would have been in danger had he not been hell-bent on catching the assassin in the first place. Cameron's apology may have been unnecessary, but his own was still due.

While making little attempt to do so carefully, Cameron began roughly pulling the killer's lifeless body into a seated position. He had absolutely no fear of waking the sleeping monster that still haunted Nate. Or was the lack of fear actually anger? Nate could not tell. He took a moment to consider whether he should be more concerned about Cameron killing the monster, than the other way around.

With L'Eshran and L'Armin staying behind, Nate decided he was happy enough to leave Cameron with the assassin. Besides, there was something more delicate he had to attend to anyway. He still needed to get L'Eshran on board. Without his help, they were going nowhere.

Nate and Helen cautiously approached L'Eshran. Neither of them really wanted to be the one who had to speak. The anger L'Eshran had shown earlier would surely be aimed at them this time, and they would deserve it too. So when the moment came, they stopped and silently stared at each other, hoping the other would begin talking. Nate soon realised that he had no choice.

"L'Eshran? Can we have a word?" he said.

There was no reply. L'Eshran stood with his back still facing them. There was no reaction at all to their question, not even a flinch. For a little while they could only interpret and anticipate his mood. He had at least moved in the last few minutes. Although with his arms now firmly crossed, reciprocity was not in any way inferred.

"L'Eshran?" Nate said again.

Finally a reaction. L'Eshran lowered his head to meet his chest, before returning upright again seconds later. He let out a long breath and then turned to face them.

"As you wish," he said. "I will assist you. But after this you must all leave."

Nate was surprised by the sudden answer. He had not even asked anything yet. There was no time to reply either, before L'Eshran walked away to join L'Armin. The two had obviously spoken about it already, telepathically no less, and were eager to start.

After a quick hobble back, Nate and Helen were also ready to begin—although Nate had a growing sense of worry that he kept to himself. He nodded to L'Armin and L'Eshran, who both returned his gesture. If the others felt as nervous as he did, they were equally as good at hiding it.

L'Armin held his hands together and closed his eyes. He remained sitting down. A frown began to form as he concentrated hard. L'Eshran did the same but remained standing, still much straighter than was ever necessary. A bead of sweat ran down L'Armin's nose as he tried to open another rift. It would have to be the last time he asked his friend to do this, Nate decided. It was clearly taking it out of him.

The moment the rift popped open, Helen moved her hand off Nate's chest and covered her eyes. It was bright, but it was not overwhelming his sight as much as before. As he peered in he was sure he could make out more of the rift this time. However ethereal a thing it was, there was substance and possibly even a structure to it that he had not seen before.

Nate could feel the bones in Helen's shoulder as he continued to lean into her. Their muscles worked in sync, tightening every time they stepped nearer to the rift. After a few more she placed her hand back on Nate's chest for

209

extra support, sending a warmth through him. It took the edge off of the pain temporarily.

"Ready?" Nate said.

"Sure, it's the same as before. Right?" she replied, with her eyes only slightly open.

He smirked slightly as he began to lead the way forward. Helen stayed put until the last possible moment, only moving when he physically began to pull her along with him. It was then—and only then—that she reluctantly followed.

Soon her grip of him began to squeeze his chest and push forcefully against his ribs. She was not enjoying the sensation at all, Nate saw. He wrapped his arms around her protectively, to show he was still there with her. The more into the light they strayed, the more her grasp had become an embrace.

Once through they found themselves in the middle of a small crowd making its way down a long hallway. Nate had to suddenly leap to the side just to avoid them. He instantly regretted the sudden jerk he was forced to inflict on his body.

After a quick check he was thankful to see Helen was OK. She was still unwilling to let go until her sight had returned fully, but she was unharmed. Once she had regained her vision she rubbed her eyes. When she realised how close she had gotten to Nate she was compelled to create a little more distance between them. She seemed a little embarrassed.

"Where are we?" she said. After a quick look around she suddenly pointed to a plaque mounted on the wall at the end of the hallway. "This is the third floor of the hotel. Why are we here?"

Nate saw a row of lifts next to where Helen had spotted the sign. A steady flow of guests entered and exited them, all following their preordained paths. Surely the killer would not use them? No, Nate was certain.

"Because the killer is somewhere in here. This is his memory," Nate said while surveying the faces scurrying to catch one of the lifts, just in case he had been wrong to assume the killer was not there.

The doors along the hall were numbered in a few different languages. The usual selection were on display. But—as was normally the case—none of them were recognisably human. Most people would have taken this as a sign that they had ventured too far. Not so for Nate. He was used to this, after so many years far from home.

He gestured to the text above the nearest door. "They don't get many visitors from Earth here do they?"

"You're the one who asked for somewhere different," Helen replied rather sharply.

Nate brushed off Helen's change in tone and continued to assess the area. He knew that behind one of the wooden doors, inlaid with decorative brass strips, rest the final conclusive proof. But which room was it? The hall was long and with more than ten on each side, too many to search by themselves. Besides, L'Armin had warned that time was limited. They needed another way.

It occurred to him that the bastard had had the gall to use a normal visitor room. The killer was far too confident. He had never even tried to hide. This only infuriated Nate further; another irritation to accompany his many others.

"Any idea where to start? Room service?" Nate joked.

Helen threw his arm away, nearly sending him tumbling to the floor. "How should I know which bloody room it is," she said.

"I'm sorry. I didn't mean to—"

"I got what you meant. You still think I knew about all of this, don't you?"

"I don't. I mean, I didn't. Look, I know I can trust you."

"Then show it." She crossed her arms and stubbornly refused to continue any further. "What did L'Armin do earlier?"

It was hopeless. He could see he had no choice. The ambush had him completely off kilter. She had kept all of her anger squirrelled away until they were alone. All of the wriggle room he had before was now but a distant memory. Here and now, he had nowhere to go. She had him dead centre in her headlights.

If he told her, it would be a betrayal to L'Armin and L'Eshran. But equally, if he kept it from her any longer it would undermine his argument. The dilemma had him totally stymied. He had tried to bluff it earlier and failed. It came down to whose trust he would have to break. He just hoped L'Armin would understand he had no real choice. She had him trapped and time was rapidly running out.

"Fine. But this is something that cannot be shared, under any circumstances," he said, while finding something else to lean against. A small bin to his side fit the bill perfectly.

Helen's closed posture faltered slightly as the conversation shifted in tone. Her arms remained linked, but they had since dropped a few inches.

"L'Armin's people are capable of more than you know. They are the ones doing all of this, not the Beings."

"Really?" Helen said. "So it's them? Why not tell people that?"

"Because if everyone knew it would leave them open to abuse. It happened to them before. So you can't tell anybody this. Do you understand? They would lose more than you can imagine if it ever got out."

Helen nodded. Her eyes were wide with amazement as her brain feasted upon the newly gained knowledge. The secret was out. Nate just hoped it did not prove fatal. No-one gained anything from revealing it anyway, only someone spiteful would share it. He knew that was not in her nature. After all he had known her for a few years and he was sure he had an accurate depiction of her character.

He tried to move their attention away from the betrayal that ate at his insides, by approaching the nearest door and knocking politely. Immediately he missed the comforting balance the bin had afforded him. When no-one answered he gestured to Helen to do the same on the door opposite. But again there was no answer.

All of the heat in his body began to congregate in his head as he continued to struggle with his guilt. It caused the hallway to stretch and bend in front of him. He could picture L'Armin's face and he looked sad, like he had been crying. Nate wondered just how connected they had become. He could almost feel his presence in the hallway, like an ethereal mind, hovering and judging. And he was not at all happy about his secret having escaped from Nate's lips.

Behind him a door slammed shut unexpectedly. It startled him, breaking his mind free of the guilt ridden daydream. He spun around and saw that a guest had exited their room and was wandering toward the stairs, at the opposite end of the hall to the lifts.

Once satisfied that this person was not the killer, he continued his search in the other direction—with a slightly faster heartbeat than before. He could see ahead that Helen had continued knocking on doors, oblivious to his distracted state. He could also see there was no way for him to reach her quickly without doing himself more damage. Instead he tried the handle of the door he had already knocked on. Just in case it was that easy. But once again, nothing.

"Over here," Helen called to him.

Nate turned to see her following closely behind a disturbingly familiar figure, heading his way. The assassin's head was covered as expected, and with only the reflection of the lights to discern the eyes; just pin-pricks hidden beneath a veil of black. He wore the same long overcoat garment, which parted slightly with each step he took. Almost casually—even nonchalantly—he strolled along the corridor, not at all like he was planning a murder.

None of the guests reacted to him as he walked past. He had obviously exited a lift in his usual stealthy manner. Except, in the more welcoming surroundings of the hotel, he now appeared much less threatening. At least relative to the others that inhabited the hotel, in all their various shapes and colours.

The killer was once again on the loose, and worst of all, comfortable in plain sight. This filled Nate with sudden dread. He had been much closer to death then he had realised. During his first day at the hotel he may have passed the killer on multiple occasions and never known it.

It was impossible for Nate to work out when this scene had occurred. It could have been before or after the attempt on his life, he could not tell. As the killer approached, the answer mattered less and less to him. He tried his best to remind himself that this version of the monster had no teeth and was totally harmless. But it did little to stem his trepidation. Tame beasts can still turn, he thought.

"Which room is yours then, you son-of-a-bitch," he said.

With Helen in tow the killer stopped by a room, turned to face the door and produced a key. Then, with a wary look down the hall—in both directions—he unlocked the room and quickly entered, leaving the door to shut by itself. Nate and Helen followed closely behind and soon found themselves deep within the beast's lair.

Inside the room there appeared to be nothing out of the ordinary. It was fairly standard. Although not as high a standard as Nate's room. He felt a perverted sense of satisfaction at having noticed this.

The pair of them watched the assassin in silence, too scared to make a sound. He walked to a spot two or so metres from the door, and began to run his hand across the smooth surface of the wall. There was nothing there, at least that Nate could see. Yet the killer's odd procedure was purposeful and suggested otherwise, like he was searching for something.

Whatever was there took a few seconds to materialize, followed by a beam of light that emanated out to the opposite wall. It was a small box that the killer had hidden somehow. It had been invisible before.

After deactivating what Nate assumed must have been a security warning system or booby-trap, the killer headed over to the bed. There in the middle sat another device, this

214

time a small black cube no more than fifteen or so centimetres in size and with urgently flashing lights along its top edge. It sat inside a large, brushed metal case that lay open, with its hinged lid resting flat on the bed behind.

Next to it in the padded case was an empty and suspiciously shaped slot. Nate knew right away that this was where the killer's weapon would normally reside. He shuddered at the thought. His face still tingled long after the shot had gone off so close to him. It had not left any more than a mental scare, luckily.

Helen stood next to him as they continued to spy on the killer. He could feel her hand on his arm, a protective gesture that he appreciated. They watched as the killer went about his business.

He did not appear to be in any rush or panic. Everything he did was with thought and accuracy, with nothing placed randomly or even at uneven angles. Each and every item was placed exactly as the killer's compulsive nature dictated. Perhaps it was a sign of apprehension about the job he had been tasked with. This hinted to Nate that it was before the attempt on his life.

A quick peek to the window confirmed it for him. The large beam of light that had marked the start of the festival had not been lit yet. There was still time for the killer to attend to other matters.

The flashing device was next on the agenda. The assassin began by folding out the top half into two pieces. Now its surface was double the original size. It appeared to be a computer, with strange keys spread out around a coin sized lens in the middle.

After a few taps of the keys the middle section sprung into life. It projected a hovering and semi-transparent display above, with a number of busy icons all whizzing about. Every input the assassin made altered the icons in some way, causing things to shoot about the display in mid-air.

"What do you suppose he's doing?" Helen whispered.

"I have no idea," Nate said as he moved closer to the device. He tried his best to make out any words that were possibly hidden among the icons. But it was all gibberish to him, hardly recognisable as a language at all.

It meant something to the killer though. He worked with fluid motions, his hands darting from side to side. He moved things around the air like a child playing intently with its favourite toy. Every now and again he held an object for longer and studied it with his nose as much as his eyes. Nate suspected the killer was once again picking up more than was immediately apparent.

After a minute or so of tapping and swiping at the air, he finally stopped and turned his attention to something in his pocket. Whatever it was it rustled as he manipulated it. He eventually produced a piece of paper, which Helen recognised straight away.

"Wait …" she managed to say before the realisation had hit her. "I gave him that. I don't understand."

The killer flattened out the paper on the bed, patting it until satisfied with its shape. He then produced another device from the metal case, which beeped politely as he activated it. With the paper held up in his left hand, he waved the device over the paper with his right. It lit up and began to send a horizontal line of green light up and down the blank page.

Line by line an image began to form on the hovering display. Nate and Helen watched intently as the picture slowly formed in front of them. By the end of the process, a fairly detailed digital representation of the recently appointed head of Maddox Industries had appeared. Even though it was unquestionably his likeness, some small details had been lost, no doubt because of the unusual way it had reached the killer.

"No," Helen said, leaning back against the nearby wall. "I gave him the details of the hit."

Nate turned his back to the killer and focused on her. "You didn't know, Helen. The image was hidden."

216

"It doesn't matter. I was involved all along and didn't know. Stuart told me to deliver it to someone while we were here. You were right. He used me to get you killed."

"That's what we're here to prove." Nate placed a supportive hand of her shoulder and looked straight into her eyes.

She nodded but moved her gaze away at the same time. The thought of being involved was clearly a difficult one to take. Her whole demeanour changed as he held her. She appeared to shrink right in front of him, dropping her shoulders and lowering her head to escape him. Now he was propping her up more than she were him.

They remained in position for a minute or two, until she wriggled away to find a space a few feet away. There she wrapped her arms around herself tightly, closing herself off to the world. The assassin's movements did little to distract her from whatever thoughts wreaked havoc in her head.

"This isn't your fault, Helen," Nate said.

He hated to see her in such a bad way. She was always so confident and strong. This was not the Helen he knew well. This Helen was more, real. He realised that the barrier that had always stood between them had been shattered. They were no longer interacting as a boss and an employee, but friends. He wanted to help her and knew she wanted the same. He reached for her and then waited tentatively to see her reaction.

Now much closer together, she glanced up at him. Her eyes were beginning to shine behind new tears. Suddenly she threw herself forward and wrapped her arms around his middle. She squeezed tightly while she buried her head into his chest.

"I would never do this to you," she said, her words partially muffled.

"I know. I'm so sorry you were dragged into this."

She moved her head from his chest and peered deep up into his eyes. In that moment nothing else mattered to Nate. The killer could have pulled out a pistol and shot him on the spot, he did not care. Her face took up his entire world. He concentrated on each and every part of her, appreciating the uninterrupted closeness they suddenly shared. The moment lasted much longer than he thought was ever possible.

The urge to then lower his head to meet hers was too much to resist. Their foreheads rested against each other for a second, before she then moved her lips up to his and gently pressed them together. She withdrew, but the bridge had already been crossed; there was no going back now. The second touch of their lips was more forceful as they fell hopelessly into each other.

Nate's head buzzed as heat rushed about his body in a blind panic. She was soft, and the touch of her skin felt statically charged as it tingled in his hands. It was too much at once for him to concentrate on any one thing in particular. Instead he let it flow over him, carrying him along like a sweet summer breeze. However many times he had imagined this moment, it never came close to what he now felt.

But just as he felt the need to squeeze her even tighter, something disturbed them. A voice broke the moment, ushering them back to the world they had so happily escaped. It was Stuart.

Chapter 18

"**W**hy are you calling me?" Stuart's voice came through the device on the bed like the thunderous roar of an angry storm.

Nate and Helen watched as his image appeared. There was no time to consider what the kiss meant for their relationship. Instead it was put to the back of their minds as the horrific sight of Stuart's giant face hovered in front of them. He looked seriously pissed off too. The veins in the sides of his neck throbbed as he frowned.

"We need to talk," the killer said while he continued to fiddle with something on the table by the far wall. His back was turned to the display; a rude gesture not unnoticed by Stuart.

Nate and Helen held each other as the conversation played out in front of them. They were spectators to a show neither of them particular wanted to watch. But they knew they had to see it through to the end.

"I told you never to contact me, Sarl," Stuart said.

"Then it appears we have both broken our promises," the killer replied.

Stuart raised his giant left eyebrow, moving the top of its arch just out of view. "What is *that* supposed to mean?" he said.

His face was almost three times its normal size as it floated above the bed, like a decapitated ghoul. If he had moved back only two or more feet from the screen, it would

219

have been more of an acceptable size. But then he never was comfortable with technology, Nate remembered.

The killer held up the paper Helen had given him and suddenly spun around to face the display. Nate could now make out what the assassin—or Sarl—had been tampering with on the table. In his right hand was his weapon. It shined proudly after many a habitual polishing.

"The target is much higher profile than we agreed. Also, he has protection with him. Killing Nathan Maddox will cost you a lot more than our usual price," he said.

Someone knocked on Stuart's door in the background. When he gave no reply, the sound of a squeaky door handle being turned echoed through the device. To his obvious annoyance, the person had begun to enter anyway.

"Not now," he shouted. The door slammed shut again abruptly. "Fine. What will it cost? Name your price. And don't wave your gun around like that, you're not frightening anyone."

Sarl turned and delicately placed the gun back down on the table. "I want the girl," he said with his back to the display again.

Stuart leant away from the screen and angled his head back. He interlocked his fingers before moving them up and allowing his double chin to rest atop them. Then for an amount of time far too long to be considered polite, he considered Sarl's proposal in silence. A random spot above his screen attracted his sight as he did so. Classic delay tactics, Nate thought.

"What do you want with her?" he said finally.

"He's actually considering it," Helen shouted.

Sarl faced Stuart again, but he said nothing. There was no real need for words, his crooked grin made his intentions abundantly clear.

"I can't let you have her," Stuart said, his face once again filling the entire display and eclipsing his surroundings. "Tell you what, just to keep it worth your while, I'll double the pay. How's that?"

220

"Perhaps I'm not making myself clear, *Stuart*. I want the girl or the deal is off. Or would you rather Nathan Maddox lived?" Sarl began to pace up and down the room slowly. "Time is running out," he added mid-step.

"What an arsehole," Helen said.

Nate agreed with her sentiment, but he could not help but notice how utterly engrossed in the scene she had become. Her grip on him repeatedly tightened and then loosened as Stuart and Sarl spoke. Each time she squeezed his arm he felt another sudden rush of heat run through him. Their kiss had him feeling quite flustered still.

An exaggerated sigh escaped Stuart's mouth that translated into a hiss of static through the device on the bed. It was strong enough to bounce repeated around the room and almost knock over a nearby lamp. Clearly the negotiations were not going his way. He was beginning to resemble a cornered animal as he growled to clear his throat. He loosened his collar to allow the rising heat to escape. This animal, however, was well adapted to defending itself, Nate well knew.

"I'll say this once more, Sarl, then I'm going to get angry. She's not part of this deal. Get the job done and you'll be rewarded justly. Don't and I'll bury you. Understand?" Stuart said.

The second he had finished speaking, Sarl stopped and turned to the screen. His bravado had not been as effective as he had assumed it would be. If anything it had set a small fire inside Sarl that threatened to burst from his eyes.

"*You'll bury me?*" The grin vanished from Sarl's face and was replaced by a deeply troubling stare. "If you were here I'd tear you in two."

"That may be so, but I have enough information regarding your *handy-work* to have you sent to the worst shit-hole prison planet you can imagine. So don't forget who you're messing with here."

After a short deliberation Sarl loosened his face and allowed the beginnings of a smile to sneak in. "You're not the only one with a back-up plan."

Stuart's change in expression made clear just how distressed the idea of having unintentionally compromised himself had made him suddenly. He slid his chair away from the screen, accidentally bashing it into the table behind. A sloshing sound of a liquid spilling could be heard in the background. The drink he had rested on his desk had evidently been tipped over.

"You have nothing," he said.

Sarl pulled open the top of his overcoat to reveal a small emblem that looked to Nate like a dagger impaling a dragon like creature. It was definitely of huge importance to Sarl and was close to him at all times. He pulled it away from his neck. The string holding it in place snapped easily as he yanked it away suddenly. Its small size allowed it to be concealed in his palm.

"What's that?" Stuart leant forward to get a better look at the item that had him so suddenly worried.

"My back-up plan. This is a small and encrypted data storage device with all the details of *your* requested handy-work. You release yours and I'll release mine." Sarl laughed as he continued. "You humans so often think you're the only intelligent life out here."

"We've got him," Nate said, excitedly.

Just as Sarl's laughter began to dwindle, Stuart joined in. He heaved his bulbous weight into the back of the chair as his throaty chuckle built. The sudden movement put his seat under immense strain, causing it to creak and moan in chorus with his joyful motions.

"Excellent," he said.

"So then. What is your answer?"

Stuart shrugged. "Fine."

"That bastard," Helen said, again clutching Nate tightly.

"And what of this guard?" Sarl said.

Stuart's laughing stopped all of a sudden. "Cameron?" he said, surprised. "Oh, I wouldn't worry about him. He's useless. Just get the job done, and then we'll discuss the girl. Will that do?"

Nate suddenly felt like a tiny weight had been lifted off of him. Cameron was never the intended fall guy. His poor track record made him the perfect one for the job, in Stuart's eyes at least. But he was not to be framed for the murder, after all. And in reality he had proven the worst possible choice. Nate had seen that his life was never at risk so long as Cameron was there. It still felt good to know for certain.

The emblem was placed carefully onto the bed. Again Sarl left Stuart waiting for an answer. He was in no rush to agree to the terms that had been so expertly put to him. For a moment or two he thought it over. As he did he slowly crossed his arms, with his overcoat still flapping open. Underneath, his clothing stuck to his skin like a tight second layer.

"That will do," he finally said.

"I'm glad you think so. Now, don't contact me again until it's done," Stuart replied before cutting off the connection.

Nate was full of conflicting emotions. He was overjoyed at having been handed the very evidence needed to implicate Stuart in the attempt on his life. But the callous nature in which Stuart and Sarl had negotiated over Helen sickened him. He dared not think about what would have come of her if *their* plan had succeeded instead of his. It made him never want to let go of her again.

During all of the posturing, Nate had seen a side of Stuart that he was becoming quite familiar with. He realised he had never really known Stuart at all, only the well-orchestrated lie that concealed his true nature. At least Sarl had never hidden his. Somehow this made Nate more fearful of Stuart.

He had also been surprised by their interplay. Even though the two of them occupied very different worlds, they were comfortable in each other's. They had been more like two competing predators, fighting for territory, than an employer to an employee.

Something Sarl had said worried him even more deeply though: Killing Nathan Maddox will cost a lot more than the usual price, he had said. Usual price? How many killings had he been paid to carry out? Nate concluded that Sarl must have had a hand in Stuart's success over the years. Perhaps this was the reason Stuart was so good at his job in the first place. Problems possibly just *disappeared* for him.

"Nate?" Helen said.

He had slipped into another daydream. This time the monsters had been all around him, salivating at his tempting flesh. Given enough time and opportunity these two monsters would have covered their lair in the bones of their victims. His spot was where it had always been, except now a new space had opened up, for Helen. It was time to slay these particular monsters.

He snapped back to reality to find Helen pulling his head down to face hers. "Nate," she said again. "I want to leave this place."

"What? Sure, come on," he replied.

As Helen headed for the door he took one last look back. Sarl continued to prepare for the job he had ended up making a spectacular mess of. His conversation with Stuart had left a smile across his face. Nate could just imagine the depraved things the killer was planning to do to Helen.

Whatever punishment he and Stuart would get for their deeds, Nate knew it would not be nearly enough. It did not give him much comfort to think about it either. Killing him was one thing. What they had planned for Helen, however, was unforgivable and scared the life out of him. They deserved far worse than imprisonment for what they had tried to do.

Nate had seen enough, he wanted out too. He hobbled into the hallway, where the exit shined like a beacon of hope. The entire day had led to this one last struggle to the rift exit. Once through it would be finished and he could put it to rest. One last obstacle between him and the end.

Helen wandered ahead, keeping a little distance between them. He hoped it was due to an eagerness to leave

224

rather than a desire to get away from him. She approached the rift exit and disappeared back through it, never once looking back. Nate had to skip the last few steps just to keep up. Then sure enough he was once again exploring a familiar light.

As it cleared he was not greeted by the haunting red sky and barren landscape he had expected. Instead the hotel sat a few hundred metres away, in the background. It was bathed in the same pleasing glow that emanated from the rings high above. They were back among the festival goers.

Sat on the floor, no more than two metres from where the rift had been, was Sarl. He was now awake and looking wholly defeated. His legs and hands were secured with restraints made entirely out of Cameron's black shoelaces. He could not go anywhere. But just to be safe Cameron was resting his right knee against Sarl's back, to pin him in place.

"Welcome back," Cameron said with a grin. "We were beginning to worry." He prodded Sarl to coax a nod of agreement out of him. He did not get one.

L'Armin sat on the floor to the side with his eyes closed. He was engrossed in thought, so much so that he did not immediately acknowledge their return. L'Eshran was knelt down beside him and looking as concerned as ever.

"He's been like that for about ten minutes. He said something about using all of his strength to keep the rift open," Cameron said.

"It required us both," L'Eshran interrupted, never taking his eyes off of his friend for a second. "But I fear it has taken more of L'Armin than it has me."

Helen went over to check on L'Armin. She tried gently to nudge him out of his trance like state by rocking his shoulder. After a few seconds he responded and snapped his eyes open. He looked around to see that the rift had now closed. He focused then on Helen before moving onto Nate, who watched from behind.

"We got it, buddy," Nate said.

L'Armin dropped his shoulders in relief. He could finally relax.

"Then we are done here," L'Eshran said before quickly returning to his feet. To his disappointment, none of the others appeared ready to leave just yet.

There was something important Nate wanted to do and it could not wait. He moved over to Sarl. He knew the emblem would be on him somewhere, it had to be. It would not have been a very good bargaining chip if he had left it behind.

"Where's the data stick?" he said.

Sarl met Nate's angry glare and smirked. "The what?" he said, looking up from his arched position.

"Don't play dumb with me. The data stick you threatened Stuart with earlier."

"Sorry, can't help you. How's the leg, by the way?"

Nate ignored the question and gestured to Cameron to pick his prisoner up. He did so as roughly as he could manage, clearly stamping his authority on the situation. Once up, Sarl took a chance to swing his bound-up arms around in protest. It did little to free him, the shoelaces had been expertly tied after all. Even if they had snapped, nothing was about to loosen Cameron's grip on him.

Greatly adding to Nate's irritation, all of Sarl's pockets were empty. He searched every inch of them but could not find the emblem in any of them. He opened the top of Sarl's black skin-tight shirt, hoping to see the emblem hanging from his neck. But it was not there either.

"Shit, I can't find it," he said, feeling a sense of dread sneak up on him. He continued to pat Sarl down, making sure he had not missed anything. He had not.

"What does it look like?" Cameron said.

Nate continued to search, he was not about to give up just yet. Except Sarl's confident smile suggested he knew it was not anywhere near where Nate was looking.

"A little emblem, thing," Nate said. "Looks like a sword stabbing a dragon. We've got to—"

"I've got something," Helen interrupted.

They turned to see Helen standing by Sarl's overcoat, which lay loose on the cold floor. Nate suddenly remembered seeing it fall to the ground during their altercation in the bar, after it had become ensnared. He clenched his fists with excitement when he saw it, in all its ragged glory. Helen continued to pick it up with care, choosing to hang it from her fingers. She held it away from herself so it could not inadvertently touch any other part of her.

All of a sudden Sarl began to fidget on the spot. Nate swore he caught a glimpse of panic in his eyes as the overcoat became the centre of attention.

"You left it in there?" Nate said, ushering Helen over to him.

"I don't know what you're talking about," Sarl replied.

"Really? Because you look a little worried."

Sarl looked down at his feet; he did not appear to be willing to watch anymore.

Nate firmly gripped the overcoat before taking it from Helen—who became visibly relieved to have handed it away. He was so afraid it would vanish out of existence if he did not hold it tight. Everything had led to this point. It quickly began to heat up in his hand; a comforting thing to remind him it was there and not going anywhere.

The weight of it surprised him, it was much heavier than he expected. How Sarl had been able to move about so smoothly while wearing it, puzzled him. With the strain beginning to pull his arm down he wasted no time and set about rummaging through it.

After only a few light pats of the coat something immediately stuck out, something sharp. He slipped his hand into the inside left pocket and felt an oddly shaped piece of metal. With it now in his palm he could feel the string rubbing against his fingers. As he pulled the emblem out he could not help but smile. He finally had what he needed.

Once again Sarl began to squirm and wriggle. The sight of the emblem in someone else's possession appeared deeply distressing to him.

"What are you going to do with that?" he said.

Nate faced him directly and was elated to see a look of fear across his face. "I'm going to admire your handy work," Nate said. Finally the monster had been tamed.

"What? How did you … There's no way you could have known about it. I don't understand," Sarl then began to plead. "I can explain. Look I'll help you get Stuart. Just let me have the device. Please."

The emblem swung playfully from Nate's index finger, with a loop wrapped tightly around his wrist. "I've got you both," he said.

This did not go down well with Sarl. He began to thrash about violently, surprising Cameron. This time he had no chance of escaping. With a swift knee to his chest, the outburst was quickly brought to a conclusion. Cameron beamed with obvious glee at having exacted his own revenge. Service with a smile, it seemed.

"I've got you," Nate repeated.

Chapter 19

After a good few hours sleep, Nate had arisen from his hotel bed and headed straight down to the pool. He waited peacefully by the side of water for absolutely nothing to happen. The bliss he had wanted the moment he had stepped off the transport shuttle was finally his to enjoy.

The hell that had ensued soon after arriving now felt like a lifetime ago. The only lingering reminder was his leg, that still throbbed, although much less than before. A doctor had checked it over and repaired the damage as much as he could. It brought a smile to Nate's face, that even in such a technological age, a bone fracture was beyond immediate repair. It had been reset, but time was still the best fix. At least the painkillers were working.

The last he had seen of Sarl was as the nearby security station's forces had carted him off. It had still taken a couple of hours for the armoured team to arrive. Time Cameron had gladly spent *subduing* him. Nate had not wanted to know how, only that it was being handled.

The emblem had stayed with Nate. He just was not willing to part with it. During his sleep he had clutched it, keeping it close to his heart. He had wound it so tight around his arm that upon waking he had realised his hand had become totally numb. It was so important to him that he was more than happy to cut off a bit of blood supply in order to keep it safe.

At a time when he felt safely back in his own surroundings, he would spread out the evidence to all that needed it. The first would be the security force that held Sarl. Nate knew from the conversation he had witnessed that there was enough of it to see him spend the rest of his life somewhere fitting.

As he stared into space, plotting his next few moves, something caught his eye. He had spotted a pleasing figure walking casually in his direction. It instantly brought a broad smile to his face.

"Hey, how you feeling?" Helen said.

"Better, thanks," he replied, inadvertently rubbing his leg.

"Good. You ready?" Helen extended out her hand.

"You bet."

They made their way away from the pool. It was slow progress, but still much faster than before Nate's leg had been tended to. This time Helen only had to hold on to him to stop him tripping. His weight was once again his burden to bear.

Ahead, Nate could see a large gathering of people spread out before them. They watched as a lone figure addressed the calm crowd. From the back it looked like the festival was in full swing, but this was different to the one before. This time the people were still and respectful, not excited and fidgety like they had been during the opening festival. Things were drawing to a close.

The man on stage was speaking to the crowd in his best and most mystical sounding voice. As they neared the gathering Nate could see that he was of the same race, but it was not L'Armin. He had evidently given someone else the job of completing the *ceremony*. Of course, Nate knew it was all just for show; a convenient lie to protect the truth.

L'Armin and L'Eshran had left as Sarl was led away. The entire episode had drained L'Armin of his strength. He had used L'Eshran to support him after that, as even walking proved difficult. Nate just hoped they would have

230

the chance to thank him properly before he and Helen were due to leave.

Eventually they found their designated spot, as Nate was considered a VIP after all. It was about time he made the most of it, he told himself. There they stood and watched as the man atop the large plinth—or unfinished pyramid as Nate still preferred—spoke to the crowd.

"We thank the Beings of the Rings for their generous gift, bestowed upon us …" the man said. "It is now time for us to part."

The crowd cheered as he approached the large lever that had activated the beam of light at the beginning of the festival. The tower of light still reached up to the rings above, just faintly tickling their edge. He stood in front of it, creating as much suspense as he could to add to the illusion.

With all of his weight put into one exaggerated movement, the man forced the lever. It clicked and clunked as the heavy, metal mechanisms moved beneath him. Eventually it reached its final position, which deactivated the beam. The glow it had bathed the crowd in faded until only the rings remained above.

Nate felt a quietness flow over him. He stood with Helen to his side and peered up. It was beautiful. He had not been able to appreciate the view properly until now. The rings swept across the sky and cut straight through a clear horizon of stars and galaxies. He could not tell if it was Helen beside him or the thought of nearly dying that made him enjoy it so much. Maybe it did not matter.

Helen took his hand as they stood contently. He looked to her, but she was mesmerised by the view above, and her eyes were wider than he had ever seen them before. Suddenly the view above him had competition, with the sight of Helen tipping the balance just slightly. For a moment he kept his eyes in place until Helen turned to face him. He was sure he had moved his gaze away in time, but a tiny squeeze of his hand suggested otherwise.

Someone tapped him on the shoulder from behind. He turned to find Cameron, L'Armin and L'Eshran standing there. L'Armin still looked a little flushed as L'Eshran held him supportively by the arm. For the first time since meeting L'Armin, Nate thought he appeared as old as he supposedly was. Largely due to the extra wrinkles that now framed his eyes.

"How are you?" Nate asked.

L'Armin answered quickly to stop L'Eshran from doing so for him. "In time," he said, "I will be well."

Cameron leant his head back and looked up, mimicking others nearby. "Wow, what a sight," he said.

"Indeed," L'Armin replied.

L'Eshran simply grumbled.

"I've got to say, you've got a hell of a place here," Nate said.

L'Armin tipped his head to the side slightly. "I suppose we do."

"I think what Nathan is trying to say is thank-you, for everything," Helen said.

Nate laughed. "That's what I meant. I could never repay you for what you've done for me."

"That's better," she added, playfully digging her elbow into his side.

L'Armin laughed quietly as he placed a hand on Nate's shoulder and inadvertently transferred a bit too much of his weight. He was about to speak when L'Eshran interrupted.

"With everything now settled I trust you will be leaving?" he said.

"I guess so." Nate glanced at Helen. "Or we could stay a little longer?"

After one last and prolonged look at the rings hovering silently above, she answered. "No, I think there's something waiting to be done at home."

Nate nodded in agreement. "In that case," he said. "I have just one more request."

L'Eshran suddenly became more animated. He leant forward and raised his hand, giving the *Stop* signal. "No. Absolutely not. I told you this was over."

"I know, but I think L'Armin might enjoy this," Nate said.

L'Armin tugged gently on L'Eshran's sleeve and silenced his friend's anger instantly. Yet the matter was not quite settled. For a moment the two stared intensely at each other. Nate assumed they were arguing telepathically again. There were no clear signs of who was winning though.

Eventually L'Armin spoke. "We are agreed. What is your request?"

Nate smiled, but did not speak.

Chapter 20

The office was quiet, a little more so than usual. A quick look to the clock confirmed the time was now eight forty-five. Another late night of arduous labour was ahead of him, even though he had rolled in around five this morning. Stuart was still busy though, too busy to really care.

He darted about the open-plan office. His was the entire 160th level, where forty-two members of staff spent their working days. With one last check, before he returned to his desk, he confirmed that all of them had left for the evening. He was finally safe to get to his real work, the kind done outside of working hours.

Stuart was rather nervous, to say the least. He chewed his bottom lip and was again sweating right through a crisp, clean shirt. Today he had pretty much ruined two already. Never mind, he thought, he could simply buy more. He would just have to go easy on his lip, however, as he had tasted a tiny bit of blood during his last anxious chomp.

The door to his own office was made of solid mahogany and was inlaid with the finest gold décor his pay-cheque allowed. Yet *he* only noticed the creek of its hinges as he pushed it open. The bloody thing had cost him a bomb and was let down by one cheap hinge.

Once inside his office and back to safety, Stuart fumbled for his personal communication device. This was a particularly expensive piece of hand-held kit that he took pride in owning. It allowed him to speak to someone many light years away, and with less than a nanosecond of delay.

He swiped the smooth surface of the device to bring it to life. It glowed brightly in the dim lighting of his office. Across the top of the display read a message that sent a chill down his spine: "Recipient is unresponsive".

It was no good. However long he stared at it, nothing changed. He had sent countless messages over the past day, all of which came back with the same unhelpful notification. *Unresponsive*? What was Sarl doing?

In frustration he launched the device across the room. A smashing noise soon followed as his expensive toy shattered upon impact with his equally expensive and polished floor. He cared little for it now that his contact had disappeared.

His attention then turned to a small black cube, sat on the table behind his desk. He took his seat and swivelled it around to face the device. Behind this stretched a night-time scene of heavy traffic that, it could be argued, was almost beautiful. Of course *his* building towered over everything outside, a symbol of high status that he relished in.

After a few moments of being distracted by the view, he focused again on the black cube. He opened it up by folding out the top section. This device was actually more standard than his expensive hand-held one. But still its usefulness made it important to him. Even though its keys were in an alien text that he struggled to understand.

Mercifully, Sarl had shown him how to use it once before. He concentrated on his earlier lessons, running through each step in turn.

No more than three key inputs later and the device erupted into a glorious display of whizzing and whirling icons. The brightness at first caused him to shut his eyes. After a few seconds he was able to interact with the hovering holographic display as fast as he dared. This was of course much slower than he would have liked. He had important things to do, so the delay annoyed him immensely.

Eventually he managed to initiate a call to his contact. He waited patiently as it tried to connect. It buzzed repeatedly but no-one was answering.

"Dammit Sarl. Answer the call. Where the fuck are you?" he said, infuriated at the device for not doing as it was told.

His outburst sent a dull echo around the room. At first he thought this was what had caught his ear, but soon he was not so sure. From behind he heard something. He could just about make out the noise of a door slowly swinging open. The squeak from the hinge gave it away. He froze as the device in front of him continued to buzz. The office was empty, he had been certain of it only moments ago.

Facing the window, he peered into the small amount of light that reflected back at him. There was definitely someone else in the room with him, possibly more than one. As he began to lean in and squint one of them came into view. He almost jumped out of his chair when he recognised the face.

"Nathan," he said, with a certain amount of trepidation.

"Turn around, Stuart," was Nate's reply.

Stuart hesitated as he thought over what to say. He immediately noticed the downward arch of Nate's mouth, accompanied by an unnerving glare. The reflection of his boss was angry. He knew why.

"I wasn't expecting you back so soon," he said.

"Turn around," Nate again asked.

Once again Stuart was sweating, except now it was coming through his suit. The moisture was not content with having fully saturated his shirt underneath. His first instinct was to flap his suit jacket open a few times to clear some of the excess heat. After that he decided to quickly deactivate the device in front of him. The last thing he wanted was for Sarl to answer at that moment. Sweating too much was one thing. Why a murderer was calling him, on the other hand, was something altogether more difficult to explain.

His chair squeaked as he slowly rotated it. Suddenly he could see who else had entered his private sanctum unannounced. In the dim light of his office he could see Nate was joined by Helen, Cameron and two odd looking characters, both of whom were dressed like some kind of monk.

"Good to see you all," Stuart said.

The group stared at him. He could almost feel their eyes burning through him. But how much did they know? he wondered. Even if Sarl had told them, surely they would not believe any of it. After all he had worked closely with Nate and Helen for years. He was confident they would allow him to explain.

"Well. Where do I start?" he asked.

"How about with this?" Nate said.

Stuart was horrified to see Nate holding the emblem Sarl had threatened him with before. Shit, he thought. They knew everything and were there to take him in. He was facing a lynch mob.

"What's that?" he tried to say confidently but stuttered instead.

"It's what's on it that you should be worried about," Helen said.

"I have no idea what you mean, Helen. Did you both enjoy your vacation? Relaxed are we?"

They did not answer. But the two strange looking characters began to move around the table toward him, one from either side.

"I don't believe we've met," Stuart said with his hand extended, ready to greet the one to his left.

Again no-one spoke. The two continued to approach him as he leant uncomfortably in his seat. He had nowhere to go. He decided it would be best to stand and continue acting as if he had no idea about the emblem.

"Well, I must be—" Stuart managed to say before he was thrust back into his padded leather chair. "Hey," he protested.

237

The man approaching from his right, the oldest of the two, then joined his friend in holding him down. The two were not allowing him to move at all, as Nate leant on his desk.

"You've really been a lot of trouble, haven't you, Stuart?" Nate said.

"Look, I—" Again Stuart was interrupted by the two to the side of him. This time the older of the two started to grope his bald head. It was odd but only slightly threatening. "Is this supposed to scare me or something?" he said.

"No," Nate said. "My friends here are going to see what else you've been up to."

Stuart's head was now held, locked in place. "What? How?" he said with his eyes uncomfortably lodged in the top corners of their sockets, just to see Nate.

"Let's say they're good at reading people." Nate appeared to share a joke with the others, who all giggled along with him.

"Bullshit," Stuart said. They would not get anything from him, he vowed. What were they going to do, read his thoughts?

THE END

###

A Thank you

Thank you for reading my first ever novel. I sincerely hope that you enjoyed it. If you did, I'd be eternally grateful if you could take a moment to leave me a review at your favourite retailer.

I now have the writing bug, so look out for my next book sometime soon. Transitory was the start of what I hope will be a vast line-up of novels. So if you enjoyed this, then rest assured, there is certainly more to come.

Thanks!

Ian Williams

About the author

Ian Williams is a Science Fiction writer from the UK. He lives in a small town roughly 50 miles outside of London.

Although born in Barking, Ian was raised in a town in Essex called Danbury. Until the age of eleven he was an ordinary child with nothing extraordinary or particularly different about him. This changed when he was diagnosed with Becker's Muscular Dystrophy just before starting secondary school. This condition only affects around 2400 boys in the UK, making it a rather rare one.

After finishing school and sixth form, Ian went on to a career in the UK Court Service. He spent seven years working there, but had also begun to write as a hobby. When that became his everyday routine he found himself lost in a world of infinite possibilities, never able to accept just one outcome of many. In the end he chose to ride the tide of time and allowed the future to be an unknown space, where only the stories he lives can ever alter that timeline.

Sorry, I think I lost myself there for a moment. Anyway, Ian is now writing as much as his fingers will allow, or until his keyboard decides to explode from all the typing.

Other books by Ian Williams

Transitory (2014)
The Sentient Collector - Sentient Trilogy book 1 (2015)
The Sentient Mimic - Sentient Trilogy book 2 (2015)
The Sentient Corruption - Sentient Trilogy book 3 (2016)

Connect with Ian Williams

Follow me on Twitter:
http://twitter.com/iwilliams235
View my Author Profile on: Amazon
Find me on: goodreads
Facebook
Website:
http://starman8243.wix.com/iwilliamsauthorpage

Made in the USA
San Bernardino, CA
16 April 2017